"I—I had better get going. I have a beauty pageant to prepare for and all."

BeeBee struck an awkward pose with the apron clenched in one hand on her hip and the other waving at an audience that, even in her imagination, still shook its head in collective disapproval.

"Hold on," Bill said. "Didn't you say you needed a recipe for this pageant?"

"Oh, well, yeah. But if you're only in town for six weeks, I don't want to take up any more of your time."

"BeeBee," he said. "C'mon. It's you. Of course I'll make the time to help."

"If you're sure it wouldn't be too much of a bother..."

The real trick would be keeping her focus on winning the pageant and creating the water buffalo herd of her dreams. Nothing could get in the way of that.

Especially not the guy who had already left her behind once before.

Dear Reader,

Look for the helpers.

This was the advice Mr. Rogers gave children for when the world felt scary. As I got older, I found myself wanting to do more than look for the helpers. I wanted to *be* one. But how?

Like my main character, BeeBee the dairy farmer, I've struggled my entire life with social anxiety: not knowing what to say or saying the wrong thing altogether. So for me, volunteering that required any kind of social interaction wasn't going to help anyone. Like Bill, BeeBee's first love who leaves her after their golden summer together at camp, I'm terrified of making a mistake and letting people down. So how was I going to help?

Then I thought about what has always brought me joy, what has always given me a sense of peace and certainty in this frightening and unpredictable world: stories. Stories about hope and redemption, stories about silly people who fall in love and make mistakes and somehow still get their happily-ever-afters. Stories about women chasing their dreams to the moon and back and the men who will do anything to help them get there.

This is one of those stories.

I hope it brings you joy.

I hope it helps make the world a little less scary for a little while.

Happy reading!

Laurie

THE DAIRY QUEEN'S
SECOND CHANCE

LAURIE BATZEL

Harlequin

HEARTWARMING

Harlequin® HEARTWARMING™

ISBN-13: 978-1-335-05115-8

The Dairy Queen's Second Chance

Copyright © 2024 by Laurie Batzel

 Harlequin Enterprises ULC
22 Adelaide St. West, 41st Floor
Toronto, Ontario M5H 4E3, Canada
www.Harlequin.com

Printed in Lithuania

Laurie Batzel lives in the Poconos with her husband, their four two-legged children and their two four-legged children, Stuart the Corgi and Midge the Marvelous Rescue Pup. Her first book, *With My Soul*, was published in 2019 and her essays can be found in several editions of *Chicken Soup for the Soul*, as well as online at *McSweeney's Internet Tendencies*, *Longreads* and Harvard University's *Tuesday Magazine*. When not writing romance that is equal parts swoons, sniffles and smiles, she can be found watching too much TV under too many blankets, testing the acceptable limits of caffeine consumption and perfecting her recipe for chocolate chip cookies. Learn more at authorlauriebatzel.com.

Visit the Author Profile page
at Harlequin.com.

To three Virginia ladies who inspired the spirit of this
book with their heart, humor and heroism:
my mom, Gayle; my sister, Sarah; and the forever
Queen of our Hearts, Sandra Bullock.

Also...world peace.

Acknowledgments

As promised, first shout-out goes to Cameron for
providing the name (and spirit) of Jeremy Binkus.
And to Charles, Cody and Caroline for cheering
Mom on while she "worked on her computer."

To James, your life makes
(the best parts of) my life possible.

To my agent, Stacey Graham, and 3 Seas Literary
Agency, thank you for making my dream a reality.
High kicks!

To the team at Harlequin Heartwarming, especially
Johanna Raisanen and Kathleen Scheibling,
I am so grateful for your enthusiastic support
and insightful direction.

To an amazing group of writers including but
not limited to Virginia Brasch, Jamie Seitz,
Sophie Andrews, Elizabeth Sumner Wafler
and Elizabeth Penney, thank you all for the
crossed fingers and toes!

To my parents, in-laws and extended family,
thank you for being as excited for this book as I am!

Finally, and always, to CJ, thanks for today.

CHAPTER ONE

WHEN MOST PEOPLE talked about their babies, they usually mentioned whose eye color their offspring had inherited or how remarkably early they'd started babbling. Almost never did they boast about the rapid growth rate of their horns or the exceptionally soft quality of the hair coating their entire bodies.

BeeBee Long gave her water-buffalo calf a satisfied pat on its rump and rose from crouching on the barn floor. She was not most people, and that was more than fine by her.

"Good girl, Lady Rosamund," she crooned. "Almost up to two hundred pounds. I'm so proud of you."

A rustling in the hay behind her prompted BeeBee to turn and shake her head lovingly at the calf's other mama. "No need for the sass, Countess Viola. You're big and beautiful too."

Light broke through the crevasses between the wooden beams of the old barn. That meant only one thing—sunrise on another beautiful day in

Crystal Hill, New York. BeeBee pushed open the double doors of the cattle barn and walked through the straw-covered pen and into the middle of the vast grazing field until she reached the perfect viewing spot. Crystal Hill Dairy Farm was situated on two hundred and fifty acres of stream-fed valley below the foothills of the Adirondacks. Now that it was officially May, the hills had burst into a green so vibrant it was like looking through emerald-colored glasses. To see a beautiful sunset, you had to drive into town, take a right at Jane Street, the main drag, and park at Crystal Hill Lake. But the perfect sunrise? That was right here.

This morning, it was all hers.

After the sun's rays crested over the tallest fir tree, she pivoted and headed for the main gate closing off the cow pasture dotted with hay bales and roaming Holstein cattle. The dairy farm had been in the family for years—passed down through the women, as their family was particularly prodigious on that account. BeeBee chuckled to herself. The overwhelmingly high ratio of women to men born in the town had caused many to speculate that there was something in the waters here. While mineral-rich enough to provide ideal nutrition for the grass that fed their cows, BeeBee scoffed at such nonsense. True, she was one of a set of four sisters, including a pair of twins, but there was nothing supernatural about Crystal Hill. It was simply another small town in upstate New York. Rural. Peaceful. Perfect.

And her home.

She closed the wooden gate behind her, padlocked it, then walked down the dirt road leading toward their family home. Every season on the farm had its own special magic, but spring was her favorite. New life cropped up everywhere she looked, from the pregnant heifers ambling slowly in the pen to the flower boxes bursting with blue cornflowers out of every window of their white two-story farmhouse. The vines climbing up the trellis sparkled with pink buds, and even the porch swing creaking in the breeze sung with extra vigor this beautiful morning.

Kicking up dust as she walked, it didn't bother BeeBee in the slightest that her boots and jeans would be coated in yet another layer of dirt. Her older sister, Jacqueline, used to shake her head in dismay when they'd been kids each time BeeBee had materialized in the doorway looking as if she had bathed in mud. At twenty-five, Jackie was only one year older and had long since given up trying to refine her middle sister into anything other than a sentient dust cloud. The twins, who were seventeen, were so busy that they weren't home enough to have opinions on BeeBee's appearance.

Today was Sunday, however, so the dance school where Lindsay essentially lived these days was closed and the antique jewelry store where Katelyn worked wouldn't open until eleven. That meant all her sisters would be home to hear the wonderful news.

Bursting through the door of their farmhouse, BeeBee pumped her fists into the air triumphantly. "It's time!"

Jackie's fingers stilled on the keyboard of her laptop. The back of her blond head tilted to one side as if stirred from deep contemplation and trying to figure out whether the words had come from the real world or the characters who lived in her head. Apparently having decided that Bee-Bee was indeed real and not one of her romance-novel creations, Jackie twisted in her chair and draped one arm around the back.

"Time for what?" she asked absently.

A trooping of feet from the staircase around the corner of the living room heralded the twins' arrival.

Katelyn followed her mirror image with measured, careful steps, holding on to the railing and not looking up until she reached the landing. "Time to get a new watch," she quipped, pushing her glasses up her nose with one finger to punctuate her joke.

"Did someone say breakfast time?" Lindsay asked, taking the last two steps in a graceful leap that sent her curly brown hair flying behind her.

BeeBee clapped her hand to her forehead and groaned. "No puns until at least nine in the morning," she said, pointing at Katelyn before moving her finger in Lindsay's ever-shifting direction. "And no breakfast either unless one of you can magically summon cinnamon rolls from Georgia's."

Jackie was a decent cook, although she had been known more than once to wander away from an overflowing pot of oatmeal because fleeting inspiration for another novel had struck. The twins could at least make toast without setting off the sprinkler system, which was more than anyone could say for BeeBee's cooking skills. It had gotten to the point that Kit, as Katelyn was known, recorded the smoke detector on her phone and trolled BeeBee with the sound every time she offered to make anyone so much as a peanut butter sandwich.

"What time is it, BeeBee?" Jackie asked with a gentle smile.

"It's time to order the water-buffalo sperm." BeeBee folded her arms over her chest and waited for the others to share her excitement—or at the very least pretend.

Instead, the twins simply shrugged before padding into the kitchen across the room.

"I'm making coffee." Lindsay, who everyone called Lou, illustrated the statement with a yawn. "Mom's volunteering at the library this morning. Kit, can you check the board to see if she has a school-board meeting tonight?"

Kit doubled back and crossed the room to check the large white board calendar on the wall between the kitchen and the living room fireplace. Each location of activity was color coded. Their mom, a former English teacher who retired for approximately two weeks before she successfully ran for the hamlet's board of supervisors, was like a rainbow with her various town committees and volunteer work. "Yeah, she's got a meeting tonight. Dad's doing a lecture on soil samples for the community college too, so we're on our own for dinner."

"I can pick up a pizza on my way home from the dance studio, but it will be late," Lou called out over the hiss of the coffeepot.

"Speaking of cheese on pizza..." BeeBee raised her voice a notch in a desperate attempt to pivot the conversation. "I bet Lucas will be happy to hear that we'll be adding more buffalo milk to his supply for Mama Renata's. She said it's really much better quality than the regular stuff."

"How about a couple of hoagies from Big Joe's?" Kit countered, completely ignoring Bee-Bee as she disappeared into the kitchen. "I have my metalworking—folk art class at the community center, then a shift at the antique store, though, so it will be late. I guess we can each do our own thing for dinner like usual."

BeeBee crossed her arms and frowned. It was bad enough that everyone was so busy with their activities, including both their educator parents, that they couldn't even find time to sit down for dinner together. But the complete lack of interest in a major development on their own family farm was simply unacceptable.

"But…but the buffalo." BeeBee held out her hands helplessly. "Jackie, you write romance. This is kind of in your wheelhouse."

Jackie pursed her lips. "I'm not sure how the progeny of water buffaloes from a farm in Italy is romantic." Her blue eyes lit up. "Unless you've fallen in love with the breeder over the phone, and you're going to fly to Tuscany to meet him in person." She grabbed a small notebook from the table next to her computer and took the pen out of her bun to scribble something in it.

"Salvatore doesn't speak a word of English, and he's also one thousand years old," BeeBee pointed out. She took off her boots at the doorway and put them on the stoop, then closed the door. "Guys, Lady Rosamund is close to maturation. She's almost two. We can inseminate her and add to the herd. I really thought you guys would be more enthusiastic about this. I'm mad *and* disappointed."

Jackie crossed the room and patted BeeBee on the arm. "I'm happy you're happy about the buffalo cheese, sweetie."

"You say it, but you don't mean it," BeeBee sulked, then jabbed her thumb at the patched front pocket on her plaid work shirt. "I always mean what I say."

"Mmm-hmm." Kit walked back into the living room and blew steam off the top of her mug. "And how's that working for you?"

BeeBee sniffed. "Just fine, thank you. My life is perfect."

"Was it perfect when Mrs. Van Ressler kicked you out of the B and B's haunted house last Halloween because you said the scariest thing there was her late husband's portrait?"

"It was a joke," BeeBee protested, throwing her hands into the air. "Besides, everyone knows she hated him. She married him when she was, like, twenty and he was almost sixty. No judgment," she added with a respectful nod of her head. "The dude was loaded. Do you know how many adorable water-buffalo babies I could buy with that kind of money?" The tingly anticipation spread through her chest once more at the image of a field full of regal water buffaloes wallowing in the streams behind their fields. There was nothing like it anywhere in the tristate area. They could become a hub for supplying high-end restaurants. Crystal Hill would become a destination for more than just the shimmering clear waters of its eponymous lake.

"That's what we're talking about," Kit said, putting her coffee mug down on the end table between the couch and their dad's ancient rocking chair. "Yes, everyone knows it. But we don't say it out loud. It's called being polite."

Jackie silently picked up the mug and placed a coaster under it before turning back to face Bee-Bee. "Or like the last town hall meeting where you shot down Joe Kim's idea for the deli platter the diner was going to provide for free at *The Nutcracker* reception?"

"Oh, come on, that was just tacky." BeeBee nodded at Lindsay. "There is nothing Christmassy about a nutcracker head made out of salami. Back me up here, Lou."

Lindsay was still in the kitchen, stretching with her left foot propped on the butcher-block counter that divided the rooms. She straightened her back and gracefully lowered her leg. "It was grotesque. But there was probably a nicer way of saying it than actually using the word *grotesque*. Which you did. Repeatedly. Into the microphone."

"Whatever," BeeBee said. "I love this town, and it…has grown accustomed to me." She rolled her eyes and walked past her sisters with a huffy toss of her long chestnut-hued braid. "When you love something you're one hundred percent honest about it. That's what real love is. Now, I'm going to go order premium water-buffalo seed, and since you guys are the Nice Police, I would appreciate some positivity on this most auspicious event."

Her sisters trailed her as she walked to the computer, trying not to let their words sink indelibly into her skin. She knew they were just trying to help her. But she was different from her sisters. She didn't have Jackie's gentle way with words and angelic face, Lou's grace and charm or Kit's ability to make beauty out of literally anything. Her sisters weren't meant to stay in Crystal Hill. But BeeBee was here for the long haul. Committed.

Anyway, this town would forgive her for anything, especially when she had enough of a herd to start providing them with delicious, creamy water-buffalo milk. Milk that could be used in plump, airy balls of mozzarella, silky-smooth yogurts and a thousand other delicacies their cousin Lucas would sell at the dairy farm's retail space downtown. They didn't produce as much milk as the Holsteins, so they were still dependent on the cows to make ends meet. But today they were one step closer to their farm achieving something very few others in the United States had dared to try.

Settling into the chair, BeeBee swiveled to face the computer and muttered to herself, "Buffalo baby day, huzzah."

Somehow it just wasn't as exciting as it had been five minutes ago. Yet her soul inflated a little more once she pulled up Salvatore's website and saw the faces of his water buffalo staring back at her. With their wide inky eyes and curly horns, they were so much more majestic than the workaday cows their farm had milked for decades. This addition had been BeeBee's idea, and her mom had been more than happy to let BeeBee take on the running of the farm the minute she had graduated from her two-year degree at the community college where her father taught.

She moved her finger on the mouse to click on the email icon, then froze and let out a yelp.

"No, no, no, no, NO!" BeeBee clutched her head with her hands and pushed the rolling chair back.

"What's wrong?" Jackie placed her delicate hand on BeeBee's arm and leaned forward, searching her face. "Are you hurt? Did Salvatore jilt you?"

That was enough to calm BeeBee out of her hysterics, at least temporarily. She pointed at the image of Salvatore that flashed on the screen. "For the last time, the man is basically one of the mummified victims from Pompeii. It's not going to happen. No, Salvatore is retiring, and…" BeeBee swallowed back the bitter taste of frustration and loss. "He's selling Orlando. My perfect stud."

The sisters let out a chorus of understanding "Ooohs." Orlando—or rather Orlando's seed—had sired Lady Rosamund, the first buffalo calf BeeBee had birthed and raised all the way from infancy. Sure, it was normal to be biased with one's own babies, but Lady Rosamund was perfect. Gentle, affectionate, she followed BeeBee around wherever she went in the pastures, never leaving her side. BeeBee had hoped to create an entire herd just like her, and Orlando had been the key. She had interviewed water-buffalo breeders over the phone for months before deciding on Salvatore. How dare he retire? The man was a spring chicken. Plenty of years left in *both* his artificial hips.

"Why don't you just buy Orlando?" Lou asked.

BeeBee leapt to her feet, temporarily forgetting that she was as clumsy as Lou was graceful. Tripping over the leg of the chair, she flew forward into Jackie's arms. "Yes! We could buy Orlando."

The idea cemented instantly as the greatest suggestion since it had occurred to someone in Naples to put cheese and sauce on hot dough to make pizza.

"Can we afford him?" Kit asked.

BeeBee shrugged. "We could always apply for a grant from the dairy association. I'm sure between that and our savings we can make it work." She hugged her sisters tightly. "Dream team, right here. I'm going to call him now."

Kit reached out and took BeeBee's hand gently. "Maybe I should call him for you."

"You think I'm going to accidentally insult him and blow the sale, don't you?" BeeBee bristled.

"No," Kit protested, "because you don't speak Italian." As she turned to unplug her phone from the charging station on the desk, she added almost inaudibly, "But yes to the other thing."

BeeBee stuck out her tongue at Kit when her sister leaned back over the computer to check the number, not caring that it was juvenile and probably slightly proving her point. So what if she was outspoken? It was always better to speak the truth, in her experience. That way there was never any confusion about how she felt about something...or someone.

BeeBee followed closely behind as Kit wandered into the kitchen speaking in lyrically fluent Italian. An exceptional artist, her younger sister dreamed of an apprenticeship to a goldsmith in Florence someday, so she had started taking Italian classes from a local tutor when she'd been fourteen. BeeBee had driven her to the classes, and even though Kit would repeat what she had learned on the thirty-minute drive home, not a single word had stuck. That was okay. They supplied all the milk for Mama Renata's Italian Ristorante and Pizzeria downtown. The only Italian BeeBee would ever need to know was *spaghetti alla norma*, her favorite dish there.

As the conversation went on, BeeBee's patience waned. Finally, she placed her hands flat on the kitchen table and stage whispered, "Kit, what is he saying? How much for Orlando?"

"Scusi, per favore," Kit said into the phone before covering her end with her hand and inclining her head to BeeBee. "He says he has a buyer already interested who is willing to pay twelve thousand euros."

"Twelve thousand?" BeeBee dropped the whisper and raised her voice to a shout. "That no-good grifter. We only paid three thousand for Viola."

To be fair, she had been a rescue, but the principle was still offensive. "What's he trying to pull? Let me talk to him." She lunged for the phone, but Kit ducked and scooted to the other side of the table to create a barricade.

"Perdono," Kit said into the phone before launching into a series of murmurs. "Mmmm. Mmm-hmm. Grazie. Ciao."

BeeBee threw up her hands in despair and sank into one of the kitchen chairs. "That's it, then. No Orlando."

Jackie, who had been listening from the safe distance of the living room, crept into the kitchen and tutted sympathetically. "Poor BeeBee. I'll make you some hot cocoa."

"It's May," BeeBee muttered. "I don't need hot cocoa. I need my water buffalo."

Jackie shrugged and went to the fridge for a gallon of milk anyway.

Kit sat down at the chair opposite BeeBee and leaned back, crossing her arms over her chest. "Well, if you had waited for me to finish the conversation instead of flying off the handle, I could have told you that Salvatore is willing to hold Orlando for you since our farm is a previous customer as opposed to the other buyer."

BeeBee sat up straight and clasped her hands over her heart. "He did? Really?" She sprang from the chair and grabbed Lindsay, who had been reaching for the coffeepot. She whirled her sister around by the hands, while Jackie spread her arms in a wide protective stance in front of the china hutch next to the fridge.

"But coffee," Lou wailed, turning her head longingly toward the pot as BeeBee continued to jig her in dizzying circles around the small kitchen.

"Coffee can wait," BeeBee crowed. "I'm getting my water buffalo. I take back everything I said about Salvatore. He's an angel and the love of my life." The image of hazel eyes and a strong jawline that definitely did not belong to the wizened Salvatore flashed in her head. She dismissed the memory with a defiant toss of her braid. Releasing Lou, she continued to spin in happy circles on her own until a minor collision with the counter stopped her.

"Um, BeeBee?" Kit said quietly. "You still have to pay him twelve thousand euros. And that doesn't include transportation. We're easily looking at a total of fifteen thousand dollars to get him here." Her dark eyebrows furrowed over her glasses.

Clutching her left ribcage where she had bumped into the counter, BeeBee frowned. "Shoot. You're right. Did Salvatore say how much time he would give us to come up with the money?"

"He said two months was the longest he could do," she replied. "The other buyer wants to breed his water-buffalo heifers sometime this summer."

"Okay." BeeBee tapped her finger on her lips. "There has to be a way we can do this. Fifteen thousand dollars in two months." She looked at Lindsay. "Could you do a fundraiser at the dance studio?"

"We just did one," Lou said before taking a long sip of her coffee and sighing contentedly. "The Crystal Hill Clog for a Cause, remember?"

BeeBee shuddered. How could she forget? Lou had tap-danced through the house for twenty-four hours straight. It had been like sharing a house with an overcaffeinated woodpecker. "Okay. What about the New York Dairy Association? Don't they have a grant program for local farms?"

"I'm on the website now." Kit held up her phone. "There's no grant applications open at the moment because they give out money as part of the Dairy Royalty Pageant coming up in June."

Jackie crossed the room and peered over Kit's shoulder. "I had a friend who won Dairy Princess in high school." She looked up at BeeBee. "Maybe Kit or Lou could enter and win the money."

Kit shook her head. "It says here the winner

of the Dairy Princess pageant only wins a five-thousand-dollar grant, and it has to be used for education. But…" She scrolled down further, a terrifying smile spreading across her face. "The Queen of the Dairy Pageant awards a twenty-thousand-dollar grant to anyone ages eighteen to twenty-four who works full-time at a dairy farm. The money has to be used for something dairy-related, like farmland acquisition, milking equipment or—" she set her phone down and pushed her glasses up her nose "—livestock procurement."

Dreadful awareness blanketed BeeBee like storm clouds obscuring her beloved horizon. Her eyes dropped to the mud-encrusted hem of her jeans, the ragged cuticles on her right hand. An ache in her shoulder reminded her of where she had staggered into the doorframe leaving her bedroom this morning. All three of her sisters were staring at her as if thinking the same exact thing at once. "No. I can't. There has to be another way."

"I don't know if there is," Kit replied. "Most of our savings are tied up in the state-college funds. You can't touch those without incurring a penalty. And we're still paying down the bank loan for the new milking stand we put in last year. With interest rates being as high as they are, there's no way we could afford to go into any more debt. If you want to grow this farm—heck, even to keep it going another five years—you have to be creative."

"There's a difference between creativity and delusions of grandeur," BeeBee huffed, sinking lower into her chair. "Me winning a beauty pageant definitely falls into the latter category."

"But why?" Jackie straightened up and began ticking items on her fingers. "You're more passionate about dairy farming than anyone else on the planet. You know everything about it. You definitely don't suffer from stage fright." She nodded her head in BeeBee's direction as she concluded with "And somewhere underneath all that mud, plaid and denim is a very attractive woman. At the very least, it would be incentive to wash out whatever is permanently caked under your fingernails."

"But wouldn't I have to be, like, graceful and demure? What if there's a talent portion? The only talent I have is hand milking faster than the machine. Oh, and whistling," she added with a proud puff of her chest.

It was something she had always been able to do—whistle in perfect pitch with a volume and clarity on par with the Revolutionary War fifes the Hudson Valley Battlefield used to sell at their gift shops. At one time in her life, it had been a way to signal a certain someone she didn't think about anymore—hardly ever, anyway.

"Actually, it says there are three portions to the pageant," Kit said. "You have to do some sort of creative presentation, like a skit or an original song. There's an interview where you talk about your specific platform for your dairy, like why you need the grant money—that part is in formal wear," she added with a cringe.

BeeBee rolled her eyes so hard she felt something pop. "Because mincing around in heels and an evening gown is such an essential part of dairy farming. That's ridiculous and outdated and—stop looking at me like you're already planning how to style my hair." She whipped her head around and pointed at Lou.

"Half-up, half-down," she said with a lift to her shoulder as if it was obvious.

"Uh-oh," Kit said.

"What, *uh-oh*?" Lou put her mug down with an indignant jut of her pointed chin. "BeeBee has gorgeous hair. You just can't tell it because you never see it out of a braid."

"No." Kit shook her head and held up her phone. "The pageant requires you to submit a dairy recipe that you prepare yourself."

All four of them groaned in defeat, and Bee-Bee dropped her head. "That's the nail in the coffin, then." Cooking was the *worst*. Their dad had done most of it when the girls had been little. However, since he had accepted a job as an adjunct science professor in the community college the year after BeeBee had graduated with her associate's degree there, they had gotten in the habit of bringing home takeout a few times a week from Big Joe's Diner or Mama Renata's Italian Restaurant.

"I guess we'll just have to find another way to come up with the money, then," Kit said sadly as she set her phone down on the table.

"No," Jackie said with an uncharacteristic force in her voice. "BeeBee, you need to do this. Not just for the money. Not even for the farm, although I agree with Kit that we need some sort of financial assistance to keep it going."

"For what, then?" BeeBee asked, confused and a little frightened. Jackie usually only spoke in tones that invited woodland creatures to sit on her shoulder.

Jackie walked around the table to stand in front of BeeBee. Even though she was older, she was several inches shorter and tiny-boned like a bird. Next to her, BeeBee felt like a water buffalo herself. "For you. I worry that you spend so much time and energy on the farm that you don't take time for your own care and maintenance. I think you should use this pageant as an opportunity to focus on doing things that are good for you, like learning to cook and dressing nicely," she said, tipping her head to the side and casting a critical eye at BeeBee's boots. "Growing the farm with a water-buffalo herd will mean branching out into gourmet and niche suppliers, like restaurants and caterers in the city. You'll need to be comfortable dressing for business meetings and events. Think of this as practice."

Out of the corner of her eye, BeeBee could see the cows moving across the pasture outside the living room's bay window. The water buffaloes were out of sight, probably happily taking their mid-morning soak in the stream on the outer edges of the grazing lands. They mingled with the cattle here and there but almost always at a distance, separated as though they knew one of these things was not like the other. They weren't sleek and pretty like the Holsteins, and they moved with a distinct gait, slow and slightly uncoordinated. But inside they kept a secret treasure trove—milk that was creamier and richer than anything in the world yet with a lower lactose content to make it easier for almost anyone to digest. Water-buffalo herds were few and far between in the US, especially in the northeast where special care had to be taken for them to make it through the winter.

BeeBee knew what Jackie was saying without saying it out loud. The three of them—Jackie,

Kit and Lou—had talents that would require them to one day leave their small comfortable nest in Crystal Hill. They were bound for the biggest, brightest places the world had to offer. Short of a talent scout combing Upstate New York in search of the next World Champion Whistler, BeeBee had no such prospects. She didn't want them anyway. Why would she want to leave her perfect town with its perfect sunrises and its perfectly imperfect people who would always forgive her no matter what slipped out of her mouth?

"Let's do it," she said with a sigh. "Wash my nails, fix my hair, teach me to walk in high heels, find some cooking classes. If I want my king of the water buffaloes, then I guess I have to become a queen."

CHAPTER TWO

BILL DANZIG WRAPPED the ties of his white apron around his waist twice and tied it.

"Crystal Hill," he said to himself, shaking his head.

Of all the places in the world his work as a gourmet chef had taken him, this was the one place he never thought he would return.

It wasn't that his first time in this picturesque town had been unpleasant. In fact, in the beginning it had been one of the happiest times of his life. But the way he had left it seven years ago remained one of his saddest memories. No matter how hard he tried, he would never forget the feeling of driving on the highway back to the city and wanting with every fiber in his body to put his car—and time itself—in reverse.

Instead, he had traveled the world. Professionally, this had given him a varied toolbox of global cuisine to use in his creations. His personal goal also remained decidedly singular: to experience as much as this world had to offer by never staying in one place for longer than three months. He had his parents to thank—or blame, depending on who you asked—for his wanderlust. With a commercial-pilot dad and a travel-writer mom, the desire to see the world was a potent combination of nature and nurture he had spent the last several years indulging.

Fortunately, this gig—teaching a series of beginner cooking classes for children at the Crystal Hill Parks and Rec Center—was only for six weeks. Just enough time to hang out with his old friend, Lucas Carl, and rest up before his next charter job started up.

As if reading his mind, Lucas strolled through the double doors and into the kitchen at the back of the rec center. At five-eleven, Bill wasn't exactly short, but Lucas still towered several inches over him, walking with a lumbering gait that had prompted more than one Sasquatch joke back in their Camp Herkimer days.

"Man, it is great to see you," Lucas said as they hugged and slapped each other on the back. "How long has it been since you've been on dry land?"

"Almost three years, with some breaks here and there," he replied. "Usually I visit my folks in the city or stay with my sister in the Berkshires during the off-season. But my parents are on back-to-back cruises for the next month and my sister's got company already, so your offer came at the perfect time."

"I really appreciate you doing this." Lucas took a step back. "The Crystal Hill Small Business Association has been pushing the local stores to do community outreach. When I suggested a cheese club, there was nothing, but crickets. It was only when I mentioned my old camp counselor friend was a gourmet chef who also happens to be great with kids that I got any kind of response."

Bill waved him off with one hand. "I'm happy to do it. I owe you after all those times I crashed in your dorm at Penn State in between cooking internships and charter gigs."

"On the plus side, there are some really cute single moms out there." Lucas jerked his thumb at the door behind him.

"Oh, really?" Bill scoffed. "So why are you still single?"

"Pssht," Lucas said. "I've grown up with most of these women since I was three. Heck, I saw one of my cousins out there with her kid." He shrugged. "Anyway, I was just hoping I could get you to fall in love with one of the locals so you would stick around a little while longer. Do you know how hard it is to find guys to hang out with in a town where the women outnumber us three to one?"

"Nice try, but once European charter season starts up again this summer, I'm back out on the boat," Bill said. "It's good money, and I get to see the world, meet new people every season, experiment with my recipes. That's the dream."

"When you put it that way, it sounds pretty great." Lucas put a hand on Bill's shoulder and pushed him back to give him an appraising look. "But, uh, do you not have access to barbers out on the high seas, or are you going for a rugged-pirate look here?"

Bill scrubbed a hand over the thick stubble blanketing his chin. "A little bit of both?" He shook his head, and his hair fell over his eyebrows with the motion. Hmm. Maybe Lucas had a point about the haircut. But that was all he would concede. The hair was temporarily unkempt and could be fixed with one of his trademark bandannas.

But there was nothing temporary about a wife and kids. In this stage in his life, short-term was the best he could offer anyone. That was what he liked best about charter yachts. Everyone on the boat knew they were only there for a limited period of time. Sometimes he liked the women he worked with enough to change their relationships from professional to romantic. Since both of them knew from the get-go that it would, by definition of the peripatetic job, be short-lived, there was never any drama.

He had learned the last time he was here not to make promises he couldn't keep.

Grabbing his second-favorite bandanna—the one with tiny black dogs on it—he tied it around his head and pushed it up so that the hair was out of his eyes, took a deep breath and followed behind Lucas out into the sea of tiny humans waiting in the cafeteria. Each rectangular table had been set up with four stations equipped with utensils and ingredients for today's recipe: fruit-and-cheese kabobs with a creamy spiced dipping sauce. Rubbing his hands together, he opened his mouth to greet the kids and their parents when the smile froze on his face.

Standing in the back by the door, shock and confusion mingling on her beautiful face, was the girl who had made him want to reverse time. Except she wasn't a girl anymore. She was a woman, the strong angles of her nose and cheek-bones softened by the wisps of brown hair falling out of her braid. While the jeans and plaid shirt tied at her waist were the same as he remembered, they looked very different on her now. Her slender coltishness had been filled out with curves. Strong muscles defined her bare fore-arms and added shapely definition to the jeans covering her long legs. He had always loved that she was almost as tall as he was. BeeBee Long wasn't a woman you could break with an embrace. It was really her—although after seven years apart, she was also someone he didn't know anymore. A complete stranger who he still missed with an undefinable and absurd ache. How could you miss someone you didn't know anymore?

And more importantly, was she one of the aforementioned single moms?

He brought his fist to his lips and cleared his throat, unable to tear his gaze away for fear she might disappear like she did in his dreams. "Hi everybody," he said in the smooth-as-butter chef voice he used for wealthy charter guests. "I'm Chef Bill. I studied cooking at the Culinary Institute of America, and for the last several years I've worked as a chef on cruise ships and charter yachts. It's an awesome job because I get to meet lots of cool people and travel all over the world. Because I'm never in the same place for all that long, every cruise is like a new adventure."

Was it his imagination, or did BeeBee's lips tighten? And why was he staring at her lips?

Bill cleared his throat. "Over the next six weeks, I'm going to teach you all how to make food for yourself that is easy, healthy and, most important of all, really, really tasty. Now, show of hands. Who all here loves food?"

He counted eleven small hands shooting enthusiastically in the air plus BeeBee's much larger
one raised tentatively alongside the other smiling
parents. Bill threw both of his arms up and waved
his hands back and forth. The kids laughed. Bee-
Bee smiled, although it was a restrained version
of the unbridled grin that could light up not just
a room but an entire campground.

"That's awesome," he went on, dropping his
arms and slipping his hands in his pockets. "You
know there's a word for people like us, people
who are really passionate about food. We're called
foodies. So, my budding foodies, when I point to
you, I want you to tell me what your absolute favorite food is, the one you would take with you
to eat every day if you were stranded on a de-
serted island."

"An island made of desserts?" a boy with light
blond hair gelled up in spikes called out, giggling. "I would just eat the whole island."

Bill pointed at the kid, then back at himself.
"Kindred spirits, man. You and me are gonna
be pals—I can already tell." He looked over the
crowd. When his eyes linked with BeeBee's
once again, his smile broadened all on its own.
"Someone else. You in the front."

He bent down and nodded to a girl in the front
with red curls and big green eyes.

She looked down shyly, then whispered, "I like…pizza?"

Bill winked, then stood back up and spread his arms out. "Pizza. I mean, come on now? Pizza is the best. Bread, delicious. Sauce, amazing. And cheese? Cheese is life. Plus you can top it with anything you want. Raise your hands if you like…pepperoni on your pizza."

Most of the hands went up. He noticed Bee-Bee's stayed down. That was all right. He had a hunch what would bring that hand sky high.

"Okay, how about sausage or hamburger? Any meat lovers?"

A few, including the blond boy, raised their hands.

Bill nodded. "That's my carnivore group right there. Team T. rex in the house. Now I know I'm gonna see some hands for this one. Who here likes their pizza with…" He paused for dramatic effect, pretending to think even though he didn't have to. This order was burned in his brain, with him every time he made or ordered pizza. "Bacon, hot peppers and pineapple?"

He was met with a chorus of high-pitched "ewwws" from the throng of children encircling him, but they weren't who he was trying to impress with that one. The lift to the corner of BeeBee's lips and the softening of her large brown eyes were all he needed. The defiance with which she raised her hand reminded him of one of the things he had always liked best about her: the refusal to be anything but authentically herself no matter what others told her. That summer at camp the girls had largely divided into Team Zayn and Team Harry as the band One Direction had officially dissolved once each of the members had put out a solo album. Bee-Bee had stridently announced that Niall Horan was the real talent of the group, an opinion that had seen her demoted from team captain of the color wars.

Over the years, more than one person had commented on Bill's resemblance to the British pop star, and every time, she was the first person who'd sprung to his mind.

"All right, everyone," he announced. "Have your grown-up people help you with your apron and form a line at the sink to wash your hands. Chef lesson number one—always wash your hands with soap and water before handling food." He resisted the urge to hard stare the kid with the bowl cut with his index finger firmly lodged in his nose. "Ready, set, scatter!"

As they dispersed in a clatter of giggles and squeals, Bill approached BeeBee across the room, certain she could hear his heart thudding even from a distance. Just as he was close enough to smell the sweet mixture of hay and fresh soap that was so distinctly BeeBee, Lucas jogged up to the two of them, clapping a hand on each of their shoulders.

"Hey, guys," he said. His typically stoic demeanor had cracked with a grin so broad that Bill lost the desire to stomp on his friend's toes for interrupting the moment. "Look at that— we've got the old Camp Herkimer gang back together again. Bill, you remember my cousin BeeBee right? She was a junior counselor for the girls' camp our last year as senior counselors for the boys. You guys hung out a lot that summer, didn't you?"

Hung out, fell madly in love. They were all just words.

"Umm, yeah," Bill said, hoping he didn't sound as awkward as he felt. "I—I remember. It's been, what, seven years?"

"Something like that," BeeBee replied with a distant tone to her voice. It was almost soft enough to make him think she was reliving those days in her head the same as him. Whenever he thought about that summer, the memories were tinged with a golden light. Fireflies flickering in the woods along the lake, the glow of a campfire illuminating BeeBee's face. Everything about it had been perfect except the way it had ended.

"And look at us now," Lucas went on, completely oblivious to the magnetic forcefield he had stumbled into between them. "BeeBee's running the farm almost completely on her own, I'm full-time at the shop. Speaking of which, I've got the cheese cubes and yogurt from the shop in the fridge back there. Are you ready for me to bring them out?"

"That'd be great," Bill said. After Lucas had finally left, Bill blinked at BeeBee in amazement. "Wow. It's really you."

She bit her lip, and yet a wide smile broke across her face anyway. "I know what you mean. I can't believe—I mean, what are you doing back in Crystal Hill?"

"Lucas sent me a message on Instagram," he said. "I had posted that I was coming off a winter charter in Hawaii and was looking for a place to sublet. He asked if I would be interested in teaching these cooking classes for kids to help out his business. So, what's—what's new with you?"

Please don't say married with kids.

BeeBee's face fell, then remolded with confusion. He had always loved how expressive her face was. "Wait—this is a cooking class for kids?"

Bill looked back at the line of children ages six to eight either having their aprons tied or jostling each other in line at the sink. "I hope so because one way or another I'm giving these rugrats back after an hour."

BeeBee closed her eyes and scrunched her nose. "I feel like such an idiot."

"Why?"

She opened one eye, then turned her head to avert his gaze. "Because I need to learn how to cook to enter this beauty pageant so I can afford my water-buffalo sire and start a new kind of dairy farm," she let out all in one breath. At last meeting his eyes, she began to chuckle softly. "But of course, because it's me, nothing is going according to plan." She spread her arms out wide and shrugged.

"There's a lot to unpack there," he said slowly, digesting the delicious, unsaid hope buried like a hunk of goat cheese in her word salad. So maybe she hadn't married the high school quarterback and had kids right after graduation. "But, uh, you should stay anyway," he added, pretty sure she could see the steam coming out of his ears from the gears in his brain cranking overtime. "You could be my assistant chef."

"Um, are you sure about that?" she asked with a skeptical arch to her eyebrow. "I can't make toast without burning it. I'm pretty sure you'd be better off with Riley Brewster as your assistant, and that kid keeps his finger so far up his nose he's got a fingerprint in his gray matter."

Bill snorted. "Right?" But he wanted her to stay. "But you should stay. It'll be fun."

"I do really need this," she said hesitantly, twirling the end of her braid around one finger. "As long as you don't feel weird about...us, you know, or anyway, the us we used to be?" She shook her head. "I promise I don't usually speak in riddles that would exhaust the Sphinx."

"I've seen the Sphinx—she's pretty well-rested," Bill quipped. "I mean, I don't think it will be a problem. We're all adults here, right?"

BeeBee leaned to her right side and nodded her chin meaningfully. "You sure about that?"

Bill turned around to see a phalanx of children gathered around him with wide eyes and dripping hands. He swiveled back in time to see BeeBee throw her head back and laugh, that big, unabashed laugh that filled a room and never failed to make him laugh too.

Nope. No problems here at all.

CHAPTER THREE

BEEBEE PEEKED OUT of the corner of her eye at Bill Danzig from the sink as she washed her hands.

He stood at the front of the small cafeteria, arranging a small bowl of fruit on the table in front of him. It was such a strange sensation to see him again. He had changed a lot, as you would expect someone to in the years between eighteen and twenty-five. His jawline was fuller and definitely hairier. Bill had always had one of those faces that looked younger because of the wide set of his hazel eyes and the fullness of his lips. The darker hue of sandy hair coating his chin aged him well, like a perfectly ripened cave cheese. She wasn't mad about the muscles popping out from under the sleeves of his T-shirt either. Those were a new and welcome addition. Seriously, had he been on charter yachts or rowing on a crew team?

And yet with all the changes, it was still him. She would recognize that face anywhere, anytime, no matter how long it had been. Even now that face and his voice, deep and calming as a mountain lake, sent shivers up her spine. She had thought of him so often—and tried so hard not to think of him with even greater frequency. Now he was back, like a song that had been stuck in her head playing on the radio. *You're here for a reason*, BeeBee reminded herself sternly. Learning to cook, winning the pageant, buying her buffalo—these were the things she should have been thinking about, and yet only one question kept running through her mind like water through her fingers.

Was he back to stay?

"All right, everyone," his voice boomed. "Are we ready?" He twisted around so he was no longer in profile and quirked a questioning eyebrow at her. "All set, BeeBee—I mean, Assistant Chef BeeBee?"

"I'm ready." She turned off the water and shook her hands dry. The droplets of water flicking up into her face still didn't seem to break the spell he had over her. There was a time she would have followed him into fire. Well, a lot had changed since then.

Although technically she did have to follow him because she was his assistant.

And also he was holding a flaming blowtorch.

She walked around the table to stand next to him, leaning away from the open flame.

"In case any of you were thinking that cooking was another boring chore to do around the house, this, my small friends, is a blowtorch," he said, acknowledging an excited murmur ripping through the children with a bob of his head. "Just one of many of the awesome tools I get to use every day in my job as a chef. After we're done with our fruit-and-cheese skewers and our dips, I'll have each of you put a marshmallow on the end of your skewers so we don't have anyone poking each other."

BeeBee bit back a grin as he leveled Riley Brewster with a hard stare.

"Then one at a time, I'll toast your marshmallow with my blowtorch. It's not any different than the fire starters your grown-ups use to light your birthday candles, but when you're a chef, you can call it a brûlée torch and people pay you lots of money to set their food on fire with it."

It was all so familiar. BeeBee's heart ached and overflowed with the memory of that summer at camp—the way he'd charmed everyone around him so effortlessly with his slightly mischievous smile and his invitingly confident presence. He'd been every kid's favorite camp counselor, the one who had prompted more than one girl to splash around in the lake pretending to drown in hopes of his rescue despite the camp's strict requirement for proficient swimming prior to attendance. Even now, the kids completely ignored the bowl of marshmallows in front of them as they watched him pick up his shining chef knife and hold it in the air.

"Now, the most important chef's tool is his or her knife," he said, holding his in the air. "This is my paring knife, Percy."

"You named your knives?" BeeBee said out loud. "Also, Percy? Really?"

"It's short for Percival." He winked at her, and she gripped the table with both hands. "As I was saying, knives are very important for chefs, but what's even more important for chefs?" He raised his hands in the air and wiggled his fingers. "These babies. So please do not use sharp knives without your trusted grown-up's permission and supervision."

He leaned over and muttered out of the corner of his mouth to BeeBee, "Worked with a chef in Manila who only had thumbs, an index finger and a pinky. Great chef. Terrible pianist."

BeeBee laughed so hard a snort came out. Then she looked down at her station and frowned. "Excuse me. Why do I have a plastic knife like the kids?"

"Because I need you to demonstrate for them how to use their utensils," he explained. "And because I've seen you eviscerate a peanut-butter-and-jelly sandwich trying to cut it in half."

"Yeah, well, peanut butter is trickier than it looks," she muttered. She hated that he still remembered all her favorite foods. He wasn't supposed to know her inside out anymore. That privilege was reserved for people who stuck around.

Following Bill's instructions, she and the children set out their wooden skewers, fruit and blocks of cheese from the bowls at their stations. BeeBee's stomach rumbled. The fruit looked beautiful. Fragrant strawberries that gleamed like rubies, dusky-cheeked apples and her favorite—large red grapes. Unable to resist a little snack, she popped a quick handful of fruit into her mouth while Bill's back was turned.

"Now since the grapes are quite large," he called out to the children, "it's important to cut the grapes in half before we put them on our skewers."

Uh-oh. BeeBee felt the grape lodge itself in the back of her throat. She could still breathe, but it was definitely larger than she had anticipated. As if somehow aware of her distress, Bill looked directly at her, furrowed his eyebrows and asked, "BeeBee, everything all right?"

Oh no. She could not let him see that she lacked the self-control of the seven-year-olds carefully following his instructions and cutting their own grapes in half. She forced the solid lump down her throat and held a thumbs-up, despite tears watering the back of her eyes. "Fine," she rasped. "Just…a little winded from all the chopping."

He cocked his head to one side but mercifully didn't say anything more. As Bill walked around the room, encouraging the children and showing them how to hold the knife to slice their fruit, BeeBee peeked at the printed recipe next to her cutting board. After slicing the fruit and cheese, they were to mix honey, cinnamon, ginger and yogurt together to make the dip. Well, that was easy enough. Maybe she could do some version of this for the pageant. It would need to be more complicated obviously, but it seemed doable even for her.

Then again, if she found her recipe on the first day, she wouldn't need to come back for any more of the classes. The idea of only seeing Bill this one time and then simply moving on was like having only a single one of Georgia's homemade chocolate-chip-and-brown-butter-toffee cookies. It was impossible.

It didn't matter because when she had finished placing all her sliced fruit on the skewer, alternating with the cheese, and mixed all the ingredients for the dip, Bill dipped a strawberry in to taste it and made a pained face.

"What?" she asked indignantly. "It's your recipe."

He wrinkled his nose. "Why don't you try it?"

Frowning, she took one of the chopped grapes and put it in her dip and shoved it into her mouth with a defiant lift of her chin. Instantly, she grabbed a napkin and spit it out.

"Blech," she cried. "That was terrible." She shook her head and clapped her hand over her forehead. "I knew it. I'm hopeless."

Bill laughed and reached for the recipe. His hand brushed hers as it passed over, and electricity shot through her entire body, jolting and comforting all at once. He tapped on the page. "I think you mixed up the measurements for the honey and the cinnamon. It's one tablespoon of honey and one teaspoon of cinnamon." He bent over and sniffed the bowl, then wrinkled his nose. "Way too much ginger too."

"My hand slipped when I was measuring it over the bowl," BeeBee confessed. "But I like gingerbread, so I figured it would be fine."

Bill's eyes creased slightly at the corners when he smiled at her. That was different, just like the stubble. He was like a pirate treasure full of new discoveries, wrapped in an actual pirate. "It's all right," he whispered. "I'll still let you have a marshmallow at the end of class."

As she stood next to him while one by one the children held up their marshmallows for him to gently toast with his blowtorch, the smell of caramelizing sugar and smoke took her back to that perfect night at camp. The night that they had stayed out by the fire longer and later than anyone else, lying side by side with their hands brushing against each other as they both reached up to point to the shooting star at the same time. He had rolled onto his side and pressed his lips so gently on hers that it had been more of a whisper than a kiss. But that whisper had awoken in her what it meant to fall in love with the same velocity of a meteor plummeting to Earth.

"Umm, Cousin BeeBee?" Caroline, Georgia's daughter, stepped out of the line to tap her on the hand. "Are you okay?"

BeeBee swallowed hard. "I, uh, yes, I'm fine." She bent down and admired Caroline's platter with fruit sliced in perfect geometric shapes and the dip sprinkled lightly with a dusting of cinnamon. "Wow. You did great, kiddo." She straightened up and put her hands on her hips. "You sure you should be in the beginners' class? You're kind of wrecking the curve for the rest of us."

"Why does your dip smell funny?" Jeremy

Binkus said as he got to the front of the line and leaned over BeeBee's station.

"Eyes on your own plate there, buddy." Bee-Bee pointed two fingers at her eyes, then back at him.

"You know, some of our favorite foods started out as mistakes," Bill said to Jeremy as he toasted his marshmallow. "Even one of my favorites, the chocolate chip cookie, started out as an accident."

"My mom makes great chocolate chip cookies," Caroline said proudly as she took her turn holding out her skewer for Bill to toast. "She runs the bakery in town." She looked over at BeeBee with her enormous blue eyes that had seemed to understand far too much of the world since she had been a toddler. "Mom wanted me to take the class to make some new friends. She said I've been staying home too much lately."

BeeBee blinked rapidly. When Caroline's dad had passed away last year, the whole town had rallied around Georgia. That was another thing BeeBee loved about Crystal Hill. Even though they gossiped and bickered as much as any close-knit community, when one of their own was hurting everything else got pushed to the side. They took care of their own here.

"Hey, did you know that we have some new kittens at the barn?" BeeBee pushed her dip to the end of the table. As much as she hated to admit it, Jeremy Binkus was right. "Why don't you come by sometime and visit them? There's a little gray one who loves to snuggle, but I'm so busy with the farm, I don't have the time. It would be a really big help if you could give the kittens some extra love."

Caroline's face beamed, and she practically spilled her dip skipping back to her seat.

Bill turned to face BeeBee. "Wow. You really cheered her up."

She shrugged. "Well, in my experience, animals can comfort even the greatest sadness."

Like the last time you left me and it broke my heart.

She shook her head and turned to clean up the mess on the tables as the children filed out the door with their grown-ups.

"Wait," said Bill.

"Yes?" She turned around, a stack of plates stuck together with melted marshmallow fluff balanced precariously in her arms. "What is it?"

"Don't you want me to toast your marshmallow for you?"

Her breath caught. Was this really happening? Setting the plates down, she walked over to him. She was a grown woman now, an adult who ran her family's dairy farm and wrangled giant cows and water buffaloes twice her size.

But one look from him and all the heady giddiness of being a seventeen-year-old in love for the first time came rushing back in a single, resonant heartbeat. She plucked a marshmallow out of the bag and stuck it on a clean skewer, holding it up for him.

Facing her close enough for her to see the small mole on the side of his neck below his ear, he leaned in, switching on the blowtorch with a soft whooshing sound. "So," he said, his voice as husky as the low crackling from the flame. "What's this about beauty pageants and buffaloes?"

BeeBee watched the marshmallow turn from pristine white to a golden toasty brown, the edges puffing and turning crisp from the heat. She turned the stick to the other side and cleared her throat. "Well," she began, wondering how he could hear anything she said over the thundering of her heart, "we're—I'm trying to start a water-buffalo herd to add to our dairy. We'll still need to keep the cows, at least at first, because the water-buffalo-milk production is much lower. I started with one female that I had inseminated by a bull from Tuscany. She produced the most beautiful calf, who is almost fully mature now. I had planned to repeat the process, but my bull is being sold. I want to buy him but we need money, and the winning grant from the New

York Queen of the Dairy Pageant is so far my best option to get the money in time."

Bill arched an eyebrow but, to his credit, didn't burst out laughing at the idea of BeeBee in a beauty pageant. "Aren't there other ways to get the cash? You could rent or sell a parcel of land, couldn't you?"

"That takes too long," BeeBee said. She had thought about that while filling out the pageant application. The more she read about it, the more desperate she had become to get out of it. "And we already used the land as collateral for Jackie's college loans, so we can't do that again either. Plus I won't touch the money set aside for the twins..." She inhaled deeply the rich smell of sugar taken almost to the edge of burning. Of course he remembered just how she liked her marshmallows.

He bent forward, and for a moment, she thought he was going to kiss her. Her lips parted in anticipation, every nerve ending alert in anticipation. But then he blew on her marshmallow to cool it before straightening up with a contented expression.

"There." He nodded at her skewer. "One brûléed swiss meringue à la crème pour la mademoiselle."

"Fancy," she said, exhaling with a small chuckle to cover the sting of disappointment. "Is this how you charm the ladies—with candy and French flattery?"

Subtlety had never been her strong point. But she couldn't take not knowing whether he was single for another second.

His mouth opened, then closed, and he leaned his hands back against the table behind him. "Actually, it's pretty hard to maintain any kind of long-term relationship when you're bouncing around different gigs from country to country. The six weeks I'm gonna be here is the longest I've been in the States in three years."

"Six weeks?" Her hopes, which had bounced to the ceiling at the news that he was still single, came crashing to the floor and shattered. "So you're not—you're not staying, then?"

His cheek twitched, and he shook his head. "Nope. Once my next charter yacht contract starts end of June, I'll be back out in the Mediterranean until winter."

"Oh." BeeBee took a small bite of her perfectly cooked marshmallow, tasting nothing at all. She chewed for a moment, then set it on her plate. "Well, I guess it was good seeing you today at least. Maybe you, me and Lucas can catch up over dinner sometime while you're in town." She turned to untie her apron so he wouldn't see the bitterness forcing her features downwards.

"Hey," he said, touching her gently on the arm as she struggled with the recalcitrant knot. "Let me help you with that." As he worked the knot, the warmth of his fingers brushing against the thin cotton of her shirt sent acute tendrils of longing through her. BeeBee toyed with the hem of the apron. At least this time, the Band-Aid was being ripped off in front of her. There would be no more brutally painful surprises, no more declarations of intentions too good to be true.

"Thanks," she said as the knot finally loosened. She pulled the apron over her head and balled it in her hands, unable to look at him. "I—I had better get going. I have a beauty pageant to prepare for and all." She struck an awkward pose with the apron clenched in one hand on her hip and the other waving at an audience that, even in her imagination, still shook its head in collective disapproval.

"Hold on," he said, closing his eyes and shaking his head as if to jog a memory. "Didn't you say you needed a recipe for this pageant?"

"Oh, well, yeah," she said, dropping her hand. "But if you're only in town for a short while, I don't want to take up any more of your time."

"BeeBee," he said. "C'mon. It's you. Of course I'll help. When would be a good time to stop by the house? I'm staying with Lucas, so it will have to depend on when he could drive me over there since I don't have a car." He tipped his fingers to his bandanna in a sort of salute. "We pirate chefs don't really stay on dry land long enough to warrant paying for long-term parking or storage."

She rolled her eyes. "Okay, Captain New-Beard," she said, teasingly reaching a finger up to poke at the chin dimple she knew lay buried under his stubble. "I get it. You're living that nomadic life." She got it all right. She just wished it wasn't the complete opposite of her own. "If you're sure it wouldn't be too much of a bother, I could really use the help." Jerking her head back at the table where her complete fail of a simple dip sat, taunting her. "Or a miracle, if you've got one of those in your bag of chef's tricks."

The real trick would be keeping her focus on winning the pageant and creating the water-buffalo herd of her dreams. Nothing could get in the way of that.

Especially not the guy who had already left her behind once before.

CHAPTER FOUR

Since he and BeeBee had agreed on Saturday for the start of their Dairy Pageant Recipe Project—a phrase that grew no less silly with repetition—Bill woke up unusually early for a weekend off. Work on charter yachts, being a chef in general meant long hours and late nights. The adrenaline rush of creation and the heightened excitement of the kitchen kept him going, but when the season was over, he tended to crash.

As he threw on a T-shirt and jeans, however, that same carbonated energy he usually got from cooking bubbled up inside him. Sure, a part of it had to do with the project itself. There was nothing he liked better than a culinary challenge. But he'd be lying to himself if he didn't admit it had even more to do with seeing BeeBee again. The second he had taken up Lucas's offer to return, her face had popped into his head—and not for the first time over the years since he had been away.

It was no wonder, then, that he took the stairs

from Lucas's apartment over the dairy store two at a time.

"I'm ready to head over to the farm whenever you are," Bill said as Lucas emerged from the stockroom behind the counter. The shop had a rustic feel to it, with beamed ceilings and a red tile floor. The sweetness of the fresh milk mingled with the smell of the rosemary sprigs nestled among the daily samples set out on a high round table in the center of the room. "Thanks for driving me, by the way. And for letting me live in your spare bedroom."

This was the downside of his rootless existence. It didn't make financial sense right now to own or even rent a place of his own. Yet somehow at almost twenty-six, he was more aware than he had been three years ago of how dependent the situation had rendered him. Even though he tried to help by babysitting his sister's kids and stocking the fridge with the favorite dishes of whatever friend was kind enough to lend him a couch, it couldn't go on like this. But anytime he tried to make a permanent plan for what to do or where to live outside of charter yachts, his brain spun out like tires in the mud. It had always done that when confronted with choices, big or small.

How were you supposed to pick just one place out of this big, beautiful world to live? If he was a superhero, he would be paralyzed by decision-making the same way Superman was by kryptonite. The memory of his favorite comic-book store in the next town over would have zoned him out completely if Lucas hadn't clapped him on the shoulder.

"C'mon." Grabbing his keys off the hook next to the coat rack, he twirled them on one finger before snatching them in his fist. "Are you sure this is how you want to spend your precious time off from work?" They headed out the door to where Lucas's truck was parked outside. As Lucas grabbed a piece of chalk and scribbled *Be right back* on the chalkboard sign hanging from the door, he glanced over his shoulder. "Helping my cousin BeeBee train for a beauty pageant is the kind of task Greek Gods might use to punish disobedient mortals. I mean, I love her, but you don't know her the way I do. She's not exactly what I would call a typical beauty queen."

Bill ducked his head and ran his hand through his hair. "Thanks for the heads-up, but it's fine. I'm only teaching the kids' class one day a week and the prep isn't difficult. This will give me something to do with my time."

Usually if he had a few weeks between gigs, he filled the time with learning something new. One month he'd learned some German phrases, figuring it would come in handy if he wanted to work on a river cruise on the Danube or the Rhine. Before that, he'd taught himself how to do close-up-illusion card tricks. Being able to pull out a trick or two helped bump tips from the charter guests, plus it had helped maintain his hand dexterity for knife work. Most importantly, it kept him from being bored. There was nothing worse than boredom. Knowing BeeBee far better than Lucas realized he did, Bill was certain that helping her prepare for the pageant would be anything but boring.

They drove down Jane Street, the main three blocks that encompassed the town center, before coming to a stop at the only traffic light downtown. Everything was just as he remembered from being here for sleepaway summer camp as a kid, then as a counselor. The red brick and pastel-siding buildings with striped awnings. The sky-blue Victorian B&B at the end of the street still run by Mrs. Van Ressler, a woman who had seemed impossibly ancient to Bill even seven years ago. The old theater across the street still had a vertical marquee with one crooked letter at the end. The birch trees surrounding Crystal Hill Lake were the only things to have grown, and even those possessed a resolute familiarity as if determined to guard the town's secret ability to remain frozen in time. Bill shuddered. The only thing more unappealing than boredom was the idea of being stagnant.

He looked over at Lucas. His friend hadn't changed a bit since they had last hung out in Lucas's dorm room five years ago. He was still the guy with the uncanny ability to repair anything that broke. An incredibly talented cheesemaker too—one of the things they had bonded over as teenagers. Although they shared a love of food and the outdoors, Lucas was the kind of guy people knew they could depend on, as reliable as a German clock. That had been especially helpful since Bill was more like the cuckoo bird that popped out every so often: entertaining, sure, but with the potential to irritate if you had to hear it long-term.

"So, what's new in your life these days, man?" Bill asked as the truck turned right and rambled onto the rural road leading past the lake and into the thicketed forest. "You seeing anybody special these days?"

Lucas grunted. "You sound like my mom." He shook his head and quirked half a smile. "I've dated a little bit here and there. BeeBee told me once that my standards were, and I quote, 'stupidly impossible' and that I shouldn't expect the perfect woman to simply waltz into my cheese cave and rescue me from myself."

Bill couldn't hold back a grin. "I mean, where's the lie, though?"

"BeeBee is honest to a fault, that's for sure."

"Is she—um—seeing anyone?" Bill stared out the open passenger-side window, hoping the question would float casually on the breeze so Lucas wouldn't get suspicious. As their only male cousin, Lucas had taken on the role of big brother to all four sisters, and it was something Bill knew he took very seriously. It was why he and BeeBee had never told him they had been together back then. Or anyone.

"Not anymore," Lucas said. "She dated another dairy farmer from around Bath for a while. I think they broke up sometime last year? Uncle Jack—BeeBee's dad—had been in charge of most of the daily farm operations when we were all kids. Once he started teaching at the community college, BeeBee took on more and more responsibility. I think it was too hard to date someone who didn't live in town when the farm occupied so much of her time."

"Those long-distance things never work out," Bill said. The words echoed in his head, taunting him.

As they came out of the woods and met a dirt road with a tall fence on either side, Bill breathed a sigh of relief that Lucas didn't have a suspicious bone in his body. As the truck slowed past the fields, a few cows lifted their heads curiously at them. He couldn't see the water buffalo though. Come to think of it, he didn't really know much about the difference between the two. He had used mozzarella di bufala in several of his recipes, though, and never been disappointed in the outcome.

"The buffalo are probably out in the stream on the far end of the property." Lucas pointed to the hills covered in pine trees to the left of the pastures, as if reading his mind. "They like to wallow in the mornings. The farm is really big, so the animals have lots of room to wander, especially when the weather is nice and warm like it is now."

He stopped the truck in the driveway sandwiched between a large red barn and the two-story white farmhouse with black shutters and a sloped green roof.

Bill got out and leaned back in through the window. "You gonna come in and say hi?"

"I've got to get back to the shop," Lucas said, then wrinkled his nose. "Besides, I can hear BeeBee yelling from here. I'm out."

As Lucas backed up the truck, Bill turned his head toward the house. His friend wasn't wrong. BeeBee's unmistakably booming voice was hollering from within, interspersed with the high-pitched squeals of other girlish voices.

Bill walked up the steps with trepidation and knocked on the green door loud enough to be heard over the din.

"Hello?" he called. "Can I come in?"

"Bill," he heard BeeBee shout. "For the love of all that's holy, get your butt in here and save me from these harpies."

He reached for the doorknob, but it swung open from the other side before he could turn it. Stumbling forward a little bit, he was greeted by a woman with short silvery hair and a cane. "Hello there," she said matter-of-factly, as if there wasn't a full-scale battle erupting in the living room behind her. "You must be Bill. I'm Mrs. Long. BeeBee said you would be coming to help."

Bill blinked and leaned to his left slightly to see a hand reaching up from the couch that was quickly tackled and pushed down by a young girl shorter than BeeBee from over the arm rest.

"I, um, yes, I'm Bill," he said hesitantly. "I'm here to help BeeBee with the pageant—is everything okay back there?"

Mrs. Long leaned heavily on her cane and twisted her head to look back, then returned a complacent smile back to him. "They're just starting the pageant preparations. You're right on time. I'm heading out for the town spring-cleaning event, but make yourself at home." She brushed past him, her cane rapping loudly down the steps as she went.

Closing the door behind him, Bill wiped his sneakers on the braided floor mat. He glanced briefly at the kitchen to the right—always the first thing he noticed in any home—before approaching the melee on the couch. "BeeBee?" he called out. Back at Camp Herkimer, they had worked out a signal. He would stroll past the cabins on the pretense of doing a perimeter check. In the quiet of the night, he would hum so she could hear him coming. It was always one of the songs by ABBA they had danced to at Camp Herkimer's Back to the Seventies Night. All the camp counselors had paired up to perform hits from the Disco era and Bill had chosen ABBA for him and BeeBee. She had protested at first, but after the first few days of practicing their lip synced medley, neither could get the tunes out of their heads. What started out as an inside joke became their secret language. On charter cruises to Greek Isles, the street musicians would play songs like "Andante, Andante" or "Super Trouper" and every time he thought of her.

He hummed the first two bars of "Mamma Mia" and instantly felt like a gigantic chump. Like she'd remember it after all this time.

Her responding whistle, as clear and tuneful

as always, rang out. He ventured another step closer to the flailing female pile-up on the blue corduroy couch.

As he drew closer, BeeBee popped to sitting upright with her legs held down by a carbon copy of the girl clawing at her arms, and Bill jumped backward in shock.

She looked like an alien creature from outer space. Her face was covered in something thick and green except for small metallic patches affixed beneath her eyes that, large to begin with, were now the size of demitasse cups. Her hair was wet and plastered to her head were bits of aluminum foil.

"Bill," she gasped. "Thank goodness you're here. Someone has to save me from the Beauty Inquisitorial Squad over here."

The girl with the glasses who was restraining BeeBee's legs rolled her eyes. "It's a skin-care regimen, not an interrogation. If you would just hold still, this would be over so much faster."

"My feet are extremely ticklish and you know it," BeeBee groaned. She jerked her right foot free of the girl's hands. "Here. Grab it and drag me out of here."

"This was your idea," the girl at BeeBee's head pointed out. "You were the one who said you'd do whatever it took to win the pageant and get the money for Orlando."

"Orlando?" Bill snickered.

"Listen, Man Who Named His Knife Percival." BeeBee glared at him. Inhaling deeply, she pressed her palms down flat on the pillow over her lap. "Okay. Thinking about Orlando helps me calm dow—WHAT DID YOU DO TO MY FINGERS?" she shrieked as she held her hands up in front of her eyes.

"We buffed them with this electronic nail-care thingy Jackie got off the internet," the girl said with a shrug. "You can't have acrylics doing farm work so this is the best way to make them nice and smooth."

"But what's with all this dust?" She shook out the pillow, and what looked like a pile of sawdust flew into the air. "It looks like you shaved off my fingerprints." She threw the pillow across the room and looked wild-eyed back at him. "It's a setup, Bill. They're going to do crimes and make me the fall guy." She pointed at the girl with glasses. "You're going to rob Mr. Stevenson's jewelry store, aren't you?"

"Hold on." Bill crossed his arms. "I thought I was here to help BeeBee create a dairy-themed recipe for the pageant. How is she supposed to cook like this?"

"Look at the new guy coming in hot," the twin without glasses said, wrinkling her nose.

"It's a beauty pageant." The other girl stood

and abandoned her post by BeeBee's ankles. There were small pink wedges between each of BeeBee's toes, so there seemed little danger of her actually making a break for it. "Yeah, it's for the Queen of the Dairy Farmers, but she still has to look good. It took us half the morning just to get the layers of dirt off her face so we can start the skin-care regimen, and we have to leave the deep-conditioning treatment in her hair at least another half hour to get out years' worth of tangles from sleeping with her hair in braids. Once we get her looking more like a beauty queen and less like Bunga the Cave Girl, then you can talk recipes, mmm-kay, Billiam?"

BeeBee snorted. "Billiam. I'm using that."

A slender woman stood up from a computer in the corner, taking a stack of papers from the printer and shuffling them neatly on one end. She walked gracefully toward them and shook her head. "Kit, Lou. Stand down. He's on Team BccBcc." She smiled graciously and said in a soft voice, "I'm Jackie. It's really nice of you to help. Why don't we all calm down and go over exactly what we need to do in the next five weeks for BeeBcc to win this pageant?"

He vaguely remembered BeeBee talking about the twins, Kit and Lou, as little girls that summer. Now they each looked like high school seniors, and it hit him how much could really change in seven years. The blonde woman he knew was the oldest sister because she had picked BeeBee up on the last day, the day Bee-Bee had punched him in the arm and said the breeziest of goodbyes. The shine of leftover tears in her eyes, however, had told a different story.

Beebee swung her legs down off the end of the couch and patted the seat next to her. "You can sit here, Billiam the Conqueror," she said with a snicker.

He strode over and sank into the soft couch. He grinned at BeeBee. "William the Conqueror made some extensive sea voyages. I'll take it."

She sniffed and gave him a small smile. Fault lines cracked in the clay-like mask. "I'm glad you're here," she whispered, leaning in. "I need someone on my side."

"Always," he whispered back, holding her gaze for longer than he should have, yet unable to tear himself away from those eyes.

Jackie set the papers down on her lap, picked the top one off the stack and began to read. "'Beatrice Elizabeth Long,'" she read out loud.

"Now you know why I go by BeeBee," she muttered to him under her breath.

"'Your application for the New York Queen of the Dairy Pageant has been accepted,'" she continued. "'We are looking forward to seeing you represent your home dairy farm at the Hudson

Valley Public Television Studios on the weekend of June twentieth and twenty-first of this year.'"

"Television?" BeeBee groaned. "I didn't know this was going to be on TV."

"Now you get why the beauty part comes first?" Kit said as she flipped the pages of a notebook full of sketches of evening gowns. "She's got to be camera ready in five weeks, and I'm pretty sure that at least some of what I combed out of her head this morning was buffalo hair."

"If I may." Jackie pointed at the paper in her hand. "'Each contestant must prepare a creative presentation that will help the judges get to know who they are and why they should represent the state as a Queen of the Dairy, a model of goodwill, grace and wholesome loveliness.'"

"Yikes," Lou whispered. She had slid into a split and lifted her face off the floor to prop her chin in her hands.

"'The next stage of the pageant consists of the contestant preparing their special dairy-centered recipe in the studio's on-set kitchens,'" Jackie read before looking up. "Oh, that's right. This is where they film that competition Dad likes to watch—*Ready, Set, Cook.*"

Bill looked over and saw the light in Bee-Bee's eyes dimming more as her sister read. He nudged her with his elbow. "Don't sweat it. I'm going to come up with a recipe so amazing they're going to crown you Empress for Life and end the pageant after this year."

"BeeBee the Great does have a nice ring to it," she joked. The set to her chin softened a little.

"'On the second day, the contestants will show off their grace and poise in formal wear. During that time, they will answer an interview question that demonstrates their passion and commitment to the animals under their care and the high quality of dairy products they provide for their community.'"

"Now that I can do," BeeBee said confidently.

"Yeah, but can you do it in heels?" Lou asked.

"Heels?" BeeBee asked, horrified. "No one said anything about heels. I'm five-ten. I've never worn heels in my life."

"You have to," Kit said emphatically. "You'll never win if you clomp across the stage in flats. Plus, you've got dynamite legs. It's about time you showed them off."

"Thanks, Kitty Cat," BeeBee said gratefully to her sister.

Bill swallowed hard at the memory of those long legs emerging from the lake. That had been the first time he had seen BeeBee, rising from the water like a majestic mermaid with her long braid coming undone over her shoulder. It had been the first time in his life he had understood what it meant to be struck breathless.

"Okay, so let's divvy up our tasks," Jackie said. "Kit, you're our creative mastermind. How would you feel about helping BeeBee with the Get to Know You presentation?"

"On it," she replied with a point of a finger gun.

"Bill, you're on recipe duty," she said with a slight inclination of her head toward him. "It has to be focused around dairy, obviously, but that shouldn't be too difficult. Also, keep in mind that our BeeBee is, how do we say this nicely, culinarily challenged?"

From the piano keyboard in the corner, three high-pitched notes sounded followed by a prolonged press of the highest of high Cs. Even with her restricted facial movements, BeeBee managed a scowl at Lou who had crept to the keyboard and made what sounded like a smoke-detector sound.

"I've got a couple recipes already in mind that are elevated versions of classic homestyle dishes," he said, pulling out his phone. "They look fancy, but they're surprisingly easy to make. I was thinking we could start with a simple croque monsieur."

"You sound like the chef from *The Little Mermaid*," BeeBee said. "English, Billerina. English."

"It's a grilled ham-and-cheese sandwich," Bill said with a wry lift of his eyebrow. "But with really good cheese and maybe pancetta instead of ham. With some fruity notes, like a plum jam."

BeeBee put her hand over her stomach. "Oh my gosh, I'm starving," she said, standing and gesturing at her sisters. "They didn't give me time to eat breakfast this morning. They just ambushed me with blow dryers and face goop the second I woke up." She patted her face with one finger. "This actually smells really good. I wonder if it's edible."

Uh-oh. BeeBee was worse than useless when she was hungry. Back in camp, he used to keep an emergency bag of trail mix in his backpack just for her. Meeting her sister's eyes, he could tell they recognized the sign of a hunger spiral too. It started with silliness like poking at her face mask, but would very rapidly devolve into fiery rage if they didn't get food in her now.

"Why don't we let New Guy go first?" Lou offered as she slunk along the back of the room toward the door. "I've got to run in to the studio for a few hours this morning to rehearse my solo for the spring recital anyway. BeeBee, just make sure you wait another ten minutes before you wash your mask off, okay?"

BeeBee looked at her watch and sighed. "Fine. I can probably squeeze some yogurt from a tube in my mouth without breaking the mask." She looked down at Bill and jerked her head to the kitchen. "This way, spatula wench."

He followed her, and as he walked by, Jackie whispered to Kit, "Well, that sounded queen-like at least."

After three croque monsieurs blackened to something resembling charcoal briquets, Bill recommended they look outside the griddle for her recipe. He made a mental note to comb through his creamy gazpacho cookbook back at Lucas's. As he watched her argue with Kit about why slam poetry was decidedly not an option for her Get to Know You segment, he heard the defeat and frustration in her voice. From out the window, he saw the water buffaloes loping back toward the barn. They were definitely different from the cows with long shaggy hair and powerful haunches much wider than a cow's.

Jackie stopped by the window next to him. "BeeBee and her buffaloes," she said with loving amusement.

He glanced back at BeeBee sitting at the kitchen table, gesticulating wildly at Kit. "Is it really worth all this?" Bill asked quietly, jerking a shoulder back at the kitchen with his hands in his pockets. "Couldn't she just find another buffalo sire from somewhere local? Wouldn't that be cheaper?"

"Sure," Jackie said. "But something tells me

that you know BeeBee very well," she said, meaningfully putting emphasis on the last two words.
"Once she latches on to something—or someone—" she added, a hardened glint of warning in
her silvery voice. "She holds on with everything
she's got. At least the attachment to her water
buffaloes is healthy for her. She knows they'll
never leave her."

"Did I hear you guys talking about my buffaloes?" BeeBee called from the table. "Are my
babies back?"

"They're on their way over to the barn now,"
Jackie answered. "Why don't you and Bill take
a little break and go check on them? I think Dad
left some treats for them by the gate when he
was out cutting the grass. We'll get back to picking out your outfits when Lou gets back."

Bill wasn't sure she even heard the last part
because she had already flown out of the kitchen,
grabbed him by the hand and pulled him out of
the door.

She let go as she clattered down the steps ahead
of him, and he laughed as he jogged to catch
up. "Slow down," he huffed. "I still have my sea
legs."

"Spoiled chef." She smirked and tossed her
braid over her shoulder.

"Beauty queen," he said when he reached her

side and swiped a patch of green left on the side of her jawline.

She rounded the curve of the driveway and slowed to a walk, narrowing her eyes at him. "I am not. I'm just faking it for a good cause." Stepping up onto the first rung of the wooden gate, she nodded her head at the animals milling happily in the muddy grassless corral in front of them. "I'm doing it for them."

The rapturous note in her voice would have made him envious if she had been looking at anything except two large beasts with faces only a mother could love. They weren't quite as shaggy as he had imagined, with hair longer and thicker on the tops of their heads and shoulders that thinned around their haunches. The snouts were longer than a cow's and wide at the end, almost like a dog's muzzle. Their tails swished happily back and forth, swatting any unsuspecting fly that dared wander too close. When BeeBee made a small clucking noise with her tongue, one of them lifted its chin and snorted loudly. The other followed suit, and they ambled gracelessly toward the gate when she reached into the bucket next to the padlocked entry.

"I have a yummy treat for you, ladies," she crooned. Withdrawing a handful of lettuce from the bucket, she held it out and the buffalo drew near enough for Bill to see the dark striations on its horns.

"The females have horns?" he asked.

She nodded. "Isn't that neat? Just another thing I love about them."

He watched her feed the other buffalo. There was something strangely relaxing about the satisfied sounds of them eating, a happy combination of chomping and snuffling. The way their horns curved upward, they almost looked like they were literally smiling from ear to ear. He hopped down off the gate and leaned back against it, crossing his arms. "I like the way you're making this place your own."

She stepped down too, facing him with one elbow resting on the fence post. "Well, my mom had a bad fall two—no, three years ago. We'd had a really bad winter, and she slipped on the ice in town while she was shoveling Mrs. Van Ressler's front walk. They had to do surgery on her hip, and it left a leg length discrepancy, which is why she still has to use the cane."

"That's terrible."

"She says the worst part about it is now everyone in town can hear her coming and hide," BeeBee said with a laugh. "Which is only partially true. Everyone in town loves her—they just don't love being wrangled into serving on one of her local planning committees or volunteer organizations."

"She should run for mayor," Bill suggested, and BeeBee mock gasped in horror.

"Please don't tell her that." She shook her head. "Anyway, between her rehabilitation and Dad's teaching schedule, I took over managing the farm. And of course, my sisters help too, when they can," she added with a slightly defensive edge to her voice.

The breeze stirred, ruffling the grass in the field behind the house like ocean waves. A longing for the smell of seawater and the excited feeling he got when he stepped onto a boat struck him. Then he looked over at BeeBee, and the feeling grew quieter.

"I know what you mean," he said. "My parents tried to get me to go to a traditional four-year school, but I already knew what I wanted to do. The idea of sitting inside in a classroom for years on end made my skin crawl."

"Hard same," BeeBee agreed. "Jackie applied for this program at the New School. She would have to spend the whole summer inside in front of a computer." She shuddered. "Sounds awful to me, but as long as she's happy."

"Are you happy?" he asked, reaching up and pulling his bandanna off before scrubbing his hand through his hair. "Lucas said you broke up with the guy you'd been seeing."

She wrinkled her long nose at him. "Do you really want to hear about this kind of thing?"

He shrugged. "I thought we were friends. Friends talk about their relationships, right?"

"We haven't seen each other in seven years," she said, pushing off the fence with her arm and putting both hands on the small of her back. "Usually friendships involve people keeping in touch and, you know, knowing what continent the other friend is currently on." BeeBee shook her head. "We're not friends, Bill."

The bald delivery of frank truths was so classically BeeBee. She had never been the type to sugarcoat things or tell people what they wanted to hear. It was a great quality, one he had always appreciated about her. But this truth hurt. Mainly because he realized all at once how much he very much wanted to be one of the lucky people in her orbit.

"But," she continued, the word trailing on the end of her speech like a delicious string of melted cheese pulling two sandwich halves together, "I'd like it if we could be. Friends, that is."

It was exactly what he had hoped to hear.

So why did the prospect leave him feeling disappointed?

CHAPTER FIVE

WHEN JACKIE SIGHED for the fifth time in half an hour, BeeBee knew something was wrong.

Nobody sighed that often, not even in Jackie's beloved romance novels.

"Okay, out with it," BeeBee said to her sister from the passenger seat. "What's the matter?"

"I don't know what you're talking about," Jackie protested. "Why would something be the matter?"

"You're breathing in a way that says there's something wrong but you don't want to say anything that might upset me right before the pageant seminar," BeeBee said as she chcckcd the GPS on her phone. They were still another thirty minutes away from the Hudson Valley. If she didn't get the truth out of Jackie soon, the truck would run out of oxygen.

Jackie kept her eyes on the road and gave a little smile. "You sound just like you did when we took road trips as kids," she teased. "You gonna call Mom and tell on me for breathing on you?"

"Don't change the subject, Jacqueline," Bee-Bee lobbed her full name for effect.

"It's just..." Jackie tightened her fingers around the steering wheel before shooting a sideways glance at BeeBee. "Are you sure that's what you wanted to wear today?"

"That's what you're hyperventilating over? My clothes?"

BeeBee looked down at her clean dark blue jeans that didn't have a single hole in them, her plum-colored button-down shirt and the clean fingernails that were still unnervingly shiny. Although the twins had been right about the skin-care stuff. Within days of using that special clarifying wash and lotion that smelled like oranges, the patches of dry skin on her cheeks had completely cleared up. Who knew that using a different soap for your face than the one for your body could make such a difference?

"I just don't want you to feel out of place if the other contestants are wearing, you know, skirts or dresses, that's all," Jackie said defensively.

For crying out loud, she had even put on their grandma's silver cuff bracelet. Okay, it was the one that said she was allergic to penicillin, but it was jewelry nonetheless. She was wearing purple and accessories. How much more girly could she get?

BeeBee rested her head back against the seat.

"The information sheet said this was an 'informal meet and greet,'" she said with an emphasis on the word *informal*. "You don't put *informal* on an invitation to a bunch of dairy farmers and expect them to show up in anything other than jeans and boots. Besides, it's not like I'm doing anything today. I'm just gonna go, listen to the former queens talk about how to smile and wave at the same time, and swap dairy shop talk with some other farmers." Her chest lifted. "Ooh, I hope there's some good snacks there. I'm starving."

"The phrase loses its hyperbolic value when you use it all the time," Jackie pointed out.

BeeBee stretched her arm out and booped her sister on the nose. "I like when you use your fancy writer words," she said with a laugh as Jackie swatted her hand away. "Thanks for driving, by the way."

"I'm happy to help," Jackie said. "Since my critique partner lives in Hudson Valley, it was a good excuse for us to get coffee and commiserate over how neither of us have heard back from the New School Scholar-in-Residence program yet."

"I'm sure you'll get it," BeeBee said. "You're an amazing writer. Although you should write more books with animals in them. People love books about animals, like the James Herriot books. Now those are classics."

Jackie shook her head. "I love those too. But they aren't romances."

BeeBee lifted a shoulder in a shrug. "Love is love, Jackie. And I love my buffaloes more than anything."

Jackie pulled up in front of the brick building that served as the home for the Hudson Valley Public Television station. She turned off the truck and folded her hands in her lap, fiddling anxiously with the pearl ring on her right hand. "Are you sure I can't interest you in some lip gloss? Or maybe we could put your hair down. I think I have a cute barrette in my purse," she said, reaching for her bag on the seat between them.

BeeBee unhooked her seat belt and opened the passenger-side door. "Oh, look at the time. I had better get in there."

"You're fifteen minutes early," Jackie looked up from her digging to call after her. "At least let me put a breath mint in your pocket."

Backing away from the truck at a rapid clip, BeeBee cupped one hand by her ear. "What? I can't hear you. You're too far away, it's like you're in Siberia," she yelled back, waving her other hand. "See you in a few hours, love you, *byyyyyyyye*—oof." Stumbling over her feet, she landed on her backside and popped back to her feet, craning her head to make sure Jackie had already driven away before she had fallen. Whew, the truck had already pulled forward.

"Are you okay?" A blond head popped up in front of BeeBee, and she jumped back.

"Yeah, I'm fine." BeeBee hadn't heard the woman approach. Who walked that quietly? A ninja, that was who. It was never a good idea to trust a ninja, even if the ninja did look exactly like one of the porcelain dolls Mrs. Van Ressler kept in the honeymoon suite at the B&B.

"I saw you fall and thought, *Gosh, that looked like it must have hurt*," the woman said with her hands on her hips. "So, I figured I'd come check and make sure you're okay. I'm Emma." She stuck out one hand, and BeeBee shook it warily.

"I'm BeeBee," she said. "Nice to meet you. And I really am fine. I've fallen on my rear end so many times they asked me to sign a print of it in concrete in front of the local movie theater."

The woman giggled. "You're funny." Her wide blue eyes lit up. "Oh, is that your creative introduction? Do you do some sort of stand-up routine?"

"Um…" BeeBee wasn't sure how much she was supposed to tell the women who were technically her competition. "Not exactly. Wow, that is a lot of sparkle you've got going on. I feel like you should have an armed guard following you around with that much bling."

Emma wore giant sparkly earrings in the shape of a yellow flower, a matching ring and necklace. The dress she wore was white but with yellow sunflowers patterned all over it. Her high heels were the same bright yellow, and BeeBee watched in awe as Emma glided toward the front door without so much as a tiny stumble in them.

Holding open the door for BeeBee, Emma put one hand over her chest and let out another musical giggle. "So. Funny. Come on, BeeBee. I'll introduce you to everyone else."

They walked into the two-story brick building with the large white satellite on top. While it looked official and bland from the outside, the inside was surprisingly homey. There was a large lobby with several high tables, couches strewn with folksy throw pillows and bucolic paintings of the Finger Lakes hung on the walls. The sound of girlish chatter filled the air, but even more importantly, BeeBee caught the smell of fresh coffee. But before she could follow her nose, Emma took her elbow with a small glittering hand and pulled her to a couch in the opposite direction.

"Everyone, this is BeeBee," she announced to the three women sitting with their legs demurely crossed. "BeeBee, this is Haven, Rebecca and Brittany."

Now BeeBee knew exactly what it must feel

like to stare directly into a rainbow. Each of the women wore pastel dresses or skirt-suit-combo thingies with shiny shoes and purses that matched the hues they wore. The redhead in the pale green dress whose name tag read *Haven* sprang to her feet and smiled at BeeBee.

"Hi, BeeBee," she said warmly. "What dairy are you from?"

"Crystal Hill Dairy in the Mohawk River Valley," she answered.

The one in the pink jacket and skirt with black hair that fell in a smooth sheet over her shoulders uncoiled her legs in long brown tights that matched her skin color perfectly. She stood gracefully. "I'm Rebecca, from Glendale Farms in Corning," she said smoothly. "Let me get you a name tag, hon. Be back in a twinkle."

The third woman, who BeeBee assumed through process of elimination was the one they called Brittany, stood and without smiling or talking, simply nodded.

Haven leaned in toward BeeBee and whispered loudly, "Brittany had her jaw wired shut a few months ago. That's why she doesn't say very much." Haven nodded at Brittany. "Don't you worry about it, sweetie. I already talked to the cook about putting your lunch order through the blender for you. We dairy gals gotta stick together."

"Poor thing," BeeBee said. "She isn't doing this to lose weight for the pageant or anything like that, is she?"

Brittany shook with silent laughter, and Haven waved her hand. "No, nothing like that. She was hand milking a cow at an elementary school demonstration, and there was a fire drill."

Cringing, BeeBee mouthed *Yikes* apologetically at Brittany, who shrugged matter-of-factly.

"BeeBee and I were just talking about our creative Get to Know You presentations," Emma said just as Rebecca returned bearing a white name-tag sticker and a pen.

"I got you purple to match your shirt," Rebecca whispered. "Is purple your signature color? It looks great with your hair and eye color."

"My signature color?" What in the world was that? BeeBee scribbled her name on the sticker and peeled the back away before slapping it onto her chest. "Not really, although I guess it helps when I've spilled grape jelly from my PB-and-J sandwiches."

All three women laughed again, even though BeeBee hadn't actually been joking that time. A smile perked at the corner of her lips. This was kind of nice. People in town didn't laugh nearly this hard at her jokes even when she made them on purpose.

"For my presentation, I'm showing a scrapbook of the history of our farm," Haven said. "My great-grandma started it with my grandpa's GI Bill from World War Two. The local paper did a story on how one of her cows got into her Victory garden, and it got picked up by the *New York Times* as a human-interest piece. The story kind of put our little town on the map, so every year our town does a little festival honoring our veterans, and they even do a little skit reenacting the Rampage of Miss Hilda." She let out a little contented sigh. "Anyway, that's how our farm got the contract to be the dairy supplier for the commissary at the local army depot. We've been so busy, I'm really hoping to win so we can hire some more folks."

"Wow," BeeBee said. "Your town does a whole festival about your farm? That's really cool." She turned to Rebecca. "What's it like in Glendale? Do they do anything special to celebrate your farm?"

"Oh, no," Rebecca wrinkled her nose and shook her head, her shoulders bouncing her curls up closer to her ears. "We're a really small farm, so our production isn't close to anything like what Haven's does."

"You are way too modest," Emma's high-pitched voice interjected. "Rebecca is like a rock star in her town."

"I wouldn't say *rock star*," Rebecca hedged. "I mean, they did give me a key to the city, but that was more symbolic than anything else."

"What did they give you the key for?" Bee-Bee asked.

"Oh, it's not that big of a deal," Rebecca said. "It was just that there was this big ice storm a few years back and one of the generators in the local hospital failed. My sister had been in the NICU there, so I knew they would be worried about being able to keep the formula and breast milk cold, and since we use dry ice to ship the dairy products, I just drove some out to them."

"She drove back and forth all night in the storm to make sure they had enough dry ice," Emma squeaked. "She was on *Good Morning America*!"

BeeBee swallowed, feeling like it was a shipment of dry ice she had just inhaled. "That's uh, that's gonna be a tough story to beat, huh, Brittany?"

She looked over at Brittany, who once again shrugged as though unimpressed. Jeepers, what was Brittany's story? She'd probably injured her jaw saving a bus full of children from the stampeding cow.

Faking it was starting to seem a lot harder than learning how to walk in high heels.

By the time they were called into the main

studio where the pageant would take place, Bee-Bee was still starving. The pastries were on the other side of the room, and she had been too afraid of running into a contestant who'd won the Nobel Prize for Farming to risk heading over there. Even worse, she had been forced to concede that Jackie had been right. No one else, not a single person, was wearing jeans.

Right as she was sitting down in a creaky folding chair, two beautiful women walked onto the stage. No, not walked—floated. They floated onto the stage with beaming white smiles and graceful hands waving as though they were actually royalty. Both women wore dresses that came to right above their knees, and on top of their perfectly shiny heads of hair sat glittering tiaras.

BeeBee leaned over to Emma and whispered, "Does the winner have to wear the crown everywhere she goes?"

"They don't have to," Emma whispered back. "But who wouldn't want to wear a sparkly tiara all the time?"

"Um." BeeBee was sure there were other people besides her for whom that would be a living nightmare. "A jewelry thief hiding from the law?"

Emma covered her mouth with her hand, trembling with laughter. "So, so funny."

One of the women onstage stepped up to the

microphone in the center and plucked it expertly from the stand. She took a step back, weaving the cord through her long, delicate fingers. "Good morning, ladies. I'd like to welcome each and every one of you to the New York State Dairy Royalty Pageant Participant Seminar."

"Bet she couldn't say that five times fast," BeeBee muttered.

"I'm Darby Sullivan, the reigning Queen of the Dairy. To my right is our reigning princess, Liana Ortiz." The younger woman with raven hair and bright red lipstick nodded and placed her hand over her heart at the mention, while the older woman—whoops, Her Majesty—continued. "Today we're going to talk a little bit about what this pageant really means, what you can expect in terms of preparation and the actual pageant itself—as well as what the lucky winner has to look forward to the moment she accepts the crown."

BeeBee's shoulders relaxed with a deep breath. That was better. Sure, the other contestants were town heroes and wunderkinds and local legacies. But she had something they didn't. She needed this more than they did. This was her chance to show her own town that she could contribute something just as valuable as the other women had to their own communities. Wasn't the drive and the hunger to prove herself enough to tip the scales in her favor just a little bit?

Speaking of hunger…

BeeBee's stomach growled loudly enough that the girl sitting in front of her actually turned her head. Her cheeks burning, BeeBee nodded at the stage. "Show some respect. Your queen is speaking."

The woman's head whipped back around so fast BeeBee actually heard her neck crack.

After talking about the pageant's history and the New York Dairy Farmers Association that sponsored it, Darby—Queen Darby—finally got to the useful information.

"Now, even though I know we've all been watching this pageant on our television screens since we were little girls making crowns out of Mama's aluminum foil—"

Oh, this was great. Trapped in a room full of people who wore tinfoil hats. Nothing at all could go wrong there.

"I'm going to go over how all of this works anyway and let you ladies in on some secret tips we picked up on our own pageant journeys," Queen Darby said with a knowing wink to Princess Liana. "Then Liana is going to select a few of you out of the audience to be our models as we show you some dos and don'ts of the interview-and-evening-gown portion. Finally, we'll all move to the kitchen for a little demonstration of the equipment. To end the day on a sweet note, I've made everyone my nana's famous mini cheese-cakes using the recipe that is my contribution to the *Queens of Dairy Winner's Circle Cookbook*, available online and in local independent book-stores throughout the region. Who's ready to get started?"

Every single hand shot up except BeeBee's, whose hands were both covering her ears to barricade them against the chorus of loud "woooo-hoooos" emanating from the room.

The first part wasn't so bad. In fact, it was both helpful and interesting to see examples of what some of the other contestants had done for their creative introduction presentations. She wished Jackie had been there to see the video of the contestant who'd done a puppet-show re-enacting scenes from *Pride and Prejudice* but with cow puppets. Since BeeBee still didn't have a clue what she was going to do beyond stepping onstage and saying *Hi, I'm BeeBee Long of Crystal Hill Dairy Farm*, it was good to see that there was no limit to what she could actually do. The bad thing was there was no limit. Thank goodness she came from a family of creative geniuses. Surely between her sisters, one of them could come up with something at least as good as *Hamilcow: An American Moo-sical*.

"So long story short, ladies, Vaseline is an absolute must," Liana was saying, so apparently BeeBee had dozed off and missed quite a bit because the last thing she had heard was Liana listing her recipe for a special tea that reduced mucus production during speeches. Unless Vaseline was one of the ingredients? They had started off by demonstrating strategic uses of Scotch tape on various body parts. Anything seemed possible in the upside-down world of beauty pageants.

"Now I bet you all are getting pretty sick of hearing us jibber jabber on and on," Darby said, making a little mouth out of her hand. With her bright red nails, even the fake mouth hand appeared to have camera-ready lipstick. "So, Liana is going to call out some seat numbers, and those ladies will come up to the stage and do a little dry run of the interview portion."

BeeBee checked the armrest of her seat. "Don't say forty-nine, please don't say forty-nine," she pleaded silently.

"Twelve, twenty-five, eight and forty-nine," Liana called out.

Dang it, Liana. BeeBee inhaled sharply and flattened her mouth into a thin, closed-lip smile to keep from groaning. Just for that she definitely wasn't going to try that Vaseline tea. Pushing to a stand, she stretched her fake smile tighter as she scooched past Emma's two thumbs up and Brittany's solemn nod of either support or sympathy—it was really hard to tell.

As she walked down the aisle to the guillotine—erm, stage—BeeBee felt every eye looking her up and down, judging her overly casual attire. She was used to standing out; after all, she had already shot up to five-eight by the time she'd been in sixth grade. Even in her family there was no point in trying to blend. Her sisters all possessed a charm that drew people to them. BeeBee could wrangle a herd of cows and charm even the most recalcitrant water buffalo away from a mid-afternoon wallow, but people were a different story. Dread filled her stomach as she trudged the steps behind the other three women who had ascended with much greater speed and enthusiasm.

"Hello, ladies," Queen Darby said with an inclination of her glittering crown. "Now, I don't want anyone to get nervous here. This is just practice. We're going to walk you through each step of the process so when it's time for the real thing, you're going to nail it."

Her Majesty strolled past the line of women, nodding and smiling at each of them, although BeeBee could have sworn both her smile and steps faltered when Darby got to her.

"Let's start with you." Darby extended her hand to BeeBee, who supposed it was better to get the torture over with rather than stand there and wait in nauseous anticipation. She squinted at BeeBee's name tag. "Barbie. Oh, that is adorable. Everyone give a big round of applause for Barbie."

She was asleep. That had to be it. Because BeeBee had had this exact nightmare before. She looked down. Nope, clothes were still on. BeeBee sighed and stepped forward. Just a few hours of dairy-princess boot camp and she would be back at her farm. She could do this. For Orlando.

"Hi. It's, uh, BeeBee, actually," she said into the microphone. Was that her voice? It sounded so strange amplified like that.

"Oh, I'm so sorry," Queen Darby said, covering her heart with one hand. "Well, that's even cuter. BeeBee, why don't you tell us where you're from?"

"I'm—wow, that's echoey—I'm from Crystal Hill Dairy Farm," she said, glancing back at the others for confirmation that she was doing this right because it sounded so terribly wrong. They smiled encouragingly, but she was pretty sure all of the other women had been smiling nonstop since arrival.

"What a lovely name for a town," Darby said. Her voice didn't sound echoey and weird when she spoke into the microphone. What kind of sorcery was that? "Crystal Hill. Of course, you know we love anything with crystals, right, ladies?" She touched her crown, and the audience laughed as if it was opening night at the Apollo.

"Erm, ha ha, right." BeeBee pretended to laugh. "Yes, um, I love all that shiny stuff, like, um, glitter and—and silver and, um, stainless-steel appliances," she stammered. The perma-smiles didn't waver, so BeeBee assumed they bought the act. *Crushed it.*

"So here's what we're going to do," Queen Darby said as Princess Liana emerged from behind the stage curtains with a small stool.

BeeBee's first thought was they were going to bring out a heifer for a milking demonstration, and her heart leapt. The hope and joy disappeared almost as quickly as they had arrived when Queen Darby lowered the microphone and placed it in front of the stool.

"I'm going to have you enter from the wings," she continued, gesturing like a model at a car show toward the curtains to BeeBee's left. "Walk across the front of the stage, stop, pivot and pose at the center, then come back here and sit. I'll ask you some sample questions that have been used during interviews in past pageants. Don't worry though," she added conspiratorially. "This is just for funsies. No one's judging you today."

"You wanna bet?" BeeBee muttered to herself

as she made for the curtains. Okay, what was she supposed to do again? Walk. She remembered that part. Then there was something she was supposed to do at the center of the stage. Curtsy? Salute? High kick? Oh, this was bad. This was very, very bad.

"All right, ladies and gentlemen," Queen Darby called out to the audience. "Our next contestant is BeeBee from Crystal Hill Dairy Farm."

The audience, as well as the other women onstage, applauded loudly.

"That's not going to last," BeeBee whispered to herself, taking a deep breath and striding onstage with her chin up high. There was an X taped to the center of the stage, so BeeBee went straight for where it marked the spot and prayed for a treasure chest to fall onto her head and kill her instantly. When she got to the spot, she tried desperately to remember what the queen had commanded her to do and came up completely blank. She tossed a helpless look over her shoulder at the line of women to her left. One of them made a little swirling motion with her finger. Turn? Twirling did seem like the kind of thing this crowd did on the regular.

Fortunately, she had sat through years of Lindsay's dance recitals—and had actually stayed awake through some of them. Sifting through her memories of fluffy tutus and bedazzled tap dancers, BeeBee put one foot behind her, then picked it up and spun on the front foot with her arms clutched to her chest. To her complete amazement, she did not fall onto her rear end and landed with both feet on the ground. Triumphantly, BeeBee turned her head to look at the queen. Her mouth hung open, clearly as impressed with BeeBee as BeeBee was with herself. Looking back at the audience, BeeBee waited for another round of clapping or perhaps another "wooo" or two.

Silence. There weren't even crickets chirping. Not a single cough drop unwrapped.

Finally, Queen Darby spoke.

"That was…something," she said with a long pause before the last word.

BeeBee had been called many things, mostly by her sisters and her cousin Lucas and almost always out of gentle teasing. But the inference from Darby's pause made it clear that "something" was not good.

Queen Darby turned to the audience. "Now BeeBee has chosen to put some flair on the turn, which is just fabulous," she said unconvincingly. "But really all the judges need is a simple pivot so they can see your posture and the back of your gown." She put one foot behind the other and rotated slowly and gracefully like there was a lazy Susan hidden underneath the stage.

Oh. Pivot. That was what she had wanted. Bee-Bee's face flushed so hot she was surprised—and more than a little disappointed—that the sprinkler system didn't turn on.

"Oh, pivot, yeah, yeah, sure," BeeBee said with a toss of her braid. "I can do that. No problem. Just thought I'd, you know, mix things up a little. But no problem—pivot."

"And don't forget to pose at the end," Princess Liana chimed in.

"Pose, right," BeeBee nodded. "Um, okay, here goes…my pose." Why was she rhyming? Because this was a nightmare and the only thing scarier than a room full of people staring at her was it turning into a Broadway-style musical, of course. A pose was like the way people stood for pictures or if they were being carved into statues, like George Washington crossing the Delaware. Shuffling her feet apart and bending one knee, BeeBee put her hands on her hips and looked up to the lights behind the seating as if scanning the horizon valiantly for British troops. Pageant people were all about the patriotism thing, right?

"Oh my," Queen Darby whispered. She took little mincing steps and put her hands on Bee-Bee's arms. "All right, let's relax the arms down, pull your feet together…there you go."

With Darby's prodding, BeeBee now felt like

she was posing for Dracula's coffin maker. "Um, like this?" She kept her head forward and spoke out of the corner of her mouth because if she moved any more, she would fall over like an off-balance mummy.

"Not...quite," Darby said. She proceeded to adjust BeeBee's arms and legs as if she were an actual Barbie doll, placing a hand on BeeBee's hip and pushing at the back of one of BeeBee's legs until her knee popped forward awkwardly. Finally, she stood on her toes and tipped Bee-Bee's head slightly to one side. Darby took a cautious step back, holding her hands in front of her as if expecting BeeBee to tip over at any moment. It was not out of the realm of possibility. "There—that's, uh, better."

BeeBee couldn't answer. This pose was more uncomfortable than any position she had ever held, and she had once milked a heifer so fearful that she had needed to pet the creature on the head with one hand, stroke its hindquarters gently with one foot and use the other foot to brace herself on the stool while she'd milked it with one hand. This was more precarious than that, and she wouldn't even be rewarded with a full pail of fresh milk at the end. She did manage to grit her teeth and stretch her mouth into a smile and let out a quick, "Mmm-hmm."

"Let's move on to the interview questions,

shall we?" Queen Darby said, nodding her crown at the stool behind them.

Unclenching herself from the Pose, BeeBee at last exhaled and walked back to the stool, dropping herself onto it with relief. Plopping her feet widely in front of her, BeeBee leaned her elbows on her knees and looked up at Queen Darby. "I'm ready, Your Highness. First question—fire away."

"Erm." Queen Darby tapped a long, glittery fingernail on her lips. "Yes, well, first let's try that one more time. And remember, you're going to be sitting in a long evening gown. So stand up."

BeeBee stood, giving the glowing red exit sign at the back of the auditorium a pointed stare. If she started running now, she could make it to Crystal Hill by supper time.

"Now try sitting slowly, with your feet and knees tight as if they've been tied together," Queen Darby said.

Okay, she had definitely read BeeBee's mind. So much for her escape plan. Concentrating on the instructions, BeeBee locked her legs together and lowered herself slowly onto the stool. Shooting a questioning look at Queen Darby, she allowed herself to breathe when Her Majesty gave her a satisfactory nod.

"All right, BeeBee." Darby read from a notecard. "First question. What would you say is your dairy farm's greatest contribution to your community?"

"Oh, wow, just diving right into the big stuff, huh?" BeeBee glanced out at the audience to find Haven and Emma giving her encouraging nods. "Our, uh, greatest contribution. Well, we supply milk to the local school. And let's see, what else?" They would make a contribution once she had the only full-scale working water-buffalo dairy farm in the state. But that probably wasn't going to help her if the judges thought that was the only reason she was here. She shrugged helplessly.

Queen Darby took pity on her. "That's all right. Everyone gets flustered in the hot seat once in a while. Let's try an easy one, okay?" She flipped through two more note cards before settling on another one. "Here we go. Describe your perfect day on the farm."

BeeBee practically collapsed in on herself with relief. This she could answer, no problem. "My perfect day on the farm would start at around five or six, depending on the time of year. I get up and have one of Georgia's orange sticky buns for breakfast with a big mug of fresh coffee to wash it down. Then I get out to the barn right as the sun comes up over the hills. I watch the sky turn from gray to pink to blue before I hear that special someone coming up behind me."

A chorus of "ooooohs" rose from the audience. Queen Darby leaned forward with a twinkle in her eyes. "Tell us about your special someone."

"Well, he's got jet-black hair that falls over his dark eyes," BeeBee said dreamily. "He's big too, with these massive shoulders. That's pretty typical of the guys from Italy though."

Audible sighs came from the whole front row.

"My favorite thing about him—well, one of my favorites—is the way his horns arc so long they curl at the very ends," she said with an enamored chuckle.

Darby, who had been leaning closer in with every word as if entranced, sat up suddenly. "His…horns?"

The sighs and ooohs turned into whispered confusion.

"I mean, you can't have a water buffalo without horns," BeeBee said, making a face that indicated how ridiculous just the notion was. "That would be like having a milking stool with only two legs." She snorted to herself. "Can you imagine?"

"I—um—yes, I suppose we can?" Darby's thinly plucked eyebrows peaked over her nose as she, for some reason, ended the sentence on a questioning note. "Gosh, um, let's—let's move on to the next contestant, shall we?"

Somehow, even in a room full of her fellow dairy farmers, BeeBee had managed to say the wrong thing yet again. If they gave out crowns for that, she would have the biggest one of all.

CHAPTER SIX

BILL TAGGED ALONG with Lucas the following Monday when he went to the farm to pick up a fresh supply of milk for the day. Not because he was that eager to see BeeBee or anything. It would be silly for him to get the anticipatory butterflies in his stomach about the prospect of spending more time with her. Especially since they were just…

Friends, he thought. The word sounded as bitter in his head as a burnt lemon rind.

He had just dreamed up a new recipe that he needed their kitchen to experiment in. His food often came to him in dreams, and this time it had appeared as a vision of a trifle—the traditional English dessert but with Middle Eastern flavors he remembered from a trip to Turkey. Cardamom and clove spices in the cake, an indulgent custard creamy and redolent with floral notes, and perhaps a sharp blood-orange drizzle to provide the acidic balance.

As Lucas went straight to the milking room

behind the barn, Bill made for the front door of the house. However, when he knocked, nobody answered. The muffled sound of voices coming from the barn drew his attention. Nodding genially at the cows munching in the feeding stand, he walked around the corner to find both Bee-Bee and Caroline, the little girl from his class, sitting on the floor next to one of the buffaloes who was reclining happily against a hay bale. An even larger buffalo stood a few feet away keeping a watchful maternal eye.

Caroline spotted him and waved.

BeeBee, who was wearing a hoodie and facing away from him as she stroked the buffalo's flank, started at the movement, whipped her head around, then relaxed when she saw who it was.

Her appearance, however, had the opposite effect on him.

"Um, BeeBee?" He hesitated, not wanting to make her feel awkward. "You got a little something on your face there. And there."

There were large brown stripes on her cheeks, nose and forehead. Tiny white dots formed crescents under her eyes.

She glared at him. "I was in the middle of one of those online makeup tutorials when Caroline knocked on the door and asked if she could visit the water buffaloes. Since that sounded like a much better use of my time than contouring in six easy steps…" She swept a hand in a circle directly in front of her face. "I figured I'd come with her."

"Honestly, I'm relieved to know it's just makeup and not—Well, never mind," he said, shaking his head and walking over toward them. The water buffalo raised its head in greeting, and he gave it a pat on the nose before settling down at its head.

Caroline and BeeBee resumed stroking the water buffalo, each looking decidedly glum. He knew what Caroline was sad about and would definitely make sure to make his class as cheerful a place as possible for her to be. But what was BeeBee's issue?

"What's going on, BeeBee?" he asked.

"I went to the pageant seminar on Saturday," she said flatly. "It…did not go well."

"I'm sure it went better than you think."

She pointed at her face, and he grimaced but sat silently, knowing instinctively she wouldn't be able to hold in the rest of the story. He counted down in his head. *Three…two…*

"All the other women there have been doing this kind of thing for years," she exploded. "The makeup and the hair and the clothes. They all knew just what to say and how to walk, and their towns all have statues of them made out of butter at the festivals they throw in their honor." She withdrew her hand from the buffalo and pulled her knees up to her chest to hug them tightly. "I thought that since it was a dairy pageant there would be other women farmers there, women like me."

But there's nobody in the world like you. And he had done the legwork on that—traveled the world and seen his share of women. It had been exciting, sure. But after a while, his relationships had blended into each other. The same short-term expectations. The same kinds of lifestyles. With BeeBee, every day could be full of surprises. You never knew what she would say or do next, whether it was awkwardly dancing to an ABBA song in front of a hundred campers or entering a beauty pageant to pay for an Italian water buffalo. She was a world of possibility and entertainment enough to hold even his admittedly short attention span.

"Who cares what you wear or how much makeup you put on?" he said with a ferocity that surprised even him.

"The pageant people, for one," she said. "Look, I know it seems silly, and I know you probably think that it's a lot of time and effort for one very specific, very expensive water buffalo—"

"That's not what I was thinking at all," Bill interjected quietly before she continued her tirade.

"But this is important to me, and I thought..."

Pushing to a stand, she paused to reach down and grab a bucket. "I thought that this could finally be my special thing. Like Jackie and her writing or Lou and her dancing. Kit with her jewelry and her art." She stood and swung the empty bucket at him. "You and your food."

Pulling up the stool, she sat next to the standing water buffalo.

Bill frowned. "Why are you hand milking her? Is there something wrong with the machine?"

"No, I just find it therapeutic," she said with a shrug. "Want to try?"

Bill walked in a slow circle around the buffalo and crossed his arms. "I don't know about this. She looks kicky."

BeeBee rolled her eyes. "She's not anymore kicky than the Steinberg twins, and you still managed to teach them how to swim at camp without losing a limb."

"Fair point," Bill said, and he took BeeBee's place on the stool after she stood. Inclining his head in a courtly nod to the water buffalo, he greeted her politely. "Hello, Miss Rosamund."

"Lady," BeeBee corrected him.

"Really?"

BeeBee extended her arm toward the animal's massive head. "Look at the way she carries herself. She's royalty." She dropped onto a hay bale between two of the stalls and rested her elbows on her knees with her chin in both hands. "Unlike yours truly. The closest thing I'd come to regal would be court jester."

Bill reached under the water buffalo and slid the bucket beneath her. Eyeing the countess suspiciously, he gave a tug of one of her teats and although she gave him a look of mild wariness, all four hooves remained firmly on the ground. As he fell into a rhythm—this really was quite relaxing—he looked over the buffalo's back at BeeBee.

"If you ask me, you're not giving yourself enough credit," he said. "So what if they all know makeup and hairstyles? No one knows—or cares—more about these animals than you. That's what really matters. I bet you if you just went up there and showed them who you really are, the judges would love you without any of that extra pageant stuff."

BeeBee dropped her hands between her knees and looked at them. She rose to her feet and paced with her head still bowed. At last she stopped, silhouetted in the open doors of the barn with a halo of morning sunrise. "That's..." She turned widened eyes to him, and Bill puffed his chest in anticipation of her praise. "That's terrible advice," she finished with a disappointed shake of her head.

"Excuse me?" His chest deflated.

"That's the pearl of wisdom you bring back from your voyages of the seven seas? Be yourself?" She put her head back and roared with a sardonic laugh. "That's it. You've cracked the code. Forget that I've lived in this town for twenty-four years and there are still people who tell me to be less myself because I'm 'a bit much,'" she said, making finger air quotes.

Walking away from him, she continued to chuckle. "What's your pirate ship called, the *SS Cliché*? I bet Caroline has seen more nuanced advice on afterschool specials for first graders."

Caroline appeared at his side and gazed up at him solemnly. "It is a little trite."

"*Trite*—that's exactly the word," BeeBee called over her shoulder. "That vocabulary just earned you a glass of fresh milk and a cookie. Run inside and find the jar on the counter. I'll be there in a minute."

As the little girl's strawberry-blond head streaked past them, Bill jogged and caught up to BeeBee, little droplets of milk flecking up the sides of the bucket as he carried it.

"I was only trying to help," he said with a shrug of his shoulder.

"I know you were," she said. "And it's very sweet. But being myself isn't going to win this pageant. It wasn't even enough to keep you—"

BeeBee stopped mid-sentence and mid-stride

with one foot on the first step. She turned her head so Bill could only see her profile, her long dark lashes skimming the freckles on her cheeks. Even with the comical streaks of makeup, she was striking. How could she not see that?

"You're the one who broke up with me, remember?" he said softly.

She lifted her eyes at that, turned up one side of her lips in a rueful smile and inclined her head in acknowledgment. "True. But that's all in the past." She went back to walking slowly up the steps, and he caught up with her once again.

"Water under the bridge," he agreed.

She rolled her eyes and leaned back against the post flanking the doorway. "If you give me one more well-worn platitude, I'm going to dump that bucket over your head, and you actually will be crying over spilt milk."

"Ha," he shot back, leaning against the opposite post and setting the bucket down next to his feet. "I know you. That would hurt you far worse than it would hurt me to see all that beautiful buffalo milk go to waste."

"I guess you do know me pretty well," she murmured. Clearing her throat, she squinted at the line of trees in the distance, then looked back at him. She whistled the first notes of "Take a Chance on Me."

He responded by humming the final notes of

the chorus, and for just a moment, he saw the longing in her eyes that matched his own. The big, unanswered question neither of them would ever say out loud. *What if?*

Then the moment passed and mischief lit her eyes once more. "So you got any more recipes for me to try, or did you just come by to show off your 'saying of the day' calendar?"

"I actually did have a recipe I wanted to play around with—hence the fresh milk." He hefted the bucket once more and held it aloft. "How do you feel about custard?"

"The genocidal general—hate him." BeeBee said as she pushed off the post and held the door open for him. "The creamy frozen deliciousness they mix in with the Italian ice—love it."

Bill shook his head and laughed. "Neither. I'll show you what I mean in the kitchen."

Pausing as they stood at the entryway, she put one hand on her hip. "You know, there may be a way to use your deeply awful advice."

"Gee, thanks."

"At the seminar, the other women did think I was funny," she said. "What if I really played up that part of myself in the introductory thing? Like, I could have my sisters help me act out scenes from when I've put my foot in my mouth at town events. I don't have any problem playing the well-meaning goofball. That's basically the same as being myself."

"Like the time you told Mr. Stevenson the antique garnet brooch he brought back from that estate sale reminded you of your cow's kidney stone?" Caroline called out from the kitchen.

"I just meant the color was the same, but yes, that's a perfect example," BeeBee called over her shoulder into the house.

"That's not what I meant," he muttered as he carried the bucket of milk through the door. "And you know it. You shouldn't have to camouflage or exaggerate anything about yourself, BeeBee."

"And you've traveled the world enough to know that's not how anything works," she said as she closed the door behind them.

CHAPTER SEVEN

OVER THE LAST several days, the Long family kitchen had become a kind of pageant-themed war room. The kitchen table was hidden under articles on posture and hairstyles, self-help books on public speaking and a copy of Tina Fey's autobiography. Bill had left a copy of the recipe he intended to use for the kids' class tomorrow. He called it a zabaglione, a kind of pudding, and if she could make this well enough, he said it could be part of a recipe that would seal the deal for her win at the pageant. The only way that was possible was if the vanilla beans he had her scrape out were from the same supplier as Jack's beanstalk beans, especially since the custard she'd made with him yesterday had turned into vanilla-flavored scrambled eggs. Twice.

But Bill had a way of making you believe that anything was possible. Well, almost anything. There were some things, like winning pageants and turning summer romances into lasting relationships, that not even his adorably naive optimism could manifest. What BeeBee did believe made dreams into realities was hard work and implacable, unrelenting determination. With that in mind, she had started wearing a posture-supporting girdle during her work on the farm to force herself into standing up straight.

After an entire morning of raking the dried grass and herding the cows into the milking stand, BeeBee's body ached in muscles she hadn't even realized existed. If it was possible to pull one's spleen, she was fairly certain that was what had happened. Reaching under her shirt, BeeBee undid the hooks of her "corset" as she climbed the stairs to her room. She ripped it off with an enormous sigh of relief.

Jackie poked her head out of her door. "You all right?"

"I am now." BeeBee drop kicked the girdle into the laundry room between her room and the bathroom, completely missed the hamper and allowed it to remain on the floor with a shrug. The idea of bending to pick it up might actually cause whatever was screaming with pain on her left side to rupture and put her out of her misery. "So, Kit and Lou and I were going over the script for my introduction skit for the pageant. Which do you think was funnier—when I accidentally left flower arrangements for Katrina Berger's wedding too close to the fence and the cows ate her bridal bouquet, or when I told Mr. Stevenson's husband his moustache made him look like an old-timey movie villain who ties women to train tracks?"

"Don't be so hard on yourself," Jackie said absentmindedly as she scrolled through her phone. "There was no way you could have known about the giant mole he was hiding under there."

"Thank goodness the moustache grew back," BeeBee shuddered. "Okay, what's going on? I haven't seen you this distracted by your phone since the casting of the *Persuasion* remake was announced."

Finally, Jackie set her phone down on the bed beside her and looked up. A pink flush stained her cheeks. "Well, the New School rejected me."

BeeBee shook her head and sank onto the bed next to her sister, wrapping one arm around her shoulders. "I'm so sorry. Those idiots. They're probably just intimidated by how good you are." She squeezed Jackie's shoulder, then pulled her head back to get a better look at her. "If this is bad news, why are you glowing?"

"Because after I got the rejection, I heard back from the other program I had applied to," she said, holding up her phone. "The one in England? I almost didn't apply for it because it's so far away, and when they put me on the waitlist, I didn't think about it anymore. But they've had someone drop out, and they offered me the slot. I'm going to Bath for the whole summer, and the best part is it's an all-scholarship program. I just have to pay for my flights!"

"Jackie, that's amazing." BeeBee leapt off the bed and pulled Jackie up by the hands, spinning her around the small room and miraculously only knocking over one lamp. Maybe the posture-control girdle thing was helping her balance after all. "So when do you leave?"

Jackie stopped spinning and let go of Bee-Bee's hands, twisting the ring on her right hand anxiously. "Well, that's the only bad part. This program starts earlier than the residency in New York. I would have to leave next weekend."

"But—but that means you'd be gone before the pageant," BeeBee spluttered. "A whole two weeks before. You're supposed to help me write out my answers for the list of potential questions for the interview portion. I can't answer off the cuff. Who knows what I might end up saying?"

Jackie's face twisted with guilt. "I'm so sorry. But I can still help you practice for the interview questions. There's email and video chats. We can make this work long-distance."

BeeBee knew she was being immature and selfish. This was a great opportunity for her sister. But it wasn't just that the timing was terrible. It was the familiarity of it all. The words that were no less reassuring than they had been almost eight years ago when Bill had said them to her.

It had been the last week of camp. BeeBee had waited outside her cabin for almost an hour until at last she'd heard the whistled tune—always an ABBA song that would end up stuck in her head the next day—from behind a tree. She had opened the door just a crack to give a thumbs-up to the other junior counselor who'd known about her nightly rendezvous with Bill before closing it silently and slipping into the darkened forest that separated the boys' and girls' cabins.

Once she'd reached the edge of the pine woods, Bill had reached out his hand for her and they'd sprinted down the path that led to the lake. It had been an especially beautiful night with the moon forming a perfect crescent reflected in the clear water. The trees that ringed the lake had served as shadowed chaperones who'd looked on as they'd sat on the dock with their feet hanging in the water.

Well, BeeBee had sat. Bill could barely stay still, jumping to his feet and climbing the piling as BeeBee had thrown her head back and laughed at his boundless enthusiasm. Before that summer, she had never found anyone whose energy could match her own, someone who actually found her uncensored exclamations amusing rather than exasperating. They had spent almost every evening together that summer, making campfires, walking the trails and talking about everything. That night, though, he could only talk about one thing.

"This is the most prestigious culinary school in the country," he had said, his face beaming through the darkness. "I still can't believe I got in. I mean, they have guest lectures and demonstrations by James Beard Award–winning chefs. And their graduates are practically guaranteed internships at some of the best restaurants all over the country. All over the world. I'll be able to travel everywhere, experience amazing global cuisine and get paid to do it. Can you imagine anything better?"

BeeBee had listened to him wax ecstatically about the possibilities, and yet all she'd heard was the sound of him leaving her. Just the thought had made her feel like something inside was ripping at the seams. She couldn't let him go, she just couldn't, not when she'd finally known what it felt like to find the one person who fit her like the perfect pair of jeans. Most girls— normal girls—would have played it cool. Most girls would have known it was ridiculous to plan a future with a guy she'd only known three months. *She* hurled her heart at him with all the subtlety of a javelin thrower.

"You know, it might be cool to go to college in the city," she had said, pulling her knees up to her chest and looking up at him. "There are probably some good agricultural-science programs there. Or I could even put college off for a few years and find a job waiting tables or something. It would be so awesome to get to see each other every day and not have to sneak around anymore."

He had stopped jumping from one foot to the other on the piling and stood very still like a bird startled into silence by a sense of approaching danger. After a moment, he had climbed down and stood at the edge of the dock, raking a hand through his gorgeous hair, the light brown streaked with gold from a summer in the sun.

"BeeBee, I don't want you changing your plans around just for me." He had started out facing her, then had turned away as he'd walked to the other side of the dock. "That's—that's putting a lot of pressure on me. I'm going to be crazy busy, studying and working late hours at various kitchens." He had turned around slowly, shrugging a shoulder as casually as if he hadn't realized that he had crumbled her world to dust in a single sentence. "We can still see each other though. It's not like the old days. There's email and Face-Time and texting. Let's just…keep things casual and see where it goes."

And that was when BeeBee had—for probably the first and only time in her life—kept her true thoughts and feelings to herself. "Um, relax—I was totally kidding," she had lied with a forced laugh that had echoed out into the woods, mocking her with its reverberations. "Like I'd miss all the fun of my senior year because I have some boyfriend in the city I have to drive five hours to see every other weekend? I mean, my sister Jackie would for sure, but you know I'm not that kind of clingy girly girl. I know we were just chilling for the summer."

Chill out. Be quiet. Relax. The words signaling tacit disapproval of her very nature had always stung like blackberry thorns scratching her bare ankles. She had used those words that night to protect herself from completely breaking down in front of the one person she had thought accepted her just as she was.

"Oh…okay," Bill had said. His voice had sounded thin, strained, and BeeBee had assumed it was from trying to hide his relief that she had been the one to end things. "If that's what you want. I mean, I'm not going to be that far away. I could still come back for the big things, like Homecoming or Prom if you wanted me to take you. We could make it work."

BeeBee had jumped to her feet as the tears thickened in her throat. She'd forced them down with a scoff. "You seriously think I want to get all dressed up in some uncomfortable dress and ridiculous high heels and spend the night taking awkward pictures at some stupid dance? Nightmare fuel is what that is." She had put her hands on her hips and shaken her head. If she was moving something, she could keep from crying. "I'm not the prom queen type, buddy. It's just as well this thing between us is over. Hey, I'll race you back to the cabins. First one back washes all the sheets after the kids are gone."

And with that she had taken off back down the path, running away as if the ground hadn't been falling out from under her feet.

Now, seven years later, she waved a hand at Jackie. "Long-distance stuff doesn't work for me. I have a hard enough time communicating in real time without making people mad. I'm—I'm sure I'll figure it out. Mom can help me. She'll be excited to put her English major to good use."

"Are you sure?" Jackie asked, tipping her head to one side with concern. "I know how important this is to you."

"It's nothing compared to you getting the chance to write where Jane Houston did," Bee-Bee quipped.

"It's Jane Austen and you know it." Jackie gave her a small smile. "You can't cover your feelings with humor. I know you too well."

BeeBee sighed. "I promise—I'll be fine." She checked her watch. "I've got to go. I've got to wash up before I go help Bill with the kids' cooking class this afternoon."

"You two have been spending a lot of time together."

BeeBee paused at the doorway and said without looking back, "Save the romantic fiction for England, sis. Cheerio." She started back down the stairs, then abruptly pivoted and ducked into the bathroom. When Jackie gave her a befuddling squint, she picked up the posture-control girdle off the floor and waved it in the air. "Gotta put my corset back on," she called over her shoulder. "You know, I really think it's helping my coordin—whu-oh."

And with that self-denying prophecy, she promptly tumbled down the stairs.

CHAPTER EIGHT

BILL RUBBED HIS hands together and clapped them once to marshal the kids' attention.

"All right, everyone," he announced. "Today we're going to learn how to make homemade custard." He cupped his hand around his mouth and said in a hushed voice, "It's really just pudding. The reason we're doing this recipe today is that it combines some basic cooking skills like separating and whisking eggs, measuring solids and liquids, and—with direct supervision—learning how to use the stove. We're going to do this one step at a time, so watch me closely before you start to handle the ingredients in front of you. Assistant Chef BeeBee, would you hand me my eggs, please?"

"Yes, Chef Bill," BeeBee said, looking out at the kids in front of them. She took the eggs off the counter in front of her and rotated her whole body in one stiff movement like a bad science-fiction-movie robot whose spine hadn't been given proper articulation. Turning her palm up, she offered him the eggs without looking up at him. "The recipe calls for two eggs."

Bill lifted a single eyebrow. Why was she being weird? Had he said something to upset her? They had shared a moment back at the house a few days ago. At least it had felt like a moment to him.

"Um, BeeBee?"

She had pivoted robotically back to facing the children. Wincing heavily, she rotated her entire person back to him. She didn't even lift her head to look at him. "Yes, Chef Bill?"

He leaned in and whispered out of the corner of his mouth, "Is everything okay?"

She plastered a fake smile on her face for the kids and muttered back between clenched teeth, "What do you mean?"

"You're refusing to look me in the eye, for starters," he said quietly. "Is this about the advice I gave you the other day? I know it was cheesy, but you love cheese. I've actually seen you hug a wheel of Gouda."

"It's not that," BeeBee shot back under her breath. "I fell down the stairs earlier today and jacked up my neck so bad I can't turn my head without seeing stars."

"Oh." That checked out. He picked up the eggs, then set them down again, leaned in once more and whispered, "Is that why you're moving like a mannequin coming to life for the first time?"

She pressed her lips together into a thin line of frustration as she leaned toward him one more time. "Ow. No. I'm wearing a posture-control girdle to practice for the pageant. Any more questions, Captain Billigan? I think your students are starting to get restless."

Out of the corner of his eye, Bill watched Jeremy Binkus surreptitiously stick his finger into the small bowl of sugar in front of him and lick it.

"Sorry about that, kids," Bill said, picking up an egg and holding it aloft. "Now, here's the first step to separating an egg."

After he had finished showing the kids how to separate the eggs and whisk them with the measured sugar, corn flour, vanilla and milk, they took turns one at a time at the stove as he showed them how to stir their mixtures as it cooked. From behind him, he could hear BeeBee chatting with a small group of the others as they took a snack break of milk and animal crackers.

"Animal crackers are the best snack because they had the good sense to include buffaloes in the lineup," BeeBee was saying.

"But Oreos have cream in the middle," Riley replied.

"Technically so does a water buffalo," BeeBee

countered. "Water-buffalo milk is even creamier than cow's milk and just as good for you. Because it's thicker it makes really good cheeses like mozzarella and paneer. And did you know that in some countries like Brazil, the police even use water buffalo for transportation because of their speed and ability to swim?"

"Cool," one of the boys chimed in. "Do they use the horns as weapons against bad guys?"

"No, although in the wild, they can be very dangerous animals," BeeBee cautioned.

"The ones on BeeBee's farm aren't though," Caroline added. "I was there Monday, and she let me pet them. They're so sweet, like giant dogs."

"Giant, ugly dogs," Jeremy Binkus said with a snort.

Bill whipped his head around. BeeBee was still moving pretty stiffly, but a comment like that could trigger her into hurling Jeremy out of a window, girdle be darned. Fortunately for everyone—most especially Jeremy Binkus—she merely held up a finger.

"That's strike one, Binkus," she warned. "Two more and I'm telling your mother you volunteered to help muck out the barn for a day."

Bill smiled to himself and turned back to the stove to remind the little girl next to him to keep stirring.

After the class was finished, he rummaged

around in the Parks office freezer until he found a pack of frozen peas. Wrapping a towel around it so he didn't shock her with the cold, he came up behind BeeBee at the sink as she washed the pans and touched her lightly on the arm.

"For your neck." He held up the bag, and her shoulders dropped with relief.

"Thanks," she said, scrubbing a pan with a pained expression on her face. "I'm dying here. Do you mind putting it on me?"

"Of course not." Standing behind her, he gently swept her braid from her neck to over her shoulder with a brush of his fingers. His chest brushed against the sharp wings of her shoulder blades made even more prominent by the way the girdle forced her into an exaggeratedly upright posture. Bill's own ribcage felt suddenly tight as if being so close to her had pulled some invisible laces inside him. It stole his breath, the urge to wrap her in his arms as he had before. It had been so long, yet even now he couldn't think straight whenever she was this close. With a determined shake of his head, he placed the cold bag against the enticing wisps of hair at the base of her neck and stepped back. "There you go."

She moved her head in small circles and breathed contentedly. "That feels much better. You're my hero."

"I thought that title belonged to your Italian

water-buffalo prince, Francisco," he teased, leaning his elbow on the counter next to the sink.

"It's Orlando, and you know it, Billicent," she shot back.

"Well, whatever his name is, he's going to be one well-cared-for water buffalo," he remarked, pushing off the counter and sliding the neck of his apron over his head. "I learned more about water buffaloes from you today than I did the entire time I spent cooking in Italy. The kids were enthralled. I think you're going to have more than just Caroline coming to visit you once he arrives."

"If he arrives." She shut off the water, then shook her hands dry with unnecessary force. "I still have to win the pageant and the grant money for him first."

"And you will, especially with the recipe I've worked out for you," he said. "Your custard went much better today. I can tell you've been practicing."

She lifted her chin into the air proudly before emitting a hiss of pain and clutching the bag of peas with her hand. "I guess I need to practice walking down the stairs more too. Speaking of walking, I'm going for a little stroll downtown to break in my high heels for the pageant. Want to come with me?"

"Do you really want my company, or do you

need someone to hold on to while you walk in heels?"

She pulled her face into a mask of obviously faux nonchalance. "Little of column *A*, little of column *B*. You in?"

"I'm in," he said immediately. "We can shop for your recipe ingredients together."

"Then what are we waiting for?"

"Your neck to thaw for one thing." Bill reached out to catch the bag of peas when it fell as she moved away from the sink.

A walk through downtown Crystal Hill was normally a quick and relatively uneventful promenade. After all, Jane Street was all of three blocks and one stoplight long. Today's jaunt was at the very least not going to be quick, Bill observed with amusement, as BeeBee's three-inch red heels rendered her incapable of taking steps larger than a few inches at a time.

"Are you sure this is necessary?" he asked as they rounded the corner in front of the Parks and Rec building and made their way toward Mrs. Van Ressler's inn. "I worked on a cruise through the Galápagos once, and there were tortoises sunning themselves on a rock who moved faster than this."

BeeBee narrowed her eyes at him. It was pretty much her only defense as her arms were stretched out in front of her, hands splayed like a mime trapped in an invisible box, and her feet shuffled along the pavement without more than a sliver of space between the soles and the ground. "Listen, Billy the Sailor Man. I have a little more than three weeks to learn how to walk in these torture devices with grace and freaking elegance. You got a boat to catch or something?"

"Oh, I'm in no rush at all," Bill teased. Walking backward a few paces in front of her, he held out his phone for a picture. "This is the funniest thing I've witnessed since I cooked a private dinner for Jim Gaffigan's family and their youngest kid shot a pea out of his nose."

BeeBee snorted. "Don't make me laugh. It'll throw me off. And don't you even think about posting this, or I'll share those pictures of you from the Camp Herkimer Seventies Night."

He lowered his phone. "You still have pictures from that night?"

BeeBee's eyes lowered back to the ground as flush stained her cheeks. "Maybe," she mumbled. Recovering quickly, she stopped in front of the B&B and leaned on the white-picket-fence post at the end of the walkway. "Hold on—I need a break." She inhaled deeply with her eyes closed. "Mmm. Is there anything that smells better than lilacs?"

The walkway leading up to the light blue Victorian house that was a favorite spot for honeymooners from the city was a veritable bower of the light purple blossoms. Puffy white hydrangeas occupied the flower pots hanging from the scalloped roofline of the porch, and pink climbing roses bravely summited the tower on the corner of the building. But even with the scent of blossoms beside them, the only thing Bill wanted was another draught of vintage BeeBee: Ivory soap and sweet dried grass. If he could bottle that smell and carry it with him on his ocean voyages, he would do it in a heartbeat.

A sharp voice cracked through his reverie.

"Beatrice Long." Mrs. Van Ressler appeared in the front doorway, pointing a gnarled arthritic finger at them. "What are you doing loitering around my flowerbed?"

BeeBee waved, momentarily losing her balance and tipping slightly backward.

Bill rushed behind to catch her, and if perhaps he let his hands linger on the small of her back even after she had regained her composure, it was only because his time on yachts had made him overly mindful of safety. It wasn't because being around her and not touching her was starting to feel a little torturous.

"Hi, Mrs. Van Ressler," Bee Bee called out, shading her eyes with one hand. "We just stopped to admire your flowers. They look beautiful this year."

Mrs. Van Ressler's mouth softened into what was almost a smile. She had worked in Hollywood as an understudy for the great Dorothy Dandridge and even now in her late eighties kept her hair meticulously curled and styled. Her dark eyes took BeeBee's measure and widened with alarm when they landed on BeeBee's feet.

"Oh, no." She shook her head and barred the doorway with her carved cane. "No, no, no. Don't even think about coming in here with those on."

BeeBee looked down at her feet in confusion. "What's wrong with my shoes? Lindsay said red patent leather was in this year." She reached for the fence post and turned around to smile at Bill. "I ordered a pair of Wellington boots in red to wear for the day Orlando arrives."

Bill shook his head at the same time his heart did a little skip. Only BeeBee would order a pair of farm boots especially for the arrival of a color-blind water buffalo.

"It's not the style to which I object," Mrs. Van Ressler snapped. "It's the hazardous human wearing them. The last time you came inside, you nearly dropped my Murano glass apple from Venice, and that was before you were leaning like the Tower of Pisa."

BeeBee twisted her head and whispered to Bill, "Mrs. Van Ressler spent a summer in Italy filming with a famous director in the sixties and likes to remind us at every turn." Spinning back around, she called out to the porch. "Don't worry, Mrs. Van Ressler. I'm not coming inside."

"Hmm," the older woman said, lowering her cane and slowly closing the door. "My collection of Venetian glassware is priceless."

"And everywhere in her dang inn," BeeBee said as she pushed off the fence and assumed her mincing progress down the sidewalk. "She has one room that's floor-to-ceiling breakable chotchkes. It's not my fault if I've had a few mishaps over the years."

Bill held out his hand as they reached the curb, but she swatted him away. "Nope. I've got to be able to do this myself. There are steps I'll have to do at the pageant building, and I'm pretty sure my farm boots aren't event appropriate."

"If you say so." The stubborn independence was as much classic BeeBee as her scent. "I'm just going to stand here with my arm awkwardly jutted out at the exact same height as your hand for no particular reason whatsoever."

Despite a tremulous wobble in her right knee, BeeBee stepped to the street between the sidewalks without falling and looked at him in triumph. "Ha. Look at that—a perfect dismount. Ten out of ten."

She did, however, allow him to conveniently hold out his hands for her to grab as she stepped up onto the next block only because he said he had seen it in a movie and wanted to try it, and she most graciously obliged. They stopped again at Georgia's Bakery, this time because Bill couldn't resist a black-and-white cookie.

"Georgia took over the bakery for her folks when they moved down to Florida," BeeBee explained as she opened the door and a bell tinkled cheerily over their heads. "Do you remember when we came here in the mornings before the other counselors woke up? Georgia's mom, Cindy, would give us black-and-whites to go with our coffee."

"Those were better than any I had in the city," Bill admitted. "But if you ever tell anyone I said that, I will vehemently claim never to have met you before in my life."

BeeBee chuckled. "You city people. To be fair, Cindy grew up in Midtown, so that is where the recipe originally came from. Georgia makes them the same way her mom did, so they should be just like you remember."

"Of course she does," he said with a roll of his eyes. "It's Crystal Hill, the Brigadoon of Upstate New York."

Her chin jerked back. "And what's that supposed to mean?"

They were interrupted by Georgia coming out from the back with a tray of perfectly decorated cupcakes. She almost looked like a movie star from the fifties herself, her short hair styled in a retro blond bob with curls bouncing just under her ears. "Hi there."

BeeBee tottered toward the counter eagerly, and Bill followed closely behind, concerned the lure of fresh pastries might override her careful efforts to stay upright. "Hi, Gigi. This is Bill." She chucked a thumb in his direction. "We were just talking about your mom's black-and-white recipe."

"You're in luck," Georgia said, bending down and reaching into the glass display case to her right. Pulling out a tray of cookies, she loaded four into a crinkling paper bag and folded the top over before straightening up and handing it to BeeBee. "These are so fresh the icing's barely hard." She smiled at Bill, the dark circles under her eyes disappearing briefly with the expression. "I've seen you around town. You're staying with Lucas, right?"

"He and I are old buddies from our days as Camp Herkimer counselors," he said, taking the cookies from Georgia's hand before Bee-Bee could lunge for them and go crashing to the yellow-and-white tiled floor. "I'm just visiting until the summer charter-yacht season kicks off again. I'm a chef," he added as an explanation.

"That sounds exciting," Georgia said as she

dusted flour from her hands. "The closest I get to a yacht is getting one of the pedal boats with a cup holder out on the lake."

"Oh, I used to love those things," Bill said. He nudged BeeBee with his elbow, and she nearly tipped over again but saved herself by grabbing onto the counter. He handed her the entire bag of cookies with an apologetic grimace. "Sorry. Remember when we used to do pedal-boat bumper cars? You nearly drowned me at least twice."

She sniffed and peeked over her nose into the bag of black-and-whites. "All's fair in love and pedal boating," she retorted haughtily.

The word *love* coming out of her mouth was enough to throw him off-balance even though his shoes were decidedly more sensible. They had said it to each other before, only once. Once had been more than enough, however, to send his teenage self both careening into the stratosphere with joy and spiraling into a core-deep panic attack over what those words really meant at the age of eighteen.

The doorbell chimed behind them. BeeBee whispered through a mouth full of cookie, "Who is it? I'm too afraid to turn around again."

"I don't know," Bill whispered back. "But she's brought either a very large dog or a medium-sized lion on a leash."

"Oh dear." BeeBee's breath escaped with a whoosh. "I know who that is."

"Coffee to go, please," the woman said from behind them. "Hello, BeeBee."

The woman's tone was so frosty Bill was surprised it didn't instantly freeze the latte Georgia handed her.

BeeBee pivoted in a circle with even greater trepidation than navigating the curb. "Hello, Ms. Hooker," she said after swallowing the large mouthful of cookie whole. Bending down, she held out a hand to the dog/lion. "Hi, Trevor."

With the instinctive ability to recognize good people—especially good people covered in cookie crumbs—that all animals seem to possess, the creature named Trevor stuck out an incredibly long tongue and licked BeeBee's hand. The tall thin woman holding Trevor's leash, on the other hand, was not so easily swayed by kind gestures or pastry remnants.

"Are you here to eat or to besmirch another stalwart institution with ageist accusations?"

Bill considered himself well-read and at times downright glib. But even he couldn't help saying "Huh" out loud to the woman's pretentious greeting.

Ignoring him, BeeBee stood up straight and cringed apologetically. "I'm really sorry about that, Ms. Hooker." Thrusting the hand with the bag of cookies out, she smiled. "Would you accept a black-and-white cookie as a peace offering? They're freshly baked."

The woman sniffed. "That would go nicely with my coffee."

But before the woman could reach out and accept the oven-baked olive branch, Bill stepped between them. "Just a minute. What's your problem with BeeBee?"

BeeBee tugged at the back of his shirt. "Bill, let it go," she hissed.

But he had had enough. What was wrong with the people in this town? He refused to let anyone else use BeeBee as a human punching bag.

"For starters, she vociferously proclaimed at a town function that no one read actual newspapers anymore and that the printing of one seemed like a 'waste of a good tree,'" Ms. Hooker said, making quote marks with the fingers of one hand.

"So?"

"The town function in question was the celebration of the first edition of my newspaper, the *Crystal Hill Crier*," she said, tilting her chin down so that her glasses slid down her nose. "Also, she said Trevor reminded her of a smaller version of one of her beastly water buffaloes."

"I meant that as a compliment," BeeBee cried out, raising a hand into the air, then just as quickly lowering it back down to steady herself against the curved back of one of the chairs. "He's got a beautiful mane like my Viola."

"Trevor is an AKC-certified Tibetan mastiff from a line that goes back several dynasties," Ms. Hooker said with a possessive stroke of the dog, who took that opportunity to tilt his head all the way to the right and allow his tongue to loll hilariously out of the side of his mouth.

"Come on, lady," Bill exclaimed. "I give you her timing isn't great, but she's not wrong. And even you have to admit that dog is big enough to be used as a durability test for bridges."

Ms. Hooker gasped, and BeeBee groaned at the same time. It was Ms. Hooker who regained breath enough to speak first.

"How dare you body-shame Trevor?" she said, yanking at his leash to draw him close. "Underneath his coat, he is svelte as a gazelle."

Bill looked at Trevor who, if it was at all possible, gave the canine equivalent of an eye roll.

"Ms. Hooker, Bill is from out of town," BeeBee offered as either an explanation or an apology—Bill wasn't sure which. "Plus, you know, he was on a boat for a long time. There's a chance he has scurvy and it's affected his ability to know when to mind his own business." Bill felt her push with both hands on his back, urging him toward the door. "Crystal Hill Dairy Farm is paying for a full-page ad in next week's issue. Kit will get the specs to you tomorrow. Sorry again for the disturbance—love your dog, which I know is definitely not a water buffalo. Bye-bye!"

Once they were out in the street, BeeBee planted her feet shoulder-width apart and jabbed her fists onto her hips. "What was that about?"

Bill blinked rapidly, and not just because of his eyes adjusting to the lowering sun hitting him square in the eyes. "I was defending you. Why are you mad at me and not the people in this town who insist on treating you like this community's running inside joke?"

"Because that's who I am," BeeBee exploded. "I blurt things out without thinking about them first, and sometimes I make people mad. I'm hopelessly uncoordinated off the farm and, despite my best efforts at hand washing, hopelessly smudgy. I know these things about myself, and so when I mess up, I try to laugh it off or make it right because, unlike you, I have to live in this town." She looked down at her feet and rubbed two fingers over the bridge of her nose.

"I just hate seeing you treated this way." He lowered his voice. "You're so much more than all those things. You're strong and smart and intensely dedicated to the things you care about. If the people in this town can tease you about the bad stuff, then at least let me convince you of the good stuff too. There's a lot of it."

"I understand what you're trying to say, but the thing is…" BeeBee bit her bottom lip and shook her head before lifting her eyes to meet his gaze straight on. "You're leaving. It's nice you see all these things in me, but that's not what makes long-term relationships work. Is this town or its people perfect? No, of course not. But I've put in the work to make our dairy farm a success, despite what people think of me. That investment means taking responsibility for my mistakes and earning their respect through the thing I can do better than anyone else—running a dairy farm."

"So you're saying that because I stuck up for you, I don't understand what it means to have long-term commitments?" Bill folded his arms. "That's not fair. I was eighteen when we got together. There was no way I was ready for a serious relationship then."

"Well, have you had any relationships in the last seven years that lasted longer than a summer?" She tapped the pointed toe of one shoe on the sidewalk. "And Lucas doesn't count."

Bill adjusted his bandanna uncomfortably. "I—we're not talking about me here."

"No, we were talking about me and my life in my town." She jabbed her index finger at her own chest. "And unless you plan on being a part of any of that, please don't try to butt into something you don't understand."

"Fine," he grumbled.

Turning on his heel, he started toward the grocery store, stopping when he didn't hear the tentative clicking of BeeBee's heels behind him. He suppressed an exasperated growl. Stubborn woman—she was worse than one of her beloved water buffaloes.

Bill looked over his shoulder at her. "Are we ingredient shopping, or what?"

"You know, I'm actually getting tired from walking around in these shoes, and this girdle is rolling down more by the second." She fidgeted with both hands on her waist. "I'd better get home before I start to look like the Michelin Man in a cummerbund."

"Do you want me to walk back with you?"

"No, thank you," she said in a stiff voice that would have made the imperious Ms. Hooker proud. "I can manage just fine on my own. I've gotten pretty good at it over the last few years."

Bill watched as she resumed her tiny half steps back down the sidewalk toward the Parks and Rec building. Shopwell's Grocery Market was in the opposite direction, between the diner and the barber shop, but he stood there and watched her make her way carefully down the sidewalk until she turned at the corner of Van Ressler's B&B

and disappeared from view. He wasn't worried about her falling. BeeBee's pride would keep her upright, if nothing else.

He had hoped she would turn around and give him the chance to run back to her arms like he had wanted to the first time he'd left.

CHAPTER NINE

"AND THEN HE had the nerve to offer to help me walk back," BeeBee recounted. She fiddled with the end of her braid as she talked.

It had been two days since her fight with Bill, and her stomach still roiled with such a mix of emotions she had only eaten three out of her usual five pancakes for breakfast and hadn't even touched the sausage. If she kept this up, her favorite jeans would start to get loose. Then she might actually have to go clothes shopping. Screwing up her face at the thought, BeeBee tossed her braid back over her shoulder defiantly and continued her rant. Lady Viola listened with great sympathy and understanding in her deep black eyes.

"I mean, he shows up out of the blue and acts like some knight in shining armor thinking— what? That I'll forget how he broke my heart? Ignore the fact that he's still a total commitment-phobe?"

It was the only thing that made sense for why

he was single. Bill was even better looking now than he had been as a teenager, the hardened muscles and wind-blown burnish on his skin a rugged upgrade from the clean-cut Niall Horan lookalike from Queens he was at eighteen. Women always flocked to him wherever he went, so why was he still available if not for a deep-rooted fear of being tied down?

BeeBee leaned back against the warmth of Lady Viola's torso. It was like having the world's softest beanbag with a soothing heartbeat. Forget couches—therapists should have water buffaloes in their offices. Something about their receptive sensitivity and agreeable snorts inspired confidentiality like nothing else.

"I should be relieved," she muttered, staring at the particles of dust twinkling in the shaft of light from the window. "Clearly I made the right decision ending things with him instead of trying to drag things out with some long-distance nonsense. He would have dumped me eventually, and I would have wasted months or even years of my life on someone who runs away when things get hard."

Lady Viola nudged the hay bale next to her face with her snout, which BeeBee took as the animal's endorsement of everything she had just said.

So why did she still feel like something wasn't right?

"BeeBee?" Lindsay's head poked around the edge of the barn door. "Jackie wants to know if you're ready to go over the interview questions."

BeeBee closed her eyes and groaned. "It's Friday afternoon. Can't I get a day off?"

"You can, but Jackie's leaving on Sunday," Lindsay reminded her, stepping into the doorway and crossing her right foot gracefully over her left. "It will be a lot easier to do this stuff now when you're in the same time zone."

With a reluctant grunt, BeeBee heaved herself off her water-buffalo beanbag and pushed with one hand to stand. Brushing the dirt and hay from her backside, she noticed another hole starting in the left knee of her jeans. She shrugged. That was how you knew they were comfortable.

"It will never make sense to me—" she followed Lindsay back into the pasture and toward the gate "—how people think that they need to 'broaden their horizons' by traveling all over the globe. TV shows make it seem so exotic, like if you spend a year in Tuscany or—or Timbuktu, you'll have this life-changing experience, whereas in reality you'll really have the same life and the same problems as you did in the first place, except with a language barrier. Honestly, the only movie that got it right was *The Wizard of Oz*. There really is no place like home."

BeeBee punctuated her statement with a dramatic fling of the gate, gliding smoothly through it just before it closed behind her. With her hand on the lock, she sighed. Here, on her farm, she could move with ease. Never once had she fallen or hurt herself out here. Why couldn't she be like this anywhere else? If Bill could see her out here with her animals, he would understand why this farm was so important to her.

"Speaking of ruby slippers, where are the red pumps we gave you the other day?"

"Erm…" BeeBee occupied herself by studiously checking the gate to make sure the lock had been slid into place. "I, uh, might have chucked them out of the car window and into the lake on Wednesday."

"Beatrice Elizabeth Long." Lou slapped her hands down at the side of her legs. Since she insisted on wearing gauzy skirts that gesture was sure to leave a mark, BeeBee noted with a small amount of smug satisfaction. "Why would you do something like that?"

"Because they're uncomfortable and stupid and I can't walk in them without big blisters forming on my toes." She stuck out her right foot as if the multiple Band-Aids were visible beneath her work boots. "Not all of us have years of pointe-shoe callouses to protect us, you know."

"You will have to wear heels at the pageant." Lou leaned one hand against the gate. "But for now, let's just work on your interview questions. Jackie's got a couple of scripted answers drafted for you."

BeeBee frowned. "What if they ask me a question we don't have a script for?"

"Jackie said she has some generic speeches that you can use as a template," Lou said. "How's the recipe coming with Bill?"

"We, uh, we hit a little snag." BeeBee paused at the door to look back down the driveway as if she expected to see someone. Which was silly because the only thing she saw were the cows dotted serenely against the brilliant sloping green of the hillside pasture. For the first time, the sight failed to bring her a sense of complete peace and fulfillment. BeeBee turned back and passed through the front door. It was only because Orlando wasn't there yet.

That had to be why it felt like someone was missing.

As soon as she set foot inside, Jackie spun around in her wheely chair at the computer. "There you are."

The gentle welcoming tone of her voice amplified the wave of loneliness cresting inside Bee-

Bee's chest. She knew it was inevitable that her sisters' collective brilliance would take them far away from their bubble tucked between the silent mountains. Somehow knowing it was bound to happen didn't make it any easier. The exact same way that knowing she had been right all along about Bill didn't make it hurt less to be "just friends." Why did everyone need to leave?

"Where else would I be?" She shrugged and stopped at the doorway to remove her boots, wincing as a Band-Aid shifted off a particularly nasty blister. BeeBee limped into the kitchen and snagged an apple off the counter before hobbling back into the living room and flopping her entire body onto the couch with a sigh.

"Just an expression," Jackie remarked placidly. "Anyway, I have some responses to a few of the previous years' questions all typed up." She stood and crossed the room.

BeeBee narrowed her eyes at the thick stack of papers under Jackie's arm. "Holy buckets. What is that, the Gettysburg Address?" She swung her legs around and let them fall to the floor, slouching into the plush couch cushions behind her. "You're leaving Sunday. Shouldn't you be packing or practicing your curtsy for when you meet the king?"

Jackie laughed. "I'm pretty sure the king of England doesn't attend seminars for unpublished romance writers. It wasn't any trouble. I needed a good creative challenge."

"If you say so." There was a good chance Jackie was just saying that because she felt bad about leaving. Then again, there were a lot of things in her sisters' worlds that didn't make sense to her, like how Lindsay would ever put on pointe shoes again after getting blisters like these for the first time. "Here. Let me take a looksie."

Jackie sat on the couch next to BeeBee as she handed her the sheath of paper still warm from the printer. Her lips puckered into a small knot like they did when she was anxious. "I feel awful leaving right now."

A very tiny, mean-spirited voice inside Bee-Bee whined, *Then don't leave.* Instead, she shook her head. "Don't worry about me. I'll be just fine. Anyway, I still have Lou and Kit to torment me—I mean, keep me company." The smile she gave felt only partially forced. "These answers look good. And they're short enough for me to memorize in the next two weeks. But, uh, what happens if they ask me a question that's not on the list?"

"That's why I wanted to sit down with you now," Jackie said. "I had the same thought. So I'll ask you some questions that aren't on the list, and we can practice your responses in case you have to improvise."

"In other words, prevent me from going rogue?"

"Ensure your victory so you can buy your champion water buffalo," Jackie responded with an arch lift of her brows.

"Well played," BeeBee replied. "Okay. I'm ready. Fire away."

Jackie inhaled deeply, then her shoulders fell as she lasered BeeBee with a scrutinizing stare. "Is that really how you're going to sit?"

BeeBee glared. "I spent all morning in the eighty-five degree heat trying to coax the Countess out of the watering hole. My feet look like a pepperoni pizza from Mama Renata's, and I'm pretty sure that stupid girdle punctured one of my lungs. I can either sit up straight or I can answer questions. Your pick, word jockey."

Jackie widened her eyes as she went back to her paper, silently mouthing, *Word jockey.*

"I'll let Lou work on your posture later. First question. Miss Long, what qualities do you possess that make you worthy of the title Queen of the Dairy?"

"Well, Judge Number One." BeeBee gritted her teeth. The things she had to endure for the sake of Orlando. "I'd have to say my devotion to producing top-quality dairy products and also the fact that I never miss a chance to yell *Off with their heads* if the situation demands it." A large chomp of her delightfully crisp apple punctuated the statement.

Jackie's right eye twitched once, but she stayed in character. "Judge Number Two would like you to tell us about the relationship between your dairy farm and the community it serves."

"Since our town is seventy percent female, we are instrumental in preventing the terrible scourge that is postmenopausal osteoporosis." BeeBee managed to keep a straight face right until the end when she dissolved into snickers.

"BeeBee."

"She says with the weary exasperation of someone carrying hormonally brittle bones and an AARP card."

Jackie opened her mouth to say more, then caught the clock out of the corner of her eye. "Goodness, it's already six o'clock."

"Happens twice a day." BeeBee yawned. She pushed gingerly to a stand and walked into the kitchen to toss her apple core into the garbage. "What's for dinner?"

"It's just you and me since Mom and Dad are at a PTA meeting and the twins are working. Hey, I have an idea. Let's go into town and grab something." Jackie set the papers down but refused to look BeeBee in the eye.

BeeBee frowned at Jackie's oddly stilted proposition. "Are you okay? You sound like you're reading from a script right now."

Jackie made a "psssht" noise with her lips, then jumped off the couch and rummaged in the key bowl by the door. "Don't be silly. We can take the long way around the lake. It's so pretty in early summer."

"I'll go, but only because you're acting so weird I'm afraid to let you drive without supervision," BeeBee warned, striding toward the door. "Are you nervous about the trip? You're going to be amazing. There's no one who writes romance like you."

Jackie fiddled with the keys. "That must be it. Come on—let's go."

Per Jackie's request, they took the scenic route wending around the far end of town. BeeBee turned her head to adjust the air-conditioning in the car as they passed the wooded entrance to Camp Herkimer. She didn't need the memories today.

Jackie pulled the car into a space in front of the lake. Next week, it would be June and the city tourists would be occupying every available surface from the parking lots to the restaurants. The lake would ring with the happy shrieks of the summer campers while twentysomethings wandered from tree to tree hunting for the perfect spot to take a selfie of them in the "authentic small-town experience."

"We can park here and walk downtown," Jackie said as she stepped out of the car. "Unless, you know, there's something else that keeps you here."

"Okay, this whole enigmatic thing you've got going on is starting to scare me," BeeBee said as she slammed the car door behind her. "Seriously. If you don't get back to normal after dinner, we are driving straight to the—Oh, you have got to be kidding me."

The second she had stepped onto the sidewalk, her eyes were drawn to the twinkle of multiple battery-powered tea lights shining inside a small wooden dingy with two bench seats. Holding the oars was none other than Bill Danzig. With the brilliant gold of the sunset backlighting him, he could have been a star in one of the rom-coms Jackie loved to watch on TV. BeeBee whirled around to find the aforementioned romantic schemer sneaking back toward the driver's side of the car.

Jackie bit her lower lip and lifted her eyebrows, the mischievous glint in her eyes indicating that not only had she—deliberately and with romance aforethought—set BeeBee up, she wasn't even sorry.

"Jacqueline, how could you?" BeeBee extended

a hand at her sister's retreating form. "You're supposed to be my sister."

And yet the traitor among them wasn't Jackie. It was BeeBee's heart, her stupid, never-seemed-to-learn heart that had bounded with both joy and relief the second she had seen who was waiting in that canoe.

"'What strange creatures sisters are,'" Jackie quoted blithely as she waved her keys in farewell and ducked into the car before popping her head back up only a moment later. "Actually, the quote is 'What strange creatures brothers are,' but I figured for a cause so noble Jane wouldn't have minded the artistic license."

"Jane Dallas does too mind, and she's probably almost as angry at you as I am," BeeBee retorted in a final half-hearted attempt to manifest outrage. But not even her purposeful use of the wrong Texas city name was enough to cause Jackie to do anything other than drive away like the coward that she was. BeeBee snapped her head back to the canoe bobbing peacefully next to the dock and the kidnapping pirate sitting inside it.

Bill hummed the chorus of "Take a Chance on Me," but nothing those temptingly full lips could do would change her mind about him. No, sir. Refusing to toss him the musical olive branch of her response, she forcefully clamped her lips shut.

He bobbed his head in a single nod, as if he had expected this from her. "BeeBee, can we talk?"

"Listen, Cappy," she hissed. "If you think I'm going to hop right into your windowless van—"

"We nautical folk call it a rowboat."

"Then you'd better think again because there isn't a candy tempting enough to get me to go anywhere with you."

"I thought you might say that," he said before bending over and pulling a square white box out from under the canoe bench. As soon as he opened it, the smell of Mama Renata's pizza with all of BeeBee's favorite toppings wafted through the balmy evening breeze.

BeeBee tried to hold her breath, and yet still the scent of spicy red peppers mingling with smoky bacon and sweet tangy pineapple found her. "You are a very evil pirate," she said before practically running to the dock and climbing into the row boat. It wobbled as she stepped in, but there was no way she was accepting the hand Bill offered her.

Settling herself onto the bench seat opposite him, she crossed her arms and jutted her chin stiffly in the air. "Fine. One slice. But I'm still mad at you about Wednesday."

He nodded solemnly as he reached behind him and presented a paper plate; although the amused twitch in the corner of his lip didn't escape her eye. He clearly thought he could win forgiveness with a clichéd romantic boat ride and a treat. Well, he didn't know her as intimately as he assumed because she was made of much tougher stuff than that.

Yet when he produced a bottle of her favorite grape soda, so cold that it produced vapors into the warm air, her incandescent rage began to flicker and dim.

Bill rowed them out to the center of the lake with an even grace to the strokes of the oars. It was one of those summer evenings where even the sun didn't seem to want to let go of such a fine, clear day until the last possible moment. It clung to the hills with every ray until finally allowing the weight of a softened sky to press it into well-earned sleep.

They sat in silence as they ate. With anyone else, BeeBee would have found the quiet almost unbearable. Instead, she appreciated that Bill didn't feel the need to thrust onto her some sort of defense or apology. Words were so often a landmine for her, exploding feelings out of nowhere before she could accurately gauge their impact. The intuitive simplicity of Bill's gesture allowed them both to communicate without fear of dynamiting the peace. If only it could be this easy with everyone. Or even better, if only she could be with him forever.

She leaned back on her elbows against the edge of the boat and took him in. His signature bandanna holding his thick wavy hair off his face. The satisfied look on his face as he took up the oars once more to keep them from drifting too close to the shoreline. "This works for you."

"What does?"

She made a sweeping motion with her hand that encompassed both the boat and the lake. "This. All of it. It's the pirate life for you, right Cap'n Billbeard?"

He looked down and chuckled. "I love the way you make these startlingly insightful statements, then try to cover them with jokes," he said. "But you're right. There's something about being on the water that settles me in a way. I was always the kid in class that couldn't sit still. Teachers loved me until it was time to actually pay attention and listen. I just couldn't stand the feeling of being confined, in a chair or even a single room."

"I remember how relieved you were to be done with school."

Bill exhaled an agreeing chuckle. "Not that culinary school was easy or anything," he said before draining the last drops of his orange soda from the bottle. Setting the empty into the recycling bag at his feet, he clasped his hands between his knees and leaned forward as if confessing a secret. "I actually failed my pastry final twice."

"You should have just made them one of your s'mores."

"It's funny because out of all the fancy desserts I've made for yacht clients, the thing that always goes over like gangbusters is a s'more bar," he said. "I make homemade marshmallows with an assortment of cookies and graham crackers with a choice of different gourmet Swiss chocolate."

"Remember the ones we made out of peanut-butter cups?" BeeBee allowed herself a wistful sigh. Taking in the way his smile had broadened, deep and real, she came as close as she was going to get to an apology. "I'm glad you found something you love so much."

"When I'm on the water—" he turned his head to gaze at the horizon, a sherbet of blue raspberry and pineapple gold, nodding at the colors' reflection melting below the boat "—I feel free. It's where I feel the most like myself." He wound back to face her. "The way you feel about Crystal Hill and your farm."

He was right, but only partially. "It's more than that," she started to explain, then stopped suddenly aware of the stillness her words pierced. "I know it's a small town with gossips who never let you forget your mistakes. I know it's not Paris or Rome. Someday I'd love to visit other places, to see and taste and experience new things." Bee-Bee didn't know why she was taking the time to clarify this to someone who would be leaving in a month. It felt important, though, that he understood who she was now, that the image he carried with him wasn't of the girl she used to be. "It's the choice to make this my home that makes it special. It's not perfect, obviously. I can't stand the annual tourist invasion even though I know it's good for business. But just like in a long-term relationship, you're not in it because of the way the other person makes you feel every second of the day. You make the choice every day to belong to them. I choose to belong here."

His eyes caught the glow of the tea lights, the effervescent gold warming the hazel like a forest sunrise. "I just hope that whatever it is you choose—be it person, place or water buffalo—knows how lucky it is to have someone as passionate and devoted as you."

She sat up and inched forward until their kneecaps touched. The air buzzed as if it was electrically charged by the fireflies blinking into the twilight. It had been seven years since they had last kissed, but she still remembered the way his lips had felt against hers, the way a simple, teasing brush could arrest the air in her lungs. Each nerve cell in her body tingled with its own memory of the way he had made her feel, but they all resounded the same word for that feeling.

Reckless.

This was reckless. He was leaving. If she let herself fall under his spell again, she would fall apart entirely when the end result was the same. She had spent the autumn of her senior year secretly scrolling through the pictures on his social media feeds and wondering why she wasn't good enough to make him want her back.

One kiss and she would be back to where she'd been before. Bill must have felt the same magnetic pull as he slowly moved his face toward hers.

Swallowing hard, BeeBee followed his lead, then ducked her head down at the last second. Reaching below his seat, she withdrew the pizza box and opened it as nonchalantly as if she didn't feel a thousand pinpricks of stifled yearning over her entire body.

"You know, I think this pizza is even better after it's been sitting for a few minutes," she said. "The cheese has settled, and you don't have to do that thing where you say a silent prayer for your fallen tastebuds because it's so hot."

Rambling endlessly about pizza wasn't at all

out of character for her. She could do an entire soliloquy on Mama Renata's deep-dish crust alone. But the wavering pitch of her voice, like a ferry boat stranded in a storm-tossed sea? That was new.

Fortunately, Bill didn't seem to notice. "You are right on that, although we will never, ever agree on your choice of toppings."

Bill had always been a hard no on the pine-apple-as-acceptable-pizza-topping debate. He wasn't the only one. Mama Renata refused to put it as an official topping on her menu, despite BeeBee knowing she kept it in the storeroom for her sorbet desserts.

BeeBee gave him a wicked smile as she took the largest piece out of the box. "More for me," she said, wiggling happily on her seat after taking a Loch Ness Monster—sized bite. Once she had finished chewing, she reflected, "I think there is a way to improve on it though."

"Remove the pineapple?"

"Hush," she chided, turning the slice over in her hand to inspect it. "We're talking pizza here. This is serious business. I don't have time for your scurvy-addled delusions."

He threw his head back and laughed. "Why do you keep insinuating that I have scurvy?"

"Because you're a pirate and you reject citrus fruits," she replied. "Obviously. Will you let me finish my thought please? It's about food. This is your milieu." She affected an exaggerated accent on the last word. See, he wasn't the only one with an arsenal of fancy-pants French.

Steepling his hands underneath his chin, he nodded. "Go on."

A small white scar on the underside of his pinky finger distracted her from her purpose. It was pale and delicate against the tanned roughness of the rest of his hands. The desire to trace it with her index finger, to feel the new callouses years of work had acquired against the tender skin of her cheeks, tightened inside her like a pulled lasso. She drew a sharp breath in and set her slice down firmly on the plate next to her. *No pizza until you get yourself together, young lady*, she thought sternly to herself.

"Buffalo mozzarella," she said. "Don't you think it would be perfect with those toppings? I mean, I'm not a professional chef, but I have completed over two lessons with the great Chef Bill Danzig, so I think I know what I'm talking about."

"Oh, really?" He cupped his chin with his left hand, leaning back onto the seat with his right. "It does have that creamy unctuousness that pairs nicely with the citrus. You'd have to use hotter peppers, otherwise the flavor profile is too sweet. And smoked prosciutto instead of bacon."

Ticking a finger at his cheek, he thought for just another moment before clasping one hand on each of his knees and nodding. "Okay, then. Let's do it."

"Do what?"

"Make your favorite pizza with buffalo mozzarella as your pageant recipe," Bill said.

BeeBee squinted, unsure whether he was making fun of her or if he was really serious. "But—but that will never work."

"Why not?" He frowned. "The judges will have tried a thousand different cream-based desserts and heavy casseroles. They'll be ready for something different."

"What if it's too different?" She pointed at him. "You don't even like pineapple on pizza."

"But you do, and that's the point."

"If you're circling back to your 'to thine own self be true' schtick, I'm calling Shakespeare's people."

"All I'm saying—" he blatantly ignored her idle threat "—is that the best things come from a place of authenticity. That's all. I'll bring over the ingredients tomorrow, and we can practice, okay?"

BeeBee looked down at her hands, cuffing her right with her left as though breaking in an invisible baseball mitt. "I, uh, I really am grateful for everything you're doing for me, Bill. I wish there was something I could do to pay you back."

He shrugged and took up the oars once more. "It's what friends do," he replied, a strange twist of his lips on the word *friends*.

"I mean it though," she insisted. "There's got to be something you want."

His eyes flickered toward her face, holding it with something BeeBee was too scared to name before flipping the switch back into casual humor. "Well, I have always wanted my own boat…"

"Done," BeeBee said with a smile. "It comes with its own remote control and fits in any standard-size bath tub."

"As long as it has a chef's kitchen and room for tables and chairs on the port side, sounds perfect."

The North Star winked at her from its sentinel place along the ridge of pine trees, as if granting her the one true wish her heart desired. Strangely enough, the first thing that came to her mind wasn't Orlando the majestic water buffalo. Instead, it was Bill's dream boat complete with the kitchen and restaurant-style setup, outdoor pizza oven sold separately.

What was wrong with her?

Clearing her throat, she turned away from the ridiculously romantic scenery clearly muddling her good sense with starlight and whispered sweet nothings about cheese. A new topic was what they needed, something not at all romantic.

"So, the Last Hurrah Barbecue is coming up soon," she blurted out.

He sat back and stroked the oars to pull the boat back toward the dock. "What in the world is the Last Hurrah Barbecue?"

"Oh, I forgot that you were never here for that," she said with a rush of relief and disappointment that the moment of temptation seemed to have passed. "Every year the week before Memorial Day the town has a big get-together by the gazebo to celebrate the last days before the summer tourists swoop in. I promised everyone we would do an ice-cream-sundae bar with special ice cream made out of the water buffaloes' milk, but we've got the FDA inspector coming that morning, so I'm a little worried about getting the ice cream there on time." She let out a deflated sigh. "Kit and Lou are busy with their own things, so it's all on me."

"What about Lucas?"

"He's taking his mom to a doctor's appointment in Rochester," she said. Lucas's mom, her aunt Rose, had recently been diagnosed with Parkinson's disease. "I don't want to put anything else on his plate right now if I can help it."

Bill nodded and gave another pull to the oars.

The way his muscles strained against the sleeves of his shirt clouded her mind with starlight madness again. BeeBee's heart pounded until he spoke again. "What's the big deal if there's no ice-cream-sundae bar?"

"What's the big deal?" Irritation cleared the haze almost instantly. "I made a commitment to the town. Plus, it's tradition. The farm always does some kind of booth at the Last Hurrah."

Bill sighed and set down the oars as the boat bumped gently against the dock. He tied it with swift expert ministrations and climbed up to the edge, holding his hand out to her. "Is it really this important to you?"

BeeBee tilted her chin down and stared up at him through sternly raised eyebrows. "The expectations of my town? The people who depend on me? Do you really need to ask me that?" She folded her arms and refused to stand until he admitted defeat.

His lips twitched. BeeBee knew him well enough to know he was torn between wanting to push her buttons even more and his genuine desire to please people. The latter won out as he rolled his eyes and crouched on one knee. "If I agree to do this, will you take my hand and get out of the boat?"

She sniffed haughtily. "Fine. But only because you begged."

"I didn't—" Bill dropped his head, his bandanna falling adorably askew with the motion. "You are the most stubborn creature on the planet, BeeBee Long. Including your precious water buffaloes—a match made in heaven if there ever was one."

BeeBee stood and reached up to set the bandanna right. Her fingers grazed the soft layer of stubble coating the lower half of his face. He'd shaved regularly the summer they'd been together, and this new piratic addition brought out a rush of tenderness unlike anything she'd ever known. He was still Bill, still charming and effortlessly buoyant as always. But there was a new maturity she saw stirring that she hadn't seen when he first arrived two weeks ago. It made her long for so much more than the dwindling days they had together. She wanted more time with him, time to unwrap the layers of what he had seen and done and become in their years apart. The only problem was whenever she uncovered another new facet, the more of him she wanted. It wasn't fair.

"You really promise you'll help me?" The pleading vulnerability that came out of her voice alarmed even her. BeeBee shot a longing gaze at the lake, wishing she could hurl herself into the water and wallow, invisible, until he had gone.

"Of course I will." He knelt down to unload the cooler and empty pizza boxes from the boat, then they both sat at the edge of the dock, their feet dangling over the water. Bill looked back at her with warning in those eyes that mirrored the hues of her beloved woods. "But you know the deal with my career. I have to be ready for any job the agency sends me on, anywhere in the world. I'm not in a position to promise more than tomorrow."

That was enough for now, she told herself, even as her heart still cried out more. "The barbecue is on Thursday," she said as she clambered to her feet. "I'll bring the ice cream over to the dairy Wednesday night after cooking class. If you can start setting things up, I'll bring the toppings over and help serve as soon as the inspection's done."

"It's a date." Then he flashed that grin of his with one side of his lips quirking higher than the other.

Would the day ever come when that grin didn't leave her completely unglued? Seven years apart hadn't done it. Would seventeen? The thought of seventeen years more without him made her heart sink.

Then he nudged her with his elbow and jutted his chin at the sky. "Looks like a full moon tonight." Under his breath, he hummed "I Have a Dream."

BeeBee followed his gaze upward and made just one more wish.

CHAPTER TEN

THE LAST HURRAH was appropriately named for the whole town seemed to have turned out for the celebration. As much as Bill hated to endorse Crystal Hill's ever-so-slightly unhealthy obsession with its ritual celebration of non-holidays, this one he could actually get behind.

For starters, it was all about the food. Joe Kim had a grill set up in front of his diner, and the savory smell of roasting sausages and burgers wafted across the street every time the breeze shifted. Georgia nodded at Bill as she carried an armful of freshly baked rolls from Stevenson's Antiques and Jewelry, where Mr. Stevenson, a tall thin man with a well-groomed salt-and-pepper moustache, had set up enormous platters of smoked brisket. Mama Renata busily hung entire heads of garlic from the ends of her booth as decoration, at which Bill rolled his eyes. As far as he knew, most of the vacationers the town anticipated came from the city, like his family, and not from Transylvania. Then again, given the amount of black clothing in a typical New Yorker's closet, he could understand the confusion.

Bill shook his head and smoothed the red-and-white checkered tablecloth over the table set up in front of the dairy's store. BeeBee had texted him and said she was on her way with the toppings, but simply waiting around and doing nothing had never been an option for him. What else would they need? Some of the kids from his cooking class waved merrily at him from the steps of the white gazebo at the end of the street on his right. Their faces and hands were painted bright red and yellow from the hot dogs they had devoured. Napkins.

Walking back into the store, Bill's mind wandered as he jogged between the display of cheese-wheel towers to the freezer in the back room. He might as well get the ice cream out now too so it had time to thaw. Being in the deep freezer all night would make it impossible to scoop. But when he got to the freezer drawer, it was already open. Picking up one of the cartons, he could feel the liquid ice cream soup sloshing inside. In his rush to get everything put away last night, he must have forgotten to close the drawer all the way.

Bill shut his eyes, willing time to reverse for not the first time in his life.

He crouched to shut the drawer, then a chorus

of loud voices from outside the shop drew his attention. He straightened up, turned and sprinted for the door the second he realized one of those voices was BeeBee's.

Through the large glass window in front, he could see BeeBee's tall outline and in front of it a semicircle of people with displeased expressions on their faces.

"And what is wrong with my menu?" A woman's voice asked shrilly, faint notes of a Brooklyn accent enhanced by anger.

"That's not what I meant," BeeBee protested. "All I was saying was since Mama Renata's is one of my sponsors for the pageant, it would be a real boost if you added my pizza to the official menu. After all, it hasn't changed in decades. My boy—my friend—Chef Bill…" She stumbled over the words. "He says that variety is what makes the difference between a good chef and a boring one."

"Boring!" Renata's voice ratcheted up so many notches that Bill half expected Trevor the lion dog to leap through the crowd. "My food is not boring. And if you think I'm still going to sponsor you for the pageant after this, you're dreaming. That's it. I'm taking my cannoli back to my boring restaurant."

Bill jumped back when the door opened and the rumble of the crowd grew briefly louder as

BeeBee slipped through the small gap and closed it behind her. She looked at Bill with wide, terrified eyes.

"I've done it again, Bill," she whispered, looking back over her shoulder once at the restless movement on the other side of the door. "Mama Renata's gone full Godfather. Now our ice-cream-sundae bar is the only dessert for the whole town."

Bill gulped as he remembered the drawer to the freezer that he had once again forgotten to close. "Um, about that."

BeeBee paced back and forth in front of the condiments shelves, too rattled to notice his despair. "I left the toppings out there. You can go get them, and I'll get the ice cream. I'll scoop quietly in the background, and you can work your Dread Pirate Charming magic on them. Hopefully we can get someone else to agree to replace Mama Renata as my sponsor, otherwise I'll have to drop out of the pageant."

"I left the freezer door open, and all the ice cream is now soup."

BeeBee stopped pacing. She looked at him with a crestfallen expression that broke his heart into a thousand pieces.

"Oh." She looked down, her entire body deflating in one ragged sigh. "Well, that's not good."

"I'm so sorry," he said, taking a tentative step closer. Sad BeeBee was less dangerous than Angry BeeBee, but it was still best to approach with caution. He reached out a hand to her. "Come on. We'll sneak out the back. They'll get over it eventually."

BeeBee raised her head. "I can't just leave. I need to get another sponsor for the pageant." She reached out, took his hand and squeezed it. "Besides, running away doesn't fix anything."

She was right. He looked at her, really looked at the woman she had become—a resourceful woman with the courage to own up to her mistakes. He squeezed her hand back. If she could be this brave, so could he.

"Okay, so we need a dessert and a sponsor," he said, letting go of her hand reluctantly and turning in a slow circle to survey their resources. "I can't bake anything because there's no oven here. What can we do with melted ice cream?" If there was one thing charter-cruise cooking had taught him, it was how to improvise. "Fudge."

BeeBee rolled her eyes. "It's just us. You can use the actual curse words if you need to."

"No." He chuckled in spite of the circumstances. It was amazing how she could make him laugh even when the world felt like it was crashing down. "I can make a quick fudge with the melted ice cream and toppings. Did you bring hot fudge or chocolate chips?"

"Both," she answered.

"Perfect," he said. Rushing past her, he breezed through the door, snatched up the bags of toppings and pushed back through. "All right. Lucas has a boiler in the back. If we melt the chocolate and mix it with the ice cream, we can spread it in a pan. It should harden in less than half an hour, but there's no guarantee," he added. "The only way this works is with really high-quality ice cream."

BeeBee's chest puffed. "It's made with milk from my water buffaloes. You don't get higher quality than that."

He nodded. "It's worth a shot anyway." Hoisting the bags, he turned and headed for the freezer.

"What can I do to help?"

Bill jutted his chin at the window. "Get back out there, Your Highness. Start working the crowd. Maybe you'll win over a new sponsor before the fudge is cooled."

"Because my personality is famously winning," she retorted sarcastically.

"It won me over," he said softly, turning before she could make another joke.

She had been right about the quality of her ice cream. As Bill mixed the melted chocolate into the rich frothy cream, his chef's intuition told him this was going to work. The high fat content of the water-buffalo milk would add a richness to the texture like condensed milk but without the cloying sweetness. He spread it into the pan he had chilled in the freezer to help it solidify faster, then shoved it into the fridge and closed the door with a firm reassurance.

Wiping his hands on the apron he had liberated from Lucas's supply closet, Bill walked through the store and out onto the street. The high school jazz band played a surprisingly tuneful rendition of Glenn Miller's "A String of Pearls," and the street was now blocked off from car traffic at the intersection by the lake. Children chased errant balloons across Jane Street. A large crowd hovered around Joe Kim's grill, but he didn't see BeeBee among them.

Looking to his left, he finally spotted her gazing at a velvet-covered display of jewelry in the window of the antique store. Mrs. Van Ressler stood next to her, gesturing dramatically as Bee-Bee nodded.

"Did you actually meet Fellini at the screen test in Italy?" BeeBee was asking when he walked closer.

Mrs. Van Ressler nodded proudly. "Yes. He looked me up and down, said, 'Beautiful, but no,' then walked away. Apparently he was a man who preferred pictures to words."

"You know, I could really use your movie-star expertise to help me with my poses for the evening-gown portion of the pageant," BeeBee said in an admiring voice.

The older woman's strong features cracked into a small smile. "Come by the B and B later today. I'll show you what I did when I posed nude for Modigliani."

Bill turned on his heel and moved out of eavesdropping range quickly at that, but the expression on his face in the dairy shop's window beamed. He knew she could do it. The summer they had spent together had been a whirlwind of infatuation and pure, distilled fun. Now he was glimpsing the full spectrum of BeeBee, flaws and all. Somehow, he liked her even better for the way she owned them. It made him want to do even more to show her he was more than the carefree teenager he had once been too.

When he took the fudge out of the fridge, it seemed like his food was once again the answer. It was perfect, the knife sinking in with a gentle resistance and the candy pieces, sprinkles and tiny marshmallows studding the top like edible jewels in a cavern made of chocolate. He arranged it neatly on a platter and, in a final moment of inspiration, grabbed a gallon of farm-fresh milk and a box of sample cups from the store room. BeeBee was doing great on her own, but it wouldn't hurt to remind everyone that her hard work on the farm provided a bulk of the milk for this town.

The entire thing was gone within an hour, and not only had Mr. Stevenson and Mrs. Van Ressler agreed to sponsor BeeBee for the pageant, but Renata had cooled off and agreed to add BeeBee's pizza to the menu if she won the pageant. As they cleared the table, BeeBee slid a sidelong glance at him.

"Thanks for saving the day," she said before bending down to catch an empty cup that had fallen to the sidewalk. Tossing it into the garbage can in front of the streetlight, she turned and strolled back to lean both hands on the table. "How'd you come up with the idea so quickly?"

"Improvising on the spot is an essential skill for working charter yachts." Bill wiped his forehead with the back of his arm, frowning slightly. "But I didn't save the day. I was the one who almost ruined it."

She quirked her head to one side. "You stuck around to fix it. That's all that really matters."

For a moment, the commotion around them, the music, even the smoky breeze seemed to stop. He couldn't stop his eyes from falling to her lips, wide and smiling. The longing to gather her in his arms was almost overpowering. Then she pushed her hands off the table, and he reminded himself to breathe evenly again.

"Anyway," she went on as if the world hadn't spiraled into colorful fireworks between them mere seconds ago, "I had better get back to the farm. I've got to get the heifers into the milking stand one more time today."

"Need any help?" he offered, lifting off the tablecloth and shaking out the crumbs before folding it neatly.

She threw back her head and laughed. "Stick to the kitchen, Billabelle. I'm used to tackling the farm mostly on my own."

"Just want you to know you don't have to manage everything by yourself," he said, his voice lowering with sincerity. "We make a pretty good team. Like peanut butter and jelly."

"Like pineapple on pizza?"

He pointed his left finger at the lake. "Get out."

The echoing peal of her laughter rang in his ears long after she had gone.

The next morning, a call on his cell startled Bill out of a very pleasant dream in which he had won a Nobel Prize for Cooking (Dream Bill had thought this a surprising turn of events, but since the king of Sweden had pronounced his meatballs "better than Ikea's," he had decided to just roll with it).

Rolling onto his side, Bill opened one eye and groggily felt on the floor below the futon for his phone. Seriously, who was calling him at seven in the morning? Not even his big sister would be that mean. Seeing that the number was international, however, his annoyance rapidly turned to curiosity. It was still another three weeks before he was scheduled to work his first charter yacht for the summer season, so it was a little early for a booking agent to be calling him about the details. Clearing his throat, he tapped the screen eagerly.

"Hello."

"Hello, is this Chef Bill Danzig?" A heavily accented Italian voice spoke on the other line.

"Yeah, it's me. Are you with the yacht-booking agency?"

"Actually, no, although they are who referred us to you," the woman said. "Apologies. I am Signora Del Pizo. I am the representative for the Italian Committee for Arts and Humanities. Our annual awards gala which honors notable members of the community is being held on a yacht, the *Alegria*, in two weeks. Unfortunately, our head chef had to pull out at the last minute due to a family emergency. The agency highly recommended you as a replacement."

"Really?" Bill switched the phone to his left hand and pushed himself up on his right elbow. "That's very flattering. Where and when exactly is the dinner?"

"The yacht will be docked in Marina di Portofino," she replied. "The gala is scheduled for Saturday evening of June nineteenth."

June nineteenth. Why was that date ringing alarm bells in his head? The official start to his charter season was the twenty-fifth, so that couldn't be it. Whatever it was, nothing could be more important than cooking for a prestigious organization like this. Forget the paycheck, it would be worth it for the fresh ingredients alone. Fragrant lemon groves you could smell from miles away. Juicy San Marzano tomatoes. Pillows of fresh mozzarella di bufala—oh no. Bill's heart crashed into the pit of his stomach. Now he remembered why the nineteenth was a big deal.

It was the night before BeeBee's pageant.

Not only would he miss the event itself, he would have to leave a few days before to plan the menu, formalize a list for the suppliers and meet with the staff who would be cooking under him. It would mean losing almost an entire week with her—helping her. That was what he meant.

"Could I, um, think about it and call you back?" Worried he might sound less than enthusiastic, he added, "I'm very interested—I just need to confirm a few things about my schedule with the booking agency. Can I call you back in a day, two tops?"

The woman sighed. "All right, but please let us know as soon as you're able. This is the number to reach me. Ciao."

Bill clicked End on the call and raked his hand through his hair. This was big. There would be celebrities and billionaire donors at this sort of thing, people who hired personal chefs for their holidays and vacation homes all around the world. They could afford the best ingredients, the rarest foods he had only read about in textbooks. A personal-chef gig would give him a place to land for longer than a few weeks without locking him into the nightmare of leases and the stifling repetition of a normal restaurant job. This could be the perfect stopgap until the next big exciting thing came along.

After throwing on a T-shirt and jeans and wrapping the Nittany Lions bandanna Lucas had given him around his forehead, Bill clattered down the stairs into the dairy shop. Judging by the clanging sounds coming from Lucas's "cheese lab" behind a curtain, his friend was already up and busy with his craft. Bill checked his watch and rapped on the doorframe next to the red curtain.

"Hey, man," he called into the room. "I should be heading out to the farm to help BeeBee pretty soon. Is the buffalo mozzarella ready?"

Last night, he had asked Lucas to throw together some balls of mozzarella for him and Bee-Bee to practice with. The process generally took a few hours, but Lucas was a night owl who would be up late making cheese for the local restaurants in addition to their own retail offerings. Like Bill, he was a perfectionist who hyper-focused on his passion, ignoring all else. Unlike Bill, he had deep roots here in Crystal Hill and had known exactly what he wanted to do with his life here since he'd been a little kid. It was hard not to envy someone whose path in life seemed so clear and direct. If Bill's life had a visual path, it would resemble that of an inflatable raft tossed into a storm-blown ocean.

"Almost," Lucas shouted back. "I'm rolling the last batch out of the bath now. The rest of the ingredients you asked for are in the fridge in the stock room. If you can grab those, we can head out as soon as I'm done here."

"Thanks."

Lucas walked past the counter and opened the door to the steps leading down to the basement stockroom. The shelves of the temperature-controlled room were lined with wheels of cave cheese silently waiting to be shown off in all their glory. He shivered as he opened the door to the fridge and pushed aside containers of freshly made yogurts and gallons of milk to the package wrapped in brown paper marked *Danzig*. Removing the package, he opened it with a satisfying crinkle of the paper. The prosciutto was gloriously pink with a thin strip of white marbling woven along the edge. It was vacuum-sealed shut, but the pineapple was sliced and so fresh the floral scent wafted out of the bag like a heavenly breeze. There would never be a world where he agreed that pineapple belonged in the category of pizza toppings, but if you had to do it, then it should be with a beautiful piece of fruit like this.

He folded the wrapping back over top of the produce and tucked it safely under his arm.

Lucas was out in the shop and removing the white overshirt he wore in his lab. Hanging it on the hook, he turned back and held aloft a net bag full of mozzarella. "Got the cheese. This was a really great batch. Oh, and the Calabrian chilis you wanted are on the shelf to your right. I'll make a note for Pop that we liberated it for personal use."

They went out to Lucas's truck with supplies in hand. As they drove past the lake, Bill thought about the way BeeBee had looked at him last night. Once they had moved past the fight downtown and joked their way through any lingering tension, she had regarded him with a calm he hadn't seen in her before. So much about her was the same, and yet her scattershot energy had been concentrated into a purpose. When she had talked about choosing to make Crystal Hill her place, it had been with the same meaningful intent that people talked about their marriages or their children. Someone who didn't know BeeBee might mistake her happy-go-lucky demeanor for impulsiveness. The woman didn't have an impulsive bone in her body. Everything she did was deliberate, from choosing to raise water buffaloes in a spot where the water and grass were uniquely suited for their milk to remaining in a town where people had learned over time to love her for who she really was. It all made sense now.

"You look pleased about something," Lucas remarked as the shadows of the trees allowed them to see without squinting again. "Don't tell me the elusive bachelor Bill Danzig has found love at last."

Bill barked a startled cough and turned his flaming face to the window. "I—what, no. It's work. I've had a good offer to be the head chef for a big dinner thing on a yacht in Italy in two weeks. Since that'll get me out of your hair sooner than we'd expected, that should make you happy too."

"Well, I'm happy for you." Lucas's nose wrinkled at the bridge. "Bummed for me. It's been nice having you around."

"Yeah right," Bill scoffed, half-heartedly punching Lucas in the right arm. "I know people get tired of me after a while."

Lucas snorted. "Who told you that?"

Bill shrugged even though he knew exactly who'd told him that. Every teacher who'd loved his outgoing personality until right around Christmas when the excitement of the holidays had had him wiggling like a puppy all the time. Even his grandparents who watched him and his sister when their parents travelled had little tolerance for the noise and constant motion that followed Bill like a wake after a speedboat. For nearly everyone in his life, he was basically essence of rose in a dessert—good in small amounts only and easily overwhelming.

Everyone except BeeBee.

"Eh," he grunted, turning his head to stare out the window again. "No one in particular."

"Well, I for one am glad you're here," he said. "It's the least I can do to thank you for getting my mom into your sister's clinical trials."

Bill waved his hand. "It wasn't a big deal. A couple of phone calls." And emails. And relentless texts. His sister, while an extremely brilliant neurologist, wasn't the best with communication. But this was his friend's mom. He didn't mind being a little bit more of a pain in his sister's backside than usual.

Lucas stopped the truck at the farm's gates

and looked him square in the eye. "It was a big deal." He broke his gaze away, tapping the steering wheel with the palm of his hand. "Mom was really having a hard time with the diagnosis. This trial gave her hope." Reaching into the cup holder, he took a clicker out of the cup holder and pressed it. The gates opened slowly, and Lucas put the car back into drive with a chuckle. "Did you know that your mom and my mom have become like besties?"

"No way."

"Really. Since Ma's been coming into the city for appointments, your mom meets up with her for coffee beforehand. Your folks are even talking about getting a vacation home out here so they can spend summers and holidays together."

"Huh." Bill rolled down his window and leaned his arm on the rim. The sun baked down on him with a warmth that heralded summer's arrival. He had no idea about any of this. Being out at sea meant that he talked with his folks sporadically at best—and sometimes not at all for weeks if it was a really busy charter. For the first time, he indulged in picturing a future further down the road then the next charter. Campfires with his and Lucas's families, being in the area long enough to see the explosion of color in the fall foliage. Putting decorations on an actual Christmas tree instead of making a tree-shaped garnish out of rosemary for holiday cruisers. The thought was impossibly tempting. Especially because in every scenario he pictured, BeeBee was there too.

When they got to the farm, Bill heard sounds coming from the barn, but they were too high-pitched to be any of the Long sisters. After helping Lucas load the barrels of milk from the storage area behind the milking stand into the back of his truck, he jogged up the front steps and swiped the sweat beading beneath his bandanna before coming inside.

One of the twins—the one with the glasses—sat at the table with a pile of fabric and a sewing machine in front of her. She raised an arm in greeting but didn't turn around to see who had entered.

"Hi, Bill," she called out over the clacking of the machine.

"How'd you know it was me?" he asked in a similarly raised voice.

She stopped and put a finger to her temple. "I sensed your presence," she said in a mystical voice before twisting in her chair and draping an elbow over the back rails. "Nah, just messing with you. BeeBee said you were stopping by. She's upstairs with Lou getting the beauty treatment."

"Another one?" Bill took off his shoes so he didn't track mud across the carpet, then settled himself onto the couch with a sigh. "Just so you know, I heard noises coming from the barn. Sounded like a kid's voice maybe?"

"Oh, that's just Caroline," Kit said as she pushed her glasses back up on her nose and returned to her machine. "BeeBee told her she could come by and visit the kittens this morning while the big animals were grazing. She's a good kid, and we went over all the safety stuff with her the first time she came over. But thanks for the reminder. I'll go check on her after I finish this costume."

"Costume?" He raised both eyebrows. "You got BeeBee to agree to a costume? We did a dance routine on Seventies Night at summer camp, and the closest thing to a costume she would agree on was adhesive sequins for her denim overalls."

Kit snorted. "Not for her. This is for me and Lou. For her creative introduction, we're doing a sketch sort of like that old game we used to play—Guess Who? We'll hold silhouette shadow boards over our faces and tell stories about BeeBee as people from the town. BeeBee will guess who the individual is, and we'll lower the board and pretend to surprise her. The script is hilarious. BeeBee actually wrote most of it herself."

"Self-deprecating humor is kind of her superpower," he admitted.

"She figured it was a great way to show the

judges how she doesn't take herself too seriously," Kit replied. "Kind of like a self-roast. It's clever because while all the other contestants will be humblebragging about themselves, BeeBee will do the opposite. At the very least, she'll stand out."

"As if she could ever blend in." Bill shook his head, once again in awe of the woman. He had been so concerned about her putting herself down. All the while, she had seen the winning strategy ten steps ahead. Before he could make a mental note never to go against her in a game of chess, footsteps coming down the stairs behind the fireplace drew his attention. He steeled himself for another brightly colored face mask or some sort of posture-improving contraption brought to them by the good people at Straitjackets "R" Us. But no amount of preparation could have readied him for what appeared at the bottom of the steps.

Bill's jaw went slack, and as he sat there with what was probably the world's dopiest expression on his face, BeeBee ducked her head and peered at him through eyes wide with uncertainty.

"Well, what do you think?" she asked, gesturing down her body with her hands. "Is it too much? I look ridiculous, don't I? See, Lou, I told you it was too much. I'd do my 'I told you so' dance, but I can't move in this getup."

"This getup" was a white halter-top gown that scooped low at her neckline and cinched her waist at the center with a silvery star-shaped brooch reminiscent of a jazz singer from the nineteen twenties. The gown sparkled like a freshly snow-covered field, and a high slit up one side revealed a length of suntanned leg that turned Bill's mouth to sawdust. The way her hair was gathered up at the back of her head highlighted the graceful curve of her neck. The dress, the hair, the makeup—all of it shone a spotlight on the aspects of her beauty that only someone intimately close to her might appreciate. It was just BeeBee, but on a pedestal for all the world to recognize what he did…

That she was extraordinary in every way possible.

The other twin, Lindsay, slid between BeeBee and the stair rail, hopping the last two steps as if they were nothing. She backed up a few steps and looked BeeBee up and down before turning her palms to the ceiling.

"What are you talking about, 'too much'?" She sounded exasperated, and her curly hair stuck out in wisps over her head, as if getting BeeBee into the gown had required considerable wrangling. "This dress fits you perfectly. I can't believe Kit found it lying around in the back of Stevenson's Antiques and Jewelry. It's like it was made for you. Bill, can you please tell her how gorgeous she looks?"

"Oh, I don't think he has to say anything," Kit added slyly from the kitchen. "Look at his face. He might as well have the word *Owwwoooga* typed in a thought bubble over his head."

A rosy flush speckled the front of BeeBee's chest and traveled up the side of her neck. "You guys stop picking on him," she said, biting her lower lip yet unable to stop the pleased cat-with-a-bowl-of-cream smile from pulling her cheeks outward. "He gets that goggle-eyed look a lot. It's probably the scurvy."

Bill removed the imaginary heart emojis from his eyes long enough to roll them. "For the last time, I don't have—"

The door flew open behind him, interrupting his protestation. It was Caroline. Her breath came in great, panicky heaves, and fear was written all over her face.

"Carebear, what's wrong?" BeeBee hiked her skirt up to rush to the girl's side.

Bill chuckled at the worn sneakers underneath her gown. Yup, still BeeBee.

"It's Jeremy," Caroline got out between gasps.

"Binkus?" BeeBee frowned. "What's he done now?"

"He wanted to come with me to see the animals, so my mom drove him over," Caroline admitted in a tumble of words. "He stacked the hay bales and climbed up to the beams on the loft, even though I told him you said never to do that. The hay fell over, and he's hanging from the roof. I'm afraid he's going to fall."

By the time she had finished, Bill had jumped to his feet and BeeBee had already flown out the door. With Katelyn and Lindsay behind him, he followed BeeBee through the gate and to the barn. He let out a sigh of relief to see that Jeremy was indeed still clinging to the beam of the lofted roof like a barn owl. Toppled hay bales lay scattered across the floor of the barn.

"Help," cried Jeremy, kicking his legs beneath him as he attempted to claw a tighter grip on the beam. "I'm slipping."

Like lightning, BeeBee tossed one hay bale on top of another and scrambled to the top. Bill stood below and held his arms up, ready to catch whoever fell first even if he needed to serve as a human mattress below them. Fortunately, Bee-Bee's height allowed her to reach Jeremy's waist. But he continued to flail in alarm, and when BeeBee nearly toppled as she ducked his foot, Bill's heart went to his throat. True, this wasn't a life-threatening situation. He had been involved in more than one of those on boats during some pretty severe weather conditions, and yet during each of those events, his heart had stayed put.

But this was BeeBee—his BeeBee—and seeing her in any kind of pain was not going to happen on his watch.

She put her hands down on the haybale next to her feet to steady herself, then rose back with her arms stretched outward for balance.

"Okay, Binkus," she called to him, hunching away from his feet. "I need you to stop kicking your feet so I can grab you. I'm not going to let you fall, I promise."

"I'm scared," he cried out as one hand slid lower from the edge of the beam.

"Trust me," BeeBee called back. She lifted her hands to him once more, and this time he stopped kicking. She grasped his small waist, her face clenched with determined concentration. Every muscle in her back and arms, visible in the revealing gown, strained in the effort as she lowered him down to her at the very moment the hay bales tipped over.

"Bill, get him," she yelled, pushing the boy in his direction as she lost her balance and fell when the bales gave way beneath her feet.

Jeremy came at him with the force of a small freight train, and even though Bill was able to catch him under the arms, the weight threw Bill staggering back into one of the stalls. His hamstrings screamed as he tried to slow their descent, and somehow he managed to get one arm behind him to break the fall while still holding on to Jeremy with the other. Pain shot through the other arm when the brunt of the impact went through it. Once the stars in his head had cleared, however, he was able to sit up and roll his wrist easily. What scared him more than losing his knife skills was BeeBee's prostrate form on the floor between the bales of hay. Lindsay and Katelyn were hovering over her, so all he could see was the glitter of her skirt and her sneakers laying terrifyingly still.

Wrenching his eyes away, he forced himself to focus for a moment on the boy untangling himself from the arm Bill had hooked under his shoulder.

"You okay, kid?" Bill asked in a hoarse voice. "Sit up slowly. Nice, deep breaths. Did you bump your head?"

Jeremy was pale, his face almost the same color as his white-blond hair. But he was alert and able to rise shakily to his feet. "N-no, I didn't hit my head." His eyes shifted worriedly over Bill's shoulder. "Is Farmer BeeBee okay?"

A horrified gasp from one of the twins sent Bill running to the spot where the two young women hovered over her. He grasped BeeBee's hand and brought it to his lips. "I'm here. What is it? What's wrong?"

Lindsay answered in a sorrowful moan. "The dress. It's ruined."

BeeBee pushed herself onto one elbow, wincing. "Meh. White was never really my color anyway."

Bill's entire chest felt like it caved in on itself with relief.

He and Katelyn each put a hand under her arm and eased her to her feet as she tried to wave them away. Miraculously, nothing seemed to be harmed too badly. Well, perhaps not nothing. The dress was, indeed, a disaster. One of the straps around the neckline was holding on by a tattered thread, and what had once been a twinkling field of snow now looked like it was streaked by muddy brown water-buffalo tracks. Bill heard small footsteps come up behind him.

"I'm—I'm sorry," Jeremy said in a small, scared voice behind them. "Caroline told me not to climb up there. Please don't be mad at me."

Still holding on to BeeBee's arm, Bill felt like he was looking into a mirror. How many times had something like this happened when he'd been a kid, when his energy had been too much to contain or instructions had flown out of his head the minute a potential adventure had called?

He leaned in to BeeBee to whisper to her to go easy, but as usual, she beat him to the punch.

"At ease, Binkus." She gave a small laugh, then put a hand to her side as if the movement had pained her. "I did exactly the same thing when I was your age. It's why I specifically warned Caroline about it—I learned from experience. Next time, just let us know when you come over to visit so we can give you the safety drill first, okay?"

The way the boy's face brightened instantly was enough to bring a lump of tears in Bill's throat. It would have been so easy for most adults to unleash frustration on a kid for simply being a kid and making a mistake at the very time in life when mistakes could be made with minimal harm. The margin for error narrowed so quickly the older you got. That was when you learned how hearts can be so much more fragile than bones.

"I can come back?" he asked hopefully. "Really?"

"Really," BeeBee said as she limped toward the door. "I'm gonna need more good farmhands to train as my water-buffalo herd grows. But it's really important to slow down and make good choices when you work with animals. Dresses can be replaced. Animals are one of a kind."

Jeremy nodded so solemnly. Bill could almost see the dawning comprehension spreading through the boy's mind, the same feeling he had gotten the first time he had set foot on a boat. It was the knowledge that there could be a place and a purpose for boys like him. Maybe there were other people besides BeeBee in Crystal Hill who liked having him around.

Katelyn and Lindsay relinquished BeeBee to swoop into comforting Jeremy and Caroline, who was waiting at the gate with tears streaming down her face. At the entrance to the barn, Bill tugged BeeBee's arm and pulled her back.

"What's the matter, Cap'n?" she asked, the strength in her voice returning with her sense of humor. "If you want to kidnap me, have at it. I'm pretty sure Lou and Kit will make me walk the plank for ruining this dress."

Bill ran his hands down her forearms and squeezed cach of her hands in his. "Are you sure you're okay? You're not just pretending so we don't worry?"

She quirked one eyebrow up at him. "Billifred. You know mc better than that. I never suffer in silence." Looking down at their entwined hands, the sarcastic tone in her voice lowered with unshared emotion. "It's sweet of you to be concerned though."

"Well." He should let go of her hands. He should walk away, keep this light and casual the way he had planned so no one got hurt again. But as usual, knowing what he should do didn't keep him from doing the exact opposite. Stepping closer, he skated a thumb across each of her knuckles. "That's what friends are for, right?"

"Right," she answered as if mesmerized by the same unseen magic closing in, pressing them toward one another. "We're friends."

Their bodies less than an inch apart, Bill could feel her breath rise to his cheek as she lifted her face. "Good friends," he murmured through the tightness in his throat. "Good friends who hold each other's hands. Who can hug and...and..."

He didn't need to say the word. He couldn't say the word because the feeling welling up inside him was too great for words to express.

So he kissed her.

CHAPTER ELEVEN

THE FIRST TIME Bill had kissed her, it had been late at night after their performance at Seventies Night. He had made a campfire and they had just finished their s'mores. His lips had tasted like burnt marshmallow and sweet chocolate. Only that lingering taste had convinced Bee-Bee that the moment was real, that Bill Danzig, the guy who could've had any girl at camp, was kissing her. Not Jackie, not Anna Steinberg, the head cheerleader. Her. It had felt like a fairy tale, right up until the unhappily-ever-after way it had ended.

This time, BeeBee was old enough to know better than to believe in fairy tales. She knew that a kiss was just a kiss and Prince Charmings didn't marry dirt-stained stable girls. It was just a kiss.

But this kiss.

This kiss was real. It grounded her with the realization of finally knowing exactly what she wanted and who she wanted to be with in this lifetime. Her hands found his waist as his cradled her cheeks, and they held each other so tightly there was no gap for light, no air between their lips. His fingers threaded through her hair, tipping her head back, and when his mouth moved away from hers to softly brush one temple and then the other, she clung to his shirt like a life raft. This wasn't a sweet, fairy-tale embrace.

It was perfect.

The snap of a footstep startled them into breaking apart, but it turned out to be more hoof than foot. A few of the cows had meandered back into the pen and idly chewed on hay from the red metal wheel in front of the barn.

BeeBee chuckled self-consciously and put a hand to her head. "I have more hay in my hair than they do in the feeder," she said. Her hand wandered thoughtlessly down to the tingling skin on her cheek where his stubble had grazed her. "I'm probably such a mess."

He reached out to cover her hand on her face with his, and when he looked at her, a thrill pierced her all the way through her body. "I think you've never looked more beautiful than you do right now."

Her eyes flicked down to the dirt stains covering her gown then back to his face, that face that had never truly left her mind, her dreams, her heart.

"Are you sure you didn't hit your head?" she teased, needing to break the intensity of the feelings threatening to spill into tears.

"If I did—" he bent his head to hers and took her lips in a light stroke of his own before breaking away once more "—I don't want this particular hallucination to end. I've missed you all these years, BeeBee. I didn't realize how much until just now."

BeeBee pressed her lips together and shut her eyes. If she said the wrong thing this time and ruined this moment, she would never forgive herself. But this was Bill. The one person in the world who made her feel perfect just as she was. She let the words tumble. "I tried not to miss you. I tried so hard not to think about you." She opened her eyes, and he was still there. That was all the reassurance she needed to tell him the truth. "But it didn't matter how many times I told myself you were gone. Every time I had an incredible meal or when something made me laugh really hard, you were the first person I wanted to share that moment with. Whenever I heard a dang ABBA song, I could have sworn you were right there, humming along. I couldn't let you go, Bill. A part of me always hoped..." She trailed off just before finishing the confession with the truth—that she had always hoped they would end up here. Because this was one kiss. One kiss didn't guarantee forever.

She let him fold her in his arms as if she was something tender and precious and rare. The feeling was wonderful and also terrifying because what if she broke?

Laying her cheek on the side of his neck, she let herself breathe in his comforting scent and warmth like clothes fresh from the dryer one more time. It was a refuge she didn't want to leave. She had just bared her soul, the secret thoughts she had kept to herself for the last seven years. All BeeBee knew was that she needed to be the one to break the spell first this time.

Pressing her hands lightly on his chest, Bee-Bee cleared her throat. "Um, so I guess we should probably get inside and get cleaned up. As assistant chef, I know the first rule is to never touch food before washing your hands."

"Right," he answered. Swallowing hard, he bobbed his head in a nod. "Sounds good. So, um, I guess let's head back inside?"

"Yeah," she said, surprised at how glum her voice sounded. Who could be sad about making homemade pizza? She supposed when the alternative was kissing a gorgeous pirate in your barn—everyone, probably.

Kit and Lou insisted on taking over the chores for the afternoon despite BeeBee's continual assurance that she was uninjured and perfectly capable of resuming her regular duties, thank you very much. Her protestations quieted when it occurred to her that an afternoon alone with Bill might not be such a bad thing. If her sisters saw anything hinting at romance between the two of them, they would become immediately and excessively invested. She didn't even want to think about the implications of Lucas finding out. But if the girls were out in the milking stands and the fields all day, that was a different story.

Bill showed her how to make the pizza crust from scratch, his hands gliding over hers as he stood behind her and showed her how to knead the dough without overworking it. If anyone had told her before that there was something more enticing than the smell of fried bacon, BeeBee would have denounced them as an obvious liar. That afternoon, though, she learned that stolen kisses behind the cover of the refrigerator door would prove a greater draw than the prosciutto, which burned while she was…distracted. The fact that the crust eventually suffered the same blackened fate made the afternoon no less enjoyable. Sure, the first try at her pageant pizza recipe had ended up a charred, half-risen mess. But the way Bill's lips sent tingles when he whispered instructions into her ear was more delicious than any gourmet concoction anyway.

When Kit and Lou returned at the end of the day, they sniffed the acrid smell lingering in the air and shared disappointed glances.

"Well, at least your creative presentation is good," Kit said mournfully as Lou looked in dismay at the ruined gown BeeBee had taken off and hung in the laundry room between the front door and the kitchen.

BeeBee looked over her shoulder at Bill, whose cheeks were flushed for reasons other than the heat of the oven. "I'll get the recipe right," she said, suppressing a satisfied smile. "Even if we have to work on it every single day this week."

"I can stay into the evenings if I need to," Bill added, removing his bandanna to run his hands through hair that was even more unkempt than usual.

Lou closed the laundry-room door and shook her head. "Even if you get the pizza recipe perfect, that still leaves the interview and the gown up in the air," she moaned.

"Meh." BeeBee turned around to face Kit and waved her hand, sending a cloud of flour into the air like fairy dust. "I'll go shopping next weekend and find a dress. There's probably a ton of prom dresses for sale at the big consignment shop in Binghamton. This week I should really focus on making out—I mean, making our recipe a triumph."

Behind her, Bill sounded very much like he choked on his own laughter.

The following week went by in a blur of sneaking pineapple-scented kisses between rehearsing the presentation, memorizing the new interview scripts Jackie had emailed her and Lou's addition of fifteen-minute HIIT workouts every afternoon before she left for her evening dance classes. HIIT supposedly stood for *high-intensity interval training*, although after the first day BeeBee was fairly certain the name came from the feeling that you had been quite literally hit by a freight train. The morning after she had barely been able to move off the couch. Normally she would have found this situation intolerable. However, with Bill sitting next to her, offering encouragement in the form of neck rubs, being temporarily immobilized wasn't actually so terribly after all. Even when every muscle ached each time she moved her head, he still managed to make her laugh when he read Kit's and Lou's parts of the people in town as they rehearsed her presentation.

He so quickly became part of her daily routine that when he wasn't around, she felt slightly unmoored. Even her water buffaloes, sensitive creatures who didn't adapt easily to new people, began to look behind her for Bill when she gave them their evening feedings. Three out of four nights he had stayed to cook dinner for the whole family, and BeeBee's mom had started referring to them as a unit—"Bill and the girls"—when calling everyone in to discuss the family's constantly shifting schedule of activities for the week.

If any of this caused Bill to feel smothered, he certainly didn't show it. He stayed later and later each night, walking out to the barn with her to watch the moon appear in the night sky. With his arms draped around her and the sounds of the animals shuffling gently around them in the darkness, BeeBee made a wish on every star above them that she could freeze time and live in this moment forever.

That Friday she got up extra early and started on her pizza crust dough so it would have time to rise before she started her work. Bill was helping Lucas in the shop that day. Even though a stab of missing him kept her eyes wandering to the front door, she reminded herself that he wouldn't be able to make the pizza with her at the pageant. But he would be there. That was what was important. Bill was the only thing keeping her anxiety from peaking off the charts every time she looked at the calendar and watched the days until the pageant winnowing down in large red Xs. As long as he was in the audience, she would be able to get through it without crying or jumping out of a window.

Stirring the sizzling pancetta—after several variations, they had landed on pancetta as the perfect meat topping—she smiled at the image of his face, beaming with pride when they announced her as the winner. As she rolled out the dough and dusted it with cornmeal, the fantasy continued and expanded. He would, of course, want to stay just a little longer to meet Orlando, the fruits of all their hard labor, wouldn't he? And when he saw the possibilities of a thriving water-buffalo farm, an untapped market with such a wonderful culinary product, he wouldn't walk away from it, not even for a job on a royal yacht. There were plenty of restaurants here in town, or he could even open his own. She could feel the smile widening, brimming all the way down to her toes at the thought of her getting the chance to stand by his side at his moment of glory when he cut the ribbon on his restaurant. Maybe she would even wear her crown, for fun. Three weeks ago she couldn't understand the appeal it held to the other girls at the pageant seminar. But having something—someone—to wear it for? That made all the difference.

Of course, none of that mattered unless she

got this pizza right. The very last step was nestling the beautifully soft clouds of buffalo mozzarella between the colorful array of toppings. BeeBee held her breath as she slid the pizza stone into the oven and closed the door. Catching a glimpse of her reflection in the oven door, she shook her head at Oven BeeBee. Silly Oven BeeBee, who somehow thought that the key to everything in her life was nailing this recipe. And yet she crouched in front of the oven anyway, refusing to move in case she got distracted and burned the darned thing again. Because no matter what sensible Real BeeBee told herself, a part of her truly believed if she could do this one thing right, anything was possible.

So when the oven timer beeped, she cautiously opened the door and let out a gasp of delighted surprise. It was perfect. Golden-brown crust, gooey cheese spreading into the caramelized pineapple and peppers. Her mouth watered instantly at the smell of the pancetta. With one hand, she reached for her cow-print oven mitts on the counter. BeeBee didn't want to take her eyes off the pizza. Knowing her luck, it would burst into flames the very second she looked away. She pulled the pizza stone out of the oven and gently tipped the pizza onto the cooling rack.

"I did it!" she yelled at the top of her lungs even though the house was, for once, completely empty. Not even the cats, who appeared from their various hidey holes and hunting positions in the barns whenever the oven opened.

BeeBee looked around at the stillness, her excitement deflating rapidly. This was what her life would be like soon enough—her sisters pulled across the globe by their gifts. Even her parents were talking about buying an RV and travelling once the twins left. Someday it would just be her and her animals. Removing the oven mitts, she tossed them onto the counter. For so long, she had thought that would be enough for her. But the silence hit her so differently now that it was really here. It was…lonely. She crossed her arms and blinked back tears until the pizza came back into focus. This creation really was a thing of beauty. And there was only one person who would appreciate its glory. That one person was still here. She wasn't alone—not yet and maybe not ever if she and her magic pizza could show him that life in this small town could be adventure enough for them both.

Frantically, she threw open the cabinets and drawers. She wasn't sure what she was looking for as they certainly didn't make pizza-sized Tupperware. There was, however, a portable cake stand. It was large and round. Lifting it out from the cabinet below the mixer, she twisted off the lid and set it next to the cooling rack.

"Hot, ow, hot," she muttered as she slid the pizza carefully onto the circular cake plate. In hindsight, keeping the oven mitts on would have been smart, but there was no time for that now. She placed the top back over the plate and screwed it on tightly before hoisting it in both arms and carrying it like a baby out the door. Once in the car, she strapped the seat belt over it and tucked it in tightly.

"Stay warm, little pizza baby," she said before hitting the gas.

BeeBee flew down the dirt road, honking her horn in passing at the Countess, who seemed to lift her horns in solidarity as the car went by. Pride swelled in BeeBee's heart. Soon there would be more just like her, and the fields she drove by would be full of water buffaloes as far as the eye could see. People would hear the name Crystal Hill and think of more than a summer vacation spot where they would spend a golden afternoon in the water. They would think of the dairy, of creamy mozzarella and tangy yogurt, and they would see Crystal Hill as more than just a temporary respite. They would think of Crystal Hill and they would see a home.

At least she hoped one person might see it that way.

That one person was still in the shop with Lucas since she could see his jacket hanging on the coat hook when she entered the store. Setting her pizza down on the counter, she tucked a stray hair that had come loose from her braid behind her ear and brushed the flour off her jeans. Deep male voices rumbled from the cheese room. Bee-Bee knew better than to go into Lucas's special "cheese lab" without donning the equivalent of a hazmat suit when she was wearing her farm clothes. But when she heard her name, BeeBee flattened herself against the Gouda display shelf and pressed an ear to the slight gap between the wall and the curtain.

"What—what do you mean?" Bill laughed, but the stammer gave away an unusual nervousness to his voice.

"You and BeeBee," Lucas repeated sternly. "How long have you two been seeing each other?"

"What makes you think BeeBee and I are seeing each other?"

BeeBee rolled her eyes. Bill was almost as bad a liar as she was. They were definitely busted, although Lucas was going to find out eventually anyway. Especially if the magic pizza worked and Bill stuck around for good.

"Come on, man," Lucas scoffed. "I saw you guys kissing beside the barn last night when I stopped by to drop off another round of the mozzarella balls. I'm not mad or anything. Just a little confused why you wouldn't tell me about it."

"Well, this time—"

"I'm sorry, this time?"

Bill sighed loud enough for BeeBee to hear over the slight hum of Lucas's boilers. "We started seeing each other the last summer I was a counselor at Camp Herkimer. We broke up right before I left for culinary school. It was BeeBee's senior year. We didn't say anything at the time because, you know, you were my best friend and basically the closest thing she's got to a big brother," he said, adding after Lucas huffed loudly, "You and I both know how protective you are of your family. We didn't want things to get weird—that's all. It was just a summer romance. She and I both agreed at the end it was best if we went our separate ways."

BeeBee sucked in a breath at the painful reminder.

"And what about now?" Lucas said pointedly. "Is this still just a casual thing for both of you? BeeBee doesn't do anything unless she can throw one thousand percent of herself into it."

"She isn't some fling," Bill shot back in a heated voice. "We've been spending almost every day together for the last three weeks. I care about her. A lot."

She bit her lip as a wide grin stretched her cheeks, certain her thundering heart would give her away.

"So, how's this going to work when you leave for Italy next week?" Lucas asked, closing the lid on a pot with a resounding clang. "Since you've been putting all this work in with her, I'm sure she's counting on you to be there for the pageant. She'll be crushed when she realizes you won't be there."

Italy? He was going to Italy next week? The smile fell off her face instantly. No. Lucas was mistaken about the dates. He did that all the time, so focused on his cheese that he forgot to eat lunch, let alone what day people were leaving the country. Bill wasn't scheduled to leave until the week after the pageant.

"BeeBee's stronger than you give her credit for," Bill replied. "She's not this emotional goofball everyone in this town paints her as. She knows what it means to have a goal and be dedicated to it. She's putting herself through all this effort to buy her water-buffalo sire for the dairy and this town. I know she'll be fine without me."

"I know who BeeBee is," Lucas answered. "I also remember coming home from college on fall break that year and wondering what the heck had happened to her. She was a mess. Skipping school to spend all day in the barn with the animals. She didn't want to see anyone, didn't want to talk to anyone. Her folks thought it was because Jackie had left for college, but that wasn't it. It was you she missed. You broke her heart, Bill."

"Shut up, Lucas," BeeBee couldn't stop herself from whispering. "Shut. Up."

Bill didn't need to know how hurt she had really been. He didn't need to know that she had almost failed that year because every time her school bus had passed the lake she'd felt like crying. The only place that had given her comfort had been the barn and the new water-buffalo calf her mom had bought as a rescue from a local hobby farm that had gone out of business. This would break the magic. Bill wouldn't see her as strong anymore. He would see her as this weepy, needy mess. No one wanted that—especially not a pirate with a fear of commitment and a history as a flight risk.

"I didn't know any of that," Bill said so quietly BeeBee had to strain to hear him.

"I'm not saying you shouldn't take the job in Italy," Lucas answered. "I just don't want Bee-Bee to get caught in your wake. For what it's worth—"

Then the doorbell chimed, and BeeBee jumped away from the curtain. Georgia walked in and smiled at her.

"Hi, BeeBee," she said before sniffing the air. "Ooh, something smells good in here. Did you guys order a pizza from Mama Renata's?"

"Oh, uh, no," BeeBee said, backing farther away from the scene of her crime and accidentally toppling over a display case of dried parmesan cannisters. Flustered, she stacked them back on the rack. Her fingers felt numb and even more clumsy than usual. Bill was leaving. Again. Just when she knew more than ever he was what she wanted more than anything. "It's my recipe for the dairy pageant. I'm doing a pizza with buffalo mozzarella."

"Wow, that's coming up soon, isn't it?" Georgia said. "We're all so excited. Big Joe's going to put it on the TV in the diner so we can have a watch party there. All the kids from the cooking class are making treats for it."

All BeeBee's emotions, the sadness at Bill's revelation, the warmth of the kids who apparently didn't think she was a weirdo loser who couldn't cook…it all rose to the surface and choked her from saying anything at all. Fortunately, Georgia didn't seem to notice and chatted easily, her blond curls dipping as she leaned over the cheese-of-the-day display in the center.

"Caroline has been filling me in on all your hard work," she said, picking up a cube of white cheddar and popping it into the corner of her cheek. "Mmm, this is good. Going to the farm has been so good for her. I really appreciate you letting her come and visit the animals."

"It's no problem," BeeBee replied, glancing anxiously back at the curtain. "She, uh, she didn't happen to say anything to you about what happened with Jeremy Binkus, did she?"

"As a matter of fact, she did." Georgia dipped her chin meaningfully and raised both eyebrows.

Oh no. Now everyone in town would have another story about how BeeBee had once again been careless and let kids swing around her barn like gibbon monkeys, and none of the parents would let the kids come over again. Great. The cherry tomato on top of the burnt pizza that was today. "Gigi, I'm so sorry."

Georgia's head jerked back. "What are you sorry for? From what I heard, you were the hero of the day. At one point in the story, you were flying and wearing a red cape. Half the girls in town are already talking about dressing up as Farmer BeeBee for Halloween."

"Are you serious?"

Georgia nodded. "As a heart attack. If you ask me, that's what you should tell the judges at the pageant for your introduction thing. I bet no one else at that pageant has a story like that. You'd win for sure."

She wasn't wrong. This was exactly the kind of thing the other contestants did. But BeeBee shook her head. "I couldn't do that. I don't have a problem telling embarrassing stories about myself. I couldn't go on television and tell an embarrassing story about someone else. It wouldn't be fair to throw Jeremy under the bus like that."

"Hmm," Georgia let out from lips pressed into a single line. "I see." There was such a knowing, motherly tone in her words, BeeBee was almost tempted into confessing to eavesdropping and going straight up to her room without supper. It was when she placed a hand on BeeBee's arm that the tears started to sting. "Are you all right, hon? You seem a little down."

"I—" BeeBee struggled to find the right words while fighting back tears. It became almost impossible when her blurred gaze fell on the pop of red from Bill's bandanna in the pocket of his jacket. She had to get out of there. "I'm fine. Just a lot going on with the pageant and stuff."

"Uh-huh," Georgia said with a knowing smile. How did moms do that? "You and a certain chef have been spending a lot of time together working on the pageant 'stuff.' It must be hard if you know he might have to leave soon."

Using her forearm, BeeBee swiped her eyes and started toward the door with her head down. "You know what, I should get going."

Georgia's voice stopped her at the door, low and kind. "When it comes to the people we love, it's always better to tell the truth. When they're gone, you always regret the things you didn't say."

In BeeBee's twenty-four years on this planet, she had found the opposite to be true. Most of her problems with the people in her town could have been avoided by keeping her mouth shut. Yet when she turned her head over her shoulder to look at Georgia, it seemed like this was one time where that might not be the case. "Thanks, Gigi."

At that moment when her tears bordered on unstoppable, Bill appeared from behind the curtain. "BeeBee, what are you doing here?"

"I just came to…" Her voice came out wobbly and thin from holding back the tide. Clearing her throat and blinking hard, she started over and pushed the words out in a rush. "The pizza. I got it right, so I just wanted to drop it off and thank you for all your help. I can take it from here."

Confusion muddled his features. "What do you mean you can take it from here?"

"I mean, I don't need you anymore." BeeBee's words came out firm and clear this time. "With the pizza. I don't need your help with the recipe anymore. And I know that, uh, you've got a lot on your plate, so I won't keep you." *No matter how much I want to keep you.* "So I'll see you when I see you, all right? I've gotta get going. Gigi, always a pleasure." She nodded at the second figure, who was now standing behind Bill and furrowing his dark eyebrows with concern. "Lucas. Nice hairnet."

Turning and pushing out of the door, BeeBee ran for the car. Two Truths and a Lie was a fun game to play around the campfire. Very different in real life when the lie was that she did, in fact, need him more than anyone else in the world.

CHAPTER TWELVE

BY THE TIME Bill's head stopped spinning long enough for him to jog to the door, BeeBee's car had already peeled away.

He turned around to see both Georgia and Lucas looking at him with mixtures of pity and recrimination on their faces.

"What was that all about?" Lifting his arms out to the sides, he let them fall because he already knew the answer. She must have heard him and Lucas talking about the job in Italy. He dropped his head and gave it a shake.

"She'll come around, Bill." Georgia put a gentle hand on his shoulder. "It is Bill, right? Caroline wasn't sure because BeeBee kept calling you Captain."

He nodded without looking at her. Georgia was such a quintessential mom with her soothing voice and the scent of vanilla that followed her from the bakery. The last thing he deserved right now was comforting. Fortunately, Lucas was right there with his disapproving-big-brother vibes.

"This is exactly what I told you would happen." Lucas snatched the hair covering off his head and balled it in his fist. "What were you thinking, getting her hopes up like that when you knew you were leaving?"

"I wasn't thinking." Bill glared at his friend even though he wasn't mad at Lucas at all. He was, however, furious with himself. "It's not like I planned for any of this to happen. I've been fighting these feelings for weeks now."

For longer than that, if he was honest with himself. Everywhere he went, from the Adriatic Sea to the Polynesian Islands, he carried Bee-Bee with him. Anytime he made a stupid joke, he waited for her to appear to call him on it. All these years after their first kiss, he still dreamed about the touch of her lips. No matter what his best intentions were, he had known all along it was inevitable. He could tie himself to every mast, on every ship and her siren song would still urge him to break free.

"Lucas, can you fetch me some ricotta from the back, please?" Georgia asked Lucas, who was still frowning in the doorway of his cheese lab like a menacing statue.

He narrowed his eyes at Bill, then wrenched

his hair covering back onto his head and pulled the curtain back.

Georgia tipped her head to one side and crinkled her eyes at Bill. "He'll be in a much better mood once he's back with his cheese," she said with a small laugh. "Just like BeeBee and her buffaloes. The world could be on fire, and as long as they have their happy places, they would be just fine."

"Must be nice to know exactly where your happy place is," Bill murmured under his breath, slipping the bandanna off his head to rake a hand through his hair.

"That's the point," Georgia said softly. "For them—and for most people—a happy place isn't a place at all. It's what gives you a purpose, what motivates you to go the extra mile even when it's hard or scary."

Bill wove the red bandanna through his fingers. That was it—the emotion that had been driving him all these years. It wasn't ambition or passion, even though he felt them when he was cooking. It was fear. He had always thought the water smoothed the rough edges of himself that didn't fit seamlessly with other people's expectations. But being on the water wasn't what made him feel like he belonged.

It was her.

He caught Georgia grinning at him as if she

could already read his thoughts. "I should... I have something I've got to do." Glancing back down at his hands, he pursed his lips as an idea started to take shape. "Can you tell Lucas I'll be back in a little while? I have to run a quick errand at Stevenson's Antiques and Jewelry."

"Will do." She nodded. "Good luck, Bill."

As he grabbed his jacket off the hook, he could have sworn she added under her breath, "You're gonna need it."

By the time he returned to the dairy that evening, Lucas was still as sour as the acid serum he used to curdle the milk for his cheese. After some explanations and a healthy amount of groveling, he gave Bill a gruff pat on his shoulder.

"I'm still upset that you guys kept all of this from me," he said. "But I guess the way I reacted kind of proved you weren't entirely wrong. All I want is for both of you to be happy—you know that, right?"

"I know." Bill grinned back at him. "And I am sorry I didn't tell you about me and BeeBee from the beginning."

Lucas nodded at the white box tied with a red ribbon under Bill's arm. "You sure this is the right move? BeeBee isn't exactly the type of girl you can just throw a pretty trinket at and expect her to forgive you for everything."

Bill patted the box. "I know. I'm just hoping

this will get me in the door long enough for her to hear what I've got to say."

"You do you." Lucas shrugged, then leaned across the counter and handed him the keys to his truck. "I've gotta stay and clean up. Lock the door behind you when you get home."

"Will do." Normally the word *home* would have given him a twinge of panic and a rush of longing for international waters. This time it didn't sound half bad.

He drove out to the farm as a distant rumble of thunder sounded in the distance. Bill gritted his teeth and tried not to take it as an ominous warning. The rain that poured down from the heavens at the exact moment he opened the driver's-side door was surely just a coincidence. Pulling the hood of his sweatshirt over his head, he ran for the front door and knocked, bending over slightly to catch his breath.

Lindsay opened the door. When she saw it was him, she immediately began tapping her foot on the floor in a clear, rhythmic display of unwelcome. "What do you want?"

"Is—is BeeBee there?" he asked, rain dripping from the top of his jacket onto his nose. "I just want to talk to her."

"She's not in here," Lindsay answered shortly. "And whatever you've done, it's going to take me a week to undo. Her face has been blotchy all evening, and so help me, if she gets dark circles under her eyes because she can't sleep, I'm sending my tiny dancer tap class to Lucas's for an early morning rehearsal."

"Easy, Lou," Katelyn called out from the kitchen. Coming around the corner with a bottle of soda in her hand, she leaned on the counter and raised it at Bill in greeting. "Hey there, New Guy. Fancy running into you twice in one day."

Lindsay whipped her head around at her sister. "What do you mean, twice in one day? Are you in cahoots with the enemy?"

Katelyn snorted. "Cahoots? You gotta stop watching those old movie musicals. No one says things like *cahoots* anymore." She raised her head to get a look at Bill. "She's in the barn. Let's hope that box is waterproof."

Bill tucked it under his khaki rain coat. "Thanks for your help, Katelyn." He turned to head for the barn, then whirled around quickly to stop the door from closing with one hand. "Oh, and Lindsay? If your tiny tappers do Riverdance, I'll be there bright and early. I love when they do that dancing-without-moving-their-arms thing."

He let the door close on Lindsay and Katelyn giggling together behind him.

Running through the rain to the barn, he closed the door behind him and immediately spotted BeeBee.

She had brought a battery-powered lantern and sat on the ground with her knees tucked up to her chest, a water buffalo sleeping on either side of her. Lindsay hadn't been wrong; her face was blotchy and somehow even more beautiful because of the unguarded emotion. Surprise wasn't one of those emotions, however, when she lifted her eyes and saw him. Hurt, fear and hope flashed in a single expressive wince.

"Hi" was all she said.

He knelt to the floor in front of her, setting the box carefully down on the straw-covered wood planks. "Hi." There was a lot he had to tell her, and she wasn't going to like all of it.

One of the buffaloes moved its head toward the box and sniffed mildly.

"What's in there, Bill?" BeeBee asked warily. "If it's another pizza, you can take it back. After this stupid pageant is done, I'm never eating pizza again."

"You don't mean that," Bill said as he repositioned himself to sitting on his backside with one knee propped under his hand. "You can be as mad at me as you want, but don't take it out on pizza. Anyway, that's not what's in the box. Go ahead—open it."

She sniffed like her buffalo and lifted her chin with disinterest. "I know why you're doing all this, and it's not going to work."

Bill shrugged and reached out nonchalantly to stroke the nose of the buffalo on his right. "Suit yourself."

Exactly three seconds later, she gave in and unwrapped the bow from the box. Lifting the lid with one distrustful eye on him, she looked down and her mouth fell open. Bill watched quietly as she stood, unfolding the dress to hold it against her body.

"It's perfect," she said breathlessly, smoothing the full skirt with one hand as she held the bodice to her chest with the other. "The color of the fabric looks almost like—"

"Denim," Bill finished for her. "I know." He had picked Katelyn up from Stevenson's and begged her to go with him to help him find a dress that was anything but the typical sparkly pageant dress. When Bill had spotted this dress on the mannequin, with its full skirt that came down just below the knees in a sleek blue-gray satin that was the exact shade of BeeBee's favorite jeans, he knew it was the one. Simple, bold and one of a kind. Just like his BeeBee. "There's something special about the skirt that Kit thought you would appreciate. I didn't get the big deal, but she squealed so loud when she saw, it sounded like—"

BeeBee let out a small, high-pitched shriek of delight.

"Like that," he finished, pushing to his feet and brushing the hay off his knees. Shooting an apologetic look at the water buffalo who raised its head in alarm, he folded his arms and shrugged.

"Pockets." An ecstatic grin lit her face. "It has pockets."

"There's something extra special in one of them," he said, holding back a smile of anticipation as she searched first in the right and then the left before withdrawing a long, brightly colored piece of fabric. She held the red-and-white paisley bandanna in her hand, then looked at him with eyes that shone even in the dim light.

"It's one of your bandannas," she said softly, holding it against her heart.

He swallowed hard at the way her face melted. This was the image he would carry with him across the ocean, the one that would push him to go the extra mile no matter how scared he felt. "It's my lucky bandanna—the one I wore when I passed my final culinary exam," he said, sticking his own hands into his pockets to keep from reaching out to hold her. That would only make letting go harder. "I don't expect you to wear it at the pageant or anything. But I thought since the dress has pockets and all, you could keep it in there as a good luck charm. If you get nervous, it will be like I'm there with you, holding your hand."

Her arms relaxed, and the top of the dress folded over her wrist. "You're still leaving, aren't you?" The quiver of her lips once she had stopped talking pierced him like a rapier.

"BeeBee, let me explain." He started to step closer to her, but there two water-buffalo horns blocked his path. Planting his feet, he extended a hand to her. "This dinner is a really big deal. It's on a super yacht with the kind of ingredients I might only get a chance to work with once in a career. Plus, the people I'm cooking for are important people. It's not just celebrities. It's dignitaries and ambassadors. The kind of people who hire private chefs."

She bent down and carefully placed the dress back in the box and closed the lid. When she stood up again, she held the bandanna out to him. "Take this with you, then. I don't want your good luck charm."

He shook his head and held his hands up, taking a step backward. "It was a gift for you. I care about you—more than a summer romance. I don't want things to end the way they did before."

"Why does this have to end?" she cried out, the ache in her voice rippling over the rain and thunder outside. "Why can't you stay here and be with me? There are restaurants here. There's a lake. Hundreds of lakes. The freaking Finger Lakes are half an hour's drive away. All the water you could ever ask for. So why are you running away again?"

"Because what if I'm still not ready?" he burst out. Pacing toward the door, he rubbed his forehead with one hand and turned around, trying to control the frustration that pushed him to leave before things got worse. "What if I get bored? Next thing you know my cooking gets boring. And the longer I stay in one place, the more people will expect of me. It's too much pressure not to mess anything up, especially this." He gestured between them with one hand. "It's just better if I leave now, before any of that can happen."

"That's the point," she said in an impatient groan as she slapped her forehead. Shaking her head, she half laughed, half sobbed in a sound that tore him apart even more. "People are always so afraid that if they stay in one place, it will keep them from growing. That's ridiculous. Being here with the people who know me is what pushes me to become a better version of myself. Living in Crystal Hill reminds me of where I've been, what I've done and what I've learned from all my mistakes." She dropped her hand, striding between the water buffaloes and coming to a stop an inch away from him, so close he could see the remnants of what he knew weren't raindrops on her eyelashes. "That's why I'm not going to repeat the same mistake I made seven years ago. I'm not ending things with you before I'm ready. I'm asking you to stay here with me. Because I'm in love with you. I think I've always loved you, and I don't want you to go away again without knowing the truth."

He cupped her face between his hands and kissed her, kissed her deep enough so she would know how he felt without him having to say it. He couldn't say it out loud because it still didn't change what had to happen next. With one last lingering whisper against her upper lip, he touched his forehead to hers. This hurt, more than anything—this hurt and it went against every fiber of his body. "I have to leave. I already committed to the job. I'm sorry, I—"

She pushed him back with both hands on his chest, turning away from him to face the back of the barn. "Then go. Just go. I've been doing fine without you for the last seven years. Everything I need is right here."

Same, a small voice inside him whispered. But fear and years of people shouting at him to just give them a break shoved the voice away. "You're going to make a great queen, BeeBee. I wish I could be there to see it."

When she didn't turn around, he backed slowly toward the door. Looking up at the pouring sky, he cast his eyes at her one more time. One of the water buffaloes stood and walked over to him as if to protect its mistress. It regarded him with solemn awareness in its inky dark eyes, taking measure of what he already knew full well.

That he was in the middle of his greatest mistake and nothing he could do would make it right.

CHAPTER THIRTEEN

So, IT TURNED out BeeBee had been wrong all this time.

For years she had beaten herself up over saying the wrong things. But now it was clear. It didn't matter what she said, whether it was the right thing or the wrong thing, whether it was the truth or a lie. Seven years ago, she had lied to Bill about how she felt and he left. Seven days ago, she had told him the truth—that she was in love with him.

And he'd still left.

Lucas came over that day with the expression of someone preparing to be shot for the message he bore. "BeeBee, how are you doing? I haven't seen you at the shop all week."

"I've been busy," she said dully from the couch. "Dairy farm. Pageant prep. Busy, busy, busy."

Also, moping. Moping was practically a full-time job. Coupled with actively avoiding anywhere she might run into Bill Danzig, well, there simply wasn't a spare minute.

"I just came to let you know that I dropped Bill off at the airport today," Lucas said, hesitating before sitting on the far end of the couch as if gauging how far away he needed to sit to be out of throttling range. His caution was unnecessary because BeeBee couldn't move.

She had known he was leaving. In fact, she had told him to leave. If it hadn't been for her, they could have at least had one more week together. The pain constricted around her, freezing her motionless. She wasn't sure which would have hurt worse—having that week with him knowing the whole time the clock was counting down or the quick, agonizing slice through the heart when she had looked him in the eyes and pushed him away from her forever.

"BeeBee?" Lucas probed carefully. "Are you all right?"

She turned her head a few inches over her shoulder to look at him. Even that small movement seemed to take every bit of energy she had. Somehow the knowledge that Bill was really gone drained the life out of her in one shot.

"No," she replied. "I'm not all right." Might as well tell the truth since it didn't matter anyway. There was nothing she could say or do that would stop the people she loved from leaving her.

"I'm so sorry for all of this," he said. "If I had known about you guys, I would have—"

"You would have what?" BeeBee let out a bitter bark of a laugh. "Forbade me from seeing him? Trapped him in your cheese lab until it was time for him to leave?" She went back to staring at the coal-stained fireplace. "There was nothing you could do. Just like there's nothing I can do now. He chose to leave."

"For what it's worth, he was absolutely miserable last week," Lucas said. "The only time he cooked was when he was teaching the classes at the rec center. One of the kids said he kept looking at the door. I think he was hoping you would show up."

"Even if that's true," BeeBee said, pushing wearily off the couch to stand up before pivoting slowly to look down at her cousin, "I still wasn't enough to make him want to stay. Do you know how much it hurts to know that?"

Lucas stood too and put his hand on Bee-Bee's shoulder. "BeeBee, I've known Bill for a really long time. I don't think it's that you weren't enough. It's more that he thinks he's not enough yet." He bent his head to make sure she understood. "When that happens, I'm pretty sure you're the first person he's going to call."

"Yeah, well…" BeeBee looked down at the frayed edges of her jeans and sniffed. "I'm probably going to be too busy with my water-buffalo empire to answer. Once I win the crown and I can bring Orlando home, I won't have time for things like pizza or stupid sunset boat rides." She raised her eyes to his and attempted a smile. "It was nice of you to come by, Lucas, but I'll be just fine. Don't you worry about me."

Lucas dropped his hand and inclined his head. "All right. But if you need a little therapy in the form of a nice triple-crème brie, you know where to find me, okay?"

"Got it." BeeBee almost smiled for real this time. Lucas and his cheese. Half the women in town were crazy about him, but the man couldn't take his head out of his asiago long enough to notice. As usual, her water buffaloes had the right idea. Nothing sounded better at the moment than a good wallow.

Her sisters, however, had other plans for the next seven days.

Lou plucked the hairs from BeeBee's eyebrows like she was preparing a freshly shot turkey for Thanksgiving. Her lower back ached from walking around the house in heels, and every time she moved, more bobby pins fell out of her hair. Despite the escalation in what felt like a beauty-themed hostage negotiation, when Jackie FaceTimed her to go over the interview questions one more time, the first thing out of her mouth was, "BeeBee, what's wrong? You look terrible."

Sure, she quickly followed it up by replacing *terrible* with *terribly tired*, but it didn't matter. She felt terrible, and it had nothing to do with the rash that had come after she had fallen asleep with an astringent face mask on for far too long.

"I'll be fine once the pageant is done," Bee-Bee answered. "Let's go over the questions one more time."

"I don't think we need to," Jackie replied, her face freezing briefly as their spotty connection wavered. "You know your answers word for word, and even the responses for questions we didn't practice were good. I think this is the first time I've asked you about your favorite farm duties without you giggling uncontrollably."

BeeBee sighed. It was because—for once—she didn't feel like laughing at inappropriate times. The one person she wanted to laugh with, complain to, even sit and say nothing with over a slice of homemade pizza wasn't there. She didn't feel like talking to anyone. This was exceptionally unfortunate seeing as how in less than twenty-four hours she would have to talk to the judges, a live studio audience and the people who watched a dairy royalty pageant on local public television on a beautiful Saturday in June. All eight of them.

"I'm as ready as I'm going to be," she said finally. "If this doesn't work, then Salvatore will sell Orlando to the other buyer and the farm slides one step closer to complete failure because of me." BeeBee couldn't even think about that right now, especially since she barely had the energy to get out of bed in the morning. It wasn't that there weren't other water-buffalo farms and breeders out there. But most of them were international and she had zero contacts anywhere else in the world. Ironically, Bill probably could have helped her find someone else if she hadn't been so busy giving him her heart and he hadn't been so busy ripping it to shreds. She shook her head. "I don't want to talk about me anymore. How is the writing going? Have you fallen in love with one of the other authors there and decided to move to England to be with him?"

Jackie laughed. "No. All of the other romance authors are women, and most of them aren't from the UK anyway. Not gonna lie, I had secretly hoped to be swept off my feet by a duke in disguise. It's nice here, although they weren't kidding about the rain. I can't believe the one thing I forgot was an umbrella."

"Not to rub it in, but it's a beautiful sunny day here." BeeBee pointed the phone at the window where the climbing roses peeked their yellow-kissed petals from behind the curtains. "It's almost birthing time for the heifers."

This was usually her favorite time of the year.

The longer days meant more time outside with her animals, more time walking among the herds with the smell of sweet grass filling the air. New life and hope were everywhere, yet none of it seemed to break through the loneliness.

"BeeBee," Jackie said in her sisterly advice voice, "can I offer you some sisterly advice?"

"I think I can't stop you, so go ahead."

"Lucas texted me and filled me in on what happened with Bill."

Darn it, Lucas. Nobody likes a snitch in a hairnet.

"What happened with Bill is over," BeeBee said. "There's no point in crying over spilt milk."

"You hate that aphorism," Jackie pointed out. "That's how I know you're not fine. Call him. Text him. This isn't the eighteen hundreds where physical distance meant a relationship was doomed. Look at us now." She gestured to the honey-colored stone building behind her and the black iron lamp flickering in the twilight behind her. "I'm six hours in the future from you. It's amazing what technology can do."

"Technology like the button I'm going to use to hang up on you now?" BeeBee held her index finger in front of the screen.

"I'm just saying, don't let your pride get in the way of love," Jackie admonished gently, a breeze ruffling her hair off her face. "I've never seen you look better than you have over the last few weeks. Your lips look like you haven't been biting them anymore the way you do when you're stressed. I'm pretty sure the time you spent with Bill had a little something to do with it."

BeeBee sniffed. "Could have been the makeup. I got pretty good at contouring, you know."

"No, you didn't."

"No, I didn't," BeeBee admitted. "Even if all of this is true, it doesn't change the fact that he doesn't want a life here."

"Ever or just right now?"

"I—" BeeBee's forehead wrinkled, pressing down on her still-sensitive but neatly trimmed eyebrows. "He said not yet."

"Okay, so you've got to ask yourself something," Jackie said matter-of-factly. "If this is *your* love story, what chapter are you on? Because it doesn't sound like he's closed the book on you."

"I was never very good with words," BeeBee admitted, propping her elbow on the end of the couch and rubbing her temple. Her head hurt, and for the first time in a month it had nothing to do with a bobby pin. "Writing them or saying them. I'm afraid I'll mess it up."

"You won't," Jackie said soothingly. "I know you won't. Just like I know you're going to be amazing at the pageant. How do I wish you luck for a dairy pageant? Break a leg? Break a hoof?"

BeeBee threw her head back and laughed, the first real laugh she'd had since Bill had used breadsticks as horns and pretended to be Orlando the water buffalo. She'd nearly spit out her lemonade at Big Joe's Diner, and it had been worth it. "Thanks, sis. For everything."

"Love you."

"Love you too. Tell the king I said cheerio."

Jackie rolled her eyes before signing off.

BeeBee let the phone fall to the cushion next to her. Twisting around, she looked back out the window at the fields. It was so beautiful, every single blade of jewel-green grass, every gentle hum the cows made as they nudged their calves into their first wobbly steps. This was where she wanted to be and what she wanted to do. It suddenly occurred to BeeBee what a rare luxury that was. Maybe she had reacted too quickly with Bill. It did sound like something she would do, if she was being honest with herself. Yes, people left. But sometimes they came back.

She turned back around and slowly, tentatively reached for her phone.

Just then, Lou burst through the door. "Bee-Bee, I think there's something wrong with one of the pregnant heifers," she said between gasps of air.

BeeBee leapt to her feet. "I'm coming," she

said, tossing her phone back onto the couch as she sprinted for the door.

It was probably better if she took her time and thought about what she wanted to say to Bill anyway. Maybe if she had done that the first time, they could have worked something out before he had left. He probably wouldn't answer anyway. Tonight was the big dinner.

He was probably having the time of his life right about now.

CHAPTER FOURTEEN

BILL HAD NEVER been more miserable.

He was in the exquisitely scenic Marina di Portofino, on a super yacht that was basically a floating four-star restaurant, surrounded by expertly trained staff and dream ingredients to create the menu of his design, and he was miserable. The gleaming kitchen on the yacht had a large window looking out over the coastline, the ring of pastel buildings behind which rose verdant hillsides that kissed the horizon itself. With the window cracked open, he could hear the waves cresting against the shore. This was the sound he craved in the still moments on land, the soothing lullaby that calmed him when nothing else would. But here, in this moment, it was doing absolutely nothing for him.

Switching off the water in the sink, he shook his hands dry and adjusted his bandanna. It was a new one he had bought specifically for this gig. This was the first time he had worn it, and already he hated it. He missed the worn cotton of his lucky red one almost as much as he missed Lucas's monosyllabic morning greetings as he soldiered away in his cheese lab and the smell of the fresh muffins from Georgia's Bakery that arose every morning. He even missed Kit and Lou's playful mocking.

But most of all, he missed BeeBee. He had texted her only once, but a hundred times—more than a hundred—he had picked up his phone to call her. He wanted to know everything about the final pageant preparation, wanted to tell her about the centuries-old olive press he had seen that day and his sous chef who had yet to say a word to him or anyone else. Was it because he didn't speak English? Was it because he had an embarrassingly high, squeaky voice? This was the opportunity of a lifetime, and all he wanted to do was share it with her.

Instead, he tightened the strings on his apron and blocked his feet apart, clasping his hands around his back as the team of assistant chefs and waiters stared back at him expectantly.

"All right, everyone," he announced. "The guests and honorees should be boarding in half an hour. Should I go over the menu one more time?"

He was answered by a chorus of "yes,"
"please do,"
"sì," and a long nod from the barrel-chested

sous chef who was saving his voice for his debut at La Scala? The memory of BeeBee whistling "Nessun Dorma" on a dare from her sister and nearly blacking out at the family dinner table two weeks ago appeared unbidden in his head. He cleared his throat and blinked, forcing it away.

"Here we go." He took out his phone and read from the Notes app. "We're starting with passed hors d'oeuvres during cocktail hour. Wild salmon gravlax with blood-orange reduction, wagyu tartar dusted with fried basil, olive tapenade crostini with Beluga caviar and a caprese lollipop consisting of fresh tomatoes stuffed with mozzarella di bufala." His voice cracked on the last three words. *You're blowing this*, a small voice in his head hissed. *Focus.*

"You need some water, Chef?" Jose, the head of the waitstaff, asked.

"No, thank you," Bill answered as he swallowed the familiar bitterness of frustration with himself. "Once the attendees have sat down, dinner will be served before the awards are given out. We start with tart lemon gazpacho with a red-chili coulis and crème-fraiche foam."

"Love that," Julia, the assistant chef said. "The balance of the heat with the acidic citrus and the cream from the dairy is brilliant. Where'd you come up with that, Chef?"

Crystal Hill.

"Well, you know, inspiration comes from a lot of different sources," he said, biting his lower lip before moving on. "Then we have a quail-egg custard topped with shaved Italian white truffles."

BeeBee's custard that tasted like scrambled eggs every single time she made it.

"Followed by a choice of pan-seared branzino or grass-fed Chianina ribeye in a reduction made from locally sourced cherries."

The smell of sweet grass that clung to Bee-Bee's hair.

"And for dessert, white-chocolate cheesecake bombs dusted with edible gold leaf and topped with champagne-roasted grapes."

That tasted just like BeeBee's favorite grape soda.

"Um, scusi, Chef Bill?" one of the waitstaff piped up. "Are you...okay?"

He set his phone down on the gleaming steel island, swallowed hard and wondered how on earth he could have missed that the menu that had been appearing in his dreams over and over again was all about BeeBee. She was the inspiration for it all—his muse. The part of his heart he could never grow out of and the only thing in his life he wanted to remain constant forever. It was her.

"I-I'm sorry." He tossed up a hand in the air. "I'm just a little—distracted, I suppose."

The sous chef placed a large hand on his shoulder and finally opened his mouth, a gruff Hungarian accent coming through. "It is all right," he said without a single change in his facial expression. "I know what it is to love and to lose. This is why you have been walking around like man whose dog is hit by bus, yes?"

"Is it really that obvious?" Bill turned to look at the staff.

Julia nodded her head of short-cropped pink hair. "We worked together on the *Luego* a few years back, remember? You were, like, the life of the party then. This week you've been more like the undertaker at a funeral."

"Also, you keep checking your phone every five minutes," Jose chimed in. "We played a drinking game the other night where we took shots whenever you looked at it. Amal got wasted."

"Wow," Bill said, scanning the crew's faces. "You guys must think I'm a hot mess, huh?" He shook his head. "It all started seven years ago today, the first week at summer camp."

He went through a brief summary of his and BeeBee's relationship, from their first kiss to the I'm Sorry picnic on the rowboat.

"That's so romantic." Julia sighed. "If my girlfriend ever pops the question, I hope she asks me with a candlelit boat dinner."

"That's risky business," Jose countered. "What if the person you're asking says no? Then you're either stuck on a boat with them all night or jump out and swim for shore."

"And it's less risky proposing on a jumbotron at the football game?" Julia shot back. "I'd take the gourmet dinner cruise on a lake any day."

"I don't know if you could call pizza and sodas gourmet," Bill said. "Anyway, it doesn't matter how. I chose to come here instead of staying there with her, and now she hates me. It's going to take a lot more than a canoe and a pineapple pizza to get her to even talk to me again. I'd need the *Queen Mary* and Chateaubriand at this point."

Someone cleared their throat from behind the waiters clustered in the galley pantry. When they parted, a tiny man with a shock of white hair ringing his bare scalp waded between them into the kitchen. It was Luigi Giordano, the CEO and philanthropist whose foundation was sponsoring the event. He crooked a bushy eyebrow at the staff and turned his head toward Bill.

"So this is where the party is," he said dryly. "I thought I had finally lost my mind and wandered onto the wrong boat."

"Gosh, it's getting late." Julia checked her

watch and her eyes bulged. "Let's get into positions, everyone."

Bill stepped forward as the rest scattered to start the mad preparations for the event. "I'm sorry, Mr. Giordano. It's on me that we're a bit behind. I was just—"

"Oh, I heard your story," Luigi interrupted, a twinkle lighting the darkness in his small eyes. "The only thing Italians love more than a good meal is a good tragic love story. Why do you think we write the best operas?"

Bill chuckled and ducked his head. "Can't argue with that. The dinner is going to be a success, Mr. Giordano. I promise no more distractions."

Luigi's wizened hand floated up between them, trembling slightly as he pointed his finger at Bill. "It is not your food I worry about, young man. The sample menu you provided was outstanding. I've never seen another chef who can understand flavor better."

"I—Thank you," Bill managed to get out as his heart thundered in his ears. He had no idea where this conversation was going. Mr. Giordano's delivery was so wry, it was difficult to anticipate whether the next comment was going to be a rebuke or a job offer for the winter at a villa in Lake Como.

"But from the pieces that I heard, it sounds

like you are having some trouble knowing what to do with your heart," Luigi went on. "This girl you fell in love with when you were a teenager, she is what you want, yes?"

"Yes," Bill repeated. "Which is unreal, right? No one meets the love of their life when they're eighteen. I was just a stupid kid. If we had tried to stay together back then, it would have been a disaster."

Luigi sighed and brought his hand to his forehead. "That is the funny thing about love. It doesn't care whether you are ready for it or not. It happens to you, and you have to decide what you are willing to do to keep it. Sixty-five years ago, I met a girl in Venice. We spent one week together, and I thought—like you—that I wasn't ready for love. I thought, *Hey, if it happened once, it will happen again.*" He shook his head. "I still think about her and wonder what could have been if I had had the courage to follow her back to America."

"But look at everything you've accomplished in your life," Bill protested. "None of that could have happened if you had settled down in one place with a woman and had kids at a young age. If I had stayed in Crystal Hill with BeeBee, I would have missed out on all of this." He gestured at the vista out the window, then spread his hands to the bounty of gorgeous fresh fish and produce waiting on the counter for him. "I couldn't have said no to this just to stay back in Crystal Hill and follow BeeBee around like a lovesick puppy."

"Are you sure those are your only choices?" Luigi ticked his head to one side. "You seem creative enough. You're telling me you can't have your career and be with the woman you love? This I find hard to believe."

"I—It's not that I couldn't do both," he admitted. "But what if I go back, put down roots and it doesn't work? How do I know I'm ready for…forever?"

Luigi snorted. "Nothing is forever, young man. Just when you think you know what life is about, it throws the soup out the window. That's why when you find love—real love—you do whatever it takes to hold on to it. You take whatever job you can find, you move across the ocean, you let that person know how you feel while you have the chance. You understand what I am saying?"

Bill nodded. "I do, actually. Food metaphors are like my second language."

Luigi chuckled, turned and started to shuffle back down the galley before stopping and holding out a hand. "The pizza and the boat by candlelight. This was a good idea." He turned his head over his shoulder, his sharp nose forming a stark profile. "I think I might have a way for you to—how do they say it—eat your cake and like it also?"

"Have your cake and eat it too?"

"That's the one," Luigi said. "Meet me on shore tomorrow at the pier. There is something I want to show you."

After he left, Bill stood in the kitchen for a moment, looking out the window at the expanse of blue stretching all the way out to the horizon. Out here, he was free. Free to make mistakes, free to hop from ship to ship without anyone keeping score or making a record of his wrongs. There was no community of wagging fingers, no history. There was only water to sail and food to prepare. But was that enough for him anymore?

A voice rumbled behind him, and he jumped.

"Are we going to cook, or what?" His sous chef had been standing there in silence for so long that Bill forgot he was even there.

"Right." Bill picked up his knife, Percy. The flash of the blade in the overhead lights reminded him of BeeBee, of course. Of how she made him laugh, kept him from taking himself too seriously, how she somehow changed and stayed the same in the last seven years. A piratic smile crooked his lips at the corners. "Yo ho, indeed."

CHAPTER FIFTEEN

IT WAS AMAZING how quickly everything could go wrong all at once.

Dr. Poniatowski finished her examination of the heifer and stood with a concerned look on her face. "The contractions aren't moving the calf as quickly as I'd like them to," she said as she removed her latex gloves. "It's still early, and I'm hesitant to intervene just yet given the heifer's advanced maternal age. Still, we need to keep a close eye on her."

Kit, Lou and BeeBee exchanged distressed glances. It was at the end of calving season, and the veterinary budget was dwindling. An invisible vise clamped tighter around BeeBee's head like the pressure of the crown she needed to win now more than ever. Their farm was small as it was. Losing a heifer and potentially a calf was no small thing. They were out of loan options and almost out of savings. The crown was more than a shiny object to her now. It was a breath of hope the farm desperately needed to gear up for the summer-tourist season that boosted their funds through the end of the year.

"Well, then one of us will have to stay behind," Kit said. She nudged Lou with her elbow. "You should go with BeeBee to the pageant. Since you're doing hair and makeup, you're essential personnel. I can call Lucas if I need another pair of hands."

"But what about the skit?" BeeBee asked as she crouched by the prostrate heifer and stroked her velvety nose. "Both of you are playing two different people from town."

"It'll be okay," Lou said with a confident toss of her hair. "I know the lines for all the parts. Lord knows we've practiced it enough. And I can do a quick change like nobody's business. We can go over it in the car on the way to the pageant tomorrow morning."

BeeBee nodded. Still a gnawing sense that this was only the beginning of her bad luck crept into her gut and wouldn't leave her alone. That feeling was confirmed that night when she got a call from Lou. She knew instantly from the thin tone in her sister's voice that something had happened.

"Don't panic, but, uh, they're taking me to the emergency room now," she said between gasps of pain. "I fell during jazz class, and my ankle

bent in a way that ankles are definitely not supposed to bend."

"Oh my gosh, Lou." BeeBee had been in the
middle of packing her outfits for the pageant in
a large duffel bag. "I'm on my way right now.
Which hospital are they taking you to?"

"East Valley, but don't you even think about
leaving the house," Lou said sharply. "I'm a non-
urgent patient, which means it could be hours
before I get in. You would be up all night. I-I'm
so sorry, BeeBee. I don't know what we're going
to do about the skit for the pageant. Oh no."

"What is it? Is your foot worse? Lou, are you
okay?"

"It's not my foot," Lou groaned in agony.
"Well, that does hurt like crazy. No, I just realized this means you'll have to do your own hair
and makeup."

"I couldn't care less about any of that right
now," BeeBee shouted into the phone. "Text me
as soon as you know anything, okay?"

After she hung up, BeeBee stared at the phone
for a minute. A breeze shot in from the open
window in her bedroom, lifting the dress Bill
had given her as it hung from the curtain rod.
Longing stabbed at her heart. None of this was
going the way she wanted. For all her bluster
and bravado, the cracks that had formed in her
over the years felt like they were finally giving

way. Scrolling on her phone, she tapped a new number.

Georgia picked up after two rings. "Hi, Bee-Bee, what's up?"

"I just wanted to tell you that I'm not doing the pageant tomorrow," she said quickly, as if saying it fast would make her feel like less of a quitter. "One of our heifers is going through a bad delivery and Lou's foot is on backward, and so if you can go ahead and spread the word that there's no need for everyone to go to the party at Big Joe's tomorrow, that would be super helpful."

"Slow down," Georgia said. "You can still do the pageant without your sisters there, can't you?"

"They're a huge part of the creative introduction skit I have to do," BeeBee said, crashing onto the bed with a defeated flop. "Caroline told you about it, right? How I pretend to be the host of a Guess Who? game, and the girls were supposed to be people from town behind cardboard cutouts who tell embarrassing but lovable stories about me and I guess their identity. I can't do it by myself." She was referring to the skit, but the words had a leaden heaviness as they fell out of her. This had been a test, a trial run of her future, and she had failed dismally. She couldn't do any of it alone. Bill was gone, her sisters would be next. Even if she won and Orlando was finally hers, she would probably screw that up too. Maybe Bill had the right idea after all. Maybe she should just run away and start the cycle of mistakes somewhere else.

"Hmm," Georgia murmured. "Let me make a few calls. I think we can work something out."

"I don't even have a way to get there anymore," BeeBee said. "Lou had the car, and one of the other dancers is taking her to the emergency room in it. I can't use the farm truck in case Kit needs it to take the heifer into the animal hospital for an emergency C-section."

"What about one of the other pageant girls?" Georgia asked. "Is there one that could swing by and pick you up on the way? You're all going to the same place."

"I—well, I guess that could work," BeeBee admitted reluctantly. "There is an online chat for the group that I keep getting email notifications about." That she kept ignoring email notifications about, if she was being perfectly honest. "Seriously, Gigi. Your mama-bear superpowers are getting in the way of my giving up on everything and quitting life in general. I don't even have an excuse to run away from home and join the circus now. BeeBee the Dairy Clown was going to be a real showstopper."

"There she is," Georgia said. "All right, let me work out the situation with the skit, and you get in touch with the pageant girls. If they can't drive you, I'll see if I can get Big Joe to run the watch party."

"Anything but that," BeeBee protested. "He'll make a life-size model of me out of Spam with a pimento tiara. I'll find a ride with one of the girls—promise."

She trooped downstairs, too glum to crow over the fact that she hadn't tripped over her own two feet in weeks. The house was dark, and even though her parents weren't there, she didn't bother to turn on the lights. It felt like too much effort.

After finally clicking on the email link for the dairy pageant online chat, she typed out a brief explanation of what had happened. Within seconds, the girls had agreed on a carpool, volunteered to help with her makeup and asked for her coffee-order preferences. The speed with which these women operated was both touching and a little frightening. It was a good thing their energies were focused on something as innocuous as a dairy pageant and not, say, robbing a bank. This combination of charm and efficiency could take out Fort Knox.

Georgia texted her two hours later just as she was climbing into bed. The message was simple: Problem solved. All you have to do is show up and do your skit as planned. Get your beauty rest, Your Majesty!

Beauty rest was not enough. The only thing that sounded at all appealing at the moment was to sleep until next week and wake up when all of this was over.

She woke up well before dawn to check on the birthing heifer. She was still immobile in the isolation pen and clearly in discomfort. Both the water buffaloes hovered nearby, as if they knew this wasn't something any woman should go through on her own.

BeeBee had just gotten out of the shower when her own female support system pulled up in the driveway. Hearing a chorus of girlish giggles outside, she pulled the curtain away from her window to watch Emma, Brittany and Haven pour out of a red SUV. Emma's head was topped with large pink curlers, and Haven had a pink silk kerchief covering hers. Brittany wore what looked suspiciously like a red satin Members Only jacket with the name of her dairy on the back and carried two enormous to go cups of coffee.

Shaking her head, BeeBee smiled a real smile for the first time in two weeks. These women might not have been Charlie's choice for angels, but as far as heavenly helpers went, she could do a lot worse.

Kit was downstairs chatting with the trio by the time BeeBee lugged her duffel bag down the steps, her evening gown in a dress bag slung over her shoulder. She greeted the women with a jut of her chin.

"I don't know how to thank you all for doing this," she said as Emma rushed forward to take her duffel bag.

"Oh, honey, we were happy to do it," she exclaimed, her curlers bouncing as she staggered slightly under the weight of the bag. "Wow, this is heavy."

"It's mostly the cardboard props for my skit," she said as she turned to Kit. "Georgia said she had everything taken care of for the skit. Did she fill you in on the plan?"

"Yup," answered Kit succinctly. "It's going to be great. You just show up in your first outfit and read your Guess Who? questions from our original script." She bent down in the kitchen and pulled out a cooler, handing it to BeeBee. "Here are your ingredients for your pizza. The kitchen will have the flour and the other basics, so this is just your pineapple, peppers, cheese and bacon."

"Pancetta," BeeBee corrected her, a fresh pang of missing Bill hitting her like a prick from a freshly sharpened chef's knife.

"Gesundheit," Kit said with an eye roll. "Uh,

you know I'm not one for the mushy, sentimental stuff—you can call Jackie for that nonsense—but, um, I'm really proud of you, Beebs. No matter what happens." She sniffed and adjusted her glasses. "Look at me blubbering on like this. You need to get going before you're late. I'll keep you posted on the heifer. Oh, and Lou as well. She should be back from the hospital soon. They said she tore a ligament, but they bandaged it up and she has to stay off it for a few weeks. The other dance teacher is driving her home."

"I love both of you girls, you know that?" Bee-Bee said before throwing her arms around her little sister, who clenched her entire body in protest before giving in and hugging her back. "Give Lou a hug for me too when she gets home."

"I think I've reached my hug limit for the day," Kit muttered as BeeBee released her, but she flushed with pride as she waved BeeBee on from the door. "Mom and Dad will be in the audience, and we'll all be cheering you on from home," she called out as BeeBee followed the girls to the car.

"Your parents aren't at the farm now?" Haven asked her.

"They actually aren't around much at all," BeeBee replied. "My dad used to run it when we were younger, but since he started teaching at the community college and my mom keeps busy with volunteer work, they come and go. They stayed in the Catskills for their anniversary last night. They'll drive back up for the pageant today."

"So who runs the farm?" Emma asked. "I mean, I work at my family's dairy, but only in the evenings after my college classes are done. Even then, I just help with maintaining the stalls and hooking the cows up in the milking stands."

"I've been running the farm for a while now," BeeBee said, clicking her seat belt into place and taking the coffee Brittany offered her with a grateful nod. "My sisters help, but they all have other things going on. The farm is my life. It's everything." *And so is the crown if I'm going to keep it going another year.*

Turning her head to gaze back at the cows as they drove past, she watched the grass ripple in the wind like water. This was her life and always would be. But the vision of what that life looked like had changed. She didn't want it to be alone anymore.

The drive to the pageant wasn't long, although when Emma streamed her Pageant Prep Playlist from her phone to the car, BeeBee feared it might never end. However, the enthusiasm of the other women in the car was contagious. By the third song, BeeBee found herself whistling along. Haven and Brittany harmonized in perfect pitch, Brittany's lilting soprano bursting free from her newly unwired jaw.

They pulled around to the back parking lot behind the complex of brick buildings. Walking into the dressing room area felt surreal. BeeBee had been preparing for this for weeks with equal parts dread and anticipation. Now the moment was finally here. All of the work, all of her hopes for what her farm could become rested on the outcome of this pageant.

And yet amid the chaos of women scrambling for a "lucky spot" at the long row of lighted mirrors, the beaded dresses rattling around her, the curling-iron cords being hurled like bullwhips, she kept her ear trained for the sound of an alert from her phone.

"BeeBee, what are you doing with your hair for the introduction?" Emma asked as she settled into the spot next to her and began unraveling curlers from her blond hair. "I always bring extra hair spray in case you need it."

"Oh, um…" BeeBee stammered as she unpacked a hairbrush and the packet of bobby pins from her duffel bag beneath the counter. "I'm not sure actually. My sister was going to do my hair and she injured her foot last night, so she couldn't make it."

Emma's eye grew impossibly wide. "Oh no. What are you going to do?"

Shrugging, BeeBee stared at her reflection in the mirror. "I always put my hair in a braid," she replied, holding her long plait up as evidence. "I want to look like myself out there, you know? But like the best version of myself." She wished there was a way to look the way she felt when Bill smiled at her. If they could bottle a version of that and sell it as a gel, she'd buy out the entire stock. She let her braid fall and sighed. "I guess I could do two braids. That's what I do when I have a little extra time in the morning and I feel like being fancy."

Emma tapped her chin with one finger, then smiled. "How about this?" With half her head still covered in curlers, she stood behind BeeBee and undid her braid, combing through the long strands with her fingers to part them into two pieces. BeeBee watched as her tiny hands moved like deft bluebirds, weaving the hair into two long braids, then pinning them securely over her head like a crown. Bending down, she reached into what looked like a tool kit, pulled out two pink tubes and held them up. "Glitter spray or no glitter spray?"

Staring in awe at her reflection, BeeBee turned her head from side to side. The look was so simple, the braids still felt like her, but now her neck looked long and swanlike. She felt like royalty and yet still someone who belonged on a farm.

"You know what?" she said with a lift of her chin. "Glitter. Glitter all the way."

"Yay," Emma squealed. "Close your eyes and cover your nose."

Not wanting to sneeze fairy dust for the next two weeks, BeeBee followed her instructions and as she listened for the hissing of the aerosol to stop so she could open her eyes, a familiar ding caused her heart to leap in her chest.

"My phone," she yelled and coughed as the heavily sweet scent filled her mouth and nose. "Good God, that's like liquified cotton candy. Can I open my eyes now, Emma? I need to check my phone."

"You're all done," Emma said. BeeBee opened her eyes to see the woman twirling her cannister of hairspray like a dueling pistol. Definitely a good thing the tiny woman lacked criminal intent.

Reaching for her phone, BeeBee fumbled as she scrolled to see who the message was from. Her hopes fell when she saw that it was from Kit, but they landed softly into relief. The heifer had made it through delivery safely. Lou had insisted on hobbling out to the barn on her crutches to help clean up the stall and, according to Kit, had made ten times more work than if she had just stayed inside and gone back to bed. BeeBee's heart swelled with affection for her sisters. They had known she wouldn't be able to concentrate on anything until she knew the animals were okay, and even with their bickering, a peace filtered through her.

"Do you need any help with your makeup?" Haven asked as she leaned back and poked her head out from the other side of the partition dividing the mirrors.

BeeBee shook her head. Wow, this hairstyle really did not budge. She was going to have to ask Emma where she got this stuff. "No thanks. I'm just going to keep it simple for the introduction. I'll probably sweat it all off during the cooking portion of the pageant anyway." Looking from one side to the other, she asked the girls, "What are you guys making for your dishes?"

"I'm making my famous panna cotta with a mixed berry coulis," Haven answered. "It's like an Italian version of pudding. My secret is I add limoncello to the coulis for a little kick."

"Oh dang, that sounds good." BeeBee sighed as she opened up the makeup case Lou had packed for her yesterday. Taking out lipstick and mascara, she set them down in front of her, frowned at the palette of other colorful bronzers and blushes and closed them with a defiant snap. "What about you, Emma?"

Emma grimaced nervously. "Ugh, I can't even

talk about it. Every time I think about the recipe part I start to get queasy," she said, holding her stomach. "There's so much that can go wrong."

"That's how I feel about the final interview," BeeBee said. "It feels like walking the plank over shark-infested waters, but in painful high heels and a corset."

Would the reminders of Bill ever stop? And even more to the point, would they ever stop hurting?

A tall woman with a clipboard appeared after a knock on the doorway. "Fifteen minutes until start time. Please finish getting ready and make your way backstage. The manager will place you in the correct order for your introductory presentations."

Emma and Haven both stood and made their way toward the door. BeeBee couldn't move. She didn't want to move unless it was to turn around and run through the walls, leaving a BeeBee-shaped hole. Then she would keep running until she hit ocean and then she would swim until she found him.

Biting her lip until it lost all its color, Bee-Bee gave her reflection a good hard stare. The only *him* she needed to think about now was Orlando. For him, she could stand up, walk out there and pretend to know what she was doing. She unzipped the hoodie she had put on to protect her costume from makeup or hairspray. Kit had found an incredible tailored women's jacket in navy blue. It nipped in her waist with a single button, and over a white button-down shirt topping a matching pencil skirt, the look was, according to Kit, "game show host, but make it pretty." The fluorescent lights caught the sparkle on her hair like a halo.

BeeBee didn't know what was going to happen next. But between the risk to their heifer and calf and the stories from the other dairy farmers, she was more aware than ever of what it meant to run a small dairy farm almost entirely on her own. Orlando was more than a novelty feature now. He was an insurance policy that could potentially save them from going under. It was all on her now.

From backstage, the low, rumbling chatter of the audience made it sound like there were a thousand people sitting in the stadium-style seats, even though she knew it couldn't have been more than one hundred at the most. The emcees, two hosts of a home-shopping program on the local cable channels, had already begun their spiel. From her place in the middle of the lineup, BeeBee could see nothing but the high updo of the woman in front of her. Chewing on her lip, she made a face at the taste of her lipstick.

"BeeBee, are you okay?"

The sound of Georgia's voice whispering to her left shocked BeeBee into jumping. "Gigi, what are you doing back here?"

"I came to get the cardboard cutouts for your skit," she replied with a grin. "If you can see us, it will spoil the surprise."

"Us?" BeeBee said, raising her voice slightly so Georgia could hear her over the sound of Brittany's small power tool on stage. Her introduction presentation was a demonstration of her lightning-fast butter-carving skills, and as she wheeled her creation backstage, BeeBee gave her two thumbs up before turning back around. But Georgia was gone.

The presentations were all surprisingly varied for a pageant that centered around a single theme. BeeBee whistled as hard as she could when Emma finished her parody song, "I Am the Very Model of a New York Dairy Farming Girl," and teared up as Haven read the article about when her great grand-father returned home from World War II and proposed to her great-grandmother in the middle of their Victory garden. When the last woman in front of her had finished her cowbell solo, BeeBee wiped her sweaty palms on her skirt and listened for her cue.

"And next, all the way from Crystal Hill Dairy

Farm, let's hear it for Beatrice Long," the male emcee said as he stretched his right arm out toward the curtain. "Beatrice is twenty-four years old and has three sisters. Her dream is to run the largest water-buffalo farm on the East Coast and provide high-quality gourmet dairy products to her town, a small village outside of the Adirondacks known for its history of quartz mining and pristine lakeside scenery. Here's Beatrice!"

Gritting her teeth at the repetition of her full name, BeeBee sucked in a deep breath and forced a smile. "Think of Orlando, think of Orlando," she muttered to herself before striding onto the small stage.

The emcee was a tall, good-looking guy with sandy hair and shockingly light blue eyes. He nodded and handed her the microphone.

Clearing her throat, BeeBee let out a shaky exhale. "Hi, everyone. I'm BeeBee Long, and today we're going to be playing a game of Guess Who?—the Crystal Hill version." Georgia had said stick to the script, so that was all she could do.

Then another person stepped onto the stage from the wings opposite her. They wore black pants and held the cardboard silhouette over their torso and face, so BeeBee truly had no idea who they could be. Georgia must have recruited someone else from town to read all of the parts.

The thought of one of the other members of her community taking the time out of their day to do this for her instantly eased the nerves flying around her stomach. When the person started speaking, she recognized the voice instantly.

The surprise was that they weren't reading from the script.

"I run a restaurant in downtown Crystal Hill."

She knew exactly who this was. But he wasn't one of the characters who was supposed to share a mildly yet lovably embarrassing story about her. Oh no. Was this revenge for the Great *Nutcracker* Debacle? When he lowered the placard, was he going to throw a lemon cream pie in her face?

"When I first opened my restaurant, money was really tight," Joe continued from behind his "anonymous" cardboard persona. "The first day, I ran out of cream for coffee by nine in the morning after using too much of my supply to make my famous banana-custard pies for the display case. I was a basket case, but within minutes after calling the Longs, BeeBee showed up at the diner with enough cream to get us through the rest of the day and block of cheddar as an opening-day gift. She even put on an apron and helped wash dishes when my busboy had an allergic reaction to the strawberries on top of the baked French toast. Guess who I am?"

For a moment, BeeBee was speechless. Swallowing back tears as the audience murmured among themselves, she finally found her voice. "You're Joe Kim, owner of Big Joe's Diner."

Tossing the cutout aside, Joe grinned at the audience and nodded. "That's right. Free pancakes if you vote for BeeBee, folks!"

She smiled, a real smile this time, and nodded at Joe as he left the stage. Then another disguised person took his place. There was more than one person from town helping her?

"I run the bed and breakfast in town," the familiarly creaky voice announced to the crowd. "Last year, we had an unexpected frost in April right before the Finger Lakes Garden Club was supposed to come and inspect my hydrangeas for the Spring Floral Gold Medal. BeeBee brought straw from her own stockpile to cover my beautiful garden and the grass. She even salted the front walk so the judges wouldn't slip on the stoop, as it gets quite hazardous with even the slightest bit of ice. Who am I?"

"Mrs. Van Ressler of Crystal Hill Castle B and B," BeeBee said, the emotion in her voice sounding extra thick from the volume of the microphone. "And folks, she did win that gold medal."

Mrs. Van Ressler revealed herself and inclined her head graciously at BeeBee before Joe returned to the stage to offer his arm and assist her as she walked. BeeBee mouthed a silent thank-you to them both, and yet there was still another figure who came onstage. It was definitely a man and definitely tall. Time felt like it froze as she stared at the fingers holding the cardboard, trying to see if she could catch a glimpse of a familiar scar. Her heart sank when the voice spoke.

"I've known BeeBee basically since she was born," Lucas said, his deep voice instantly recognizable and comforting the slight disappointment that it wasn't Bill after all. "She's the closest thing I have to a little sister, and she's also one of my best friends. When I graduated from college, my girlfriend had just broken up with me, and it was really devastating. Everyone around me kept offering me support and sympathy and trying to fix me up with their mother's hairdresser's daughters.

"But BeeBee knew exactly what I needed. She showed up at the retail space for the dairy with a jug of water-buffalo milk she had special ordered. She lugged it into my workroom all by herself, set it down at my feet and told me she needed me to learn how to make cheese out of it because she wanted to add a herd of water buffaloes to her farm and she wasn't going to do it until I stopped moping and got to work. See," he added after the audience stopped laughing. "BeeBee knew that the best way to get my mind off my heartache was work. She knows the people in her town and reaches out to help them whether they ask for it or not. We know we can count on everything being okay because we have her around. And I hope she knows that I'll always be there for her too. Who am I?"

"Lucas Carl," she said through a mixture of laughter and barely restrained sobs. "My cousin, my friend and the best darned cheesemaker in the whole world."

He dropped the placard and crossed the stage to wrap her up in a hug. "I'm sorry about Bill," he whispered in her ear. "I'm still rooting for you two to work it out, but I'm Team BeeBee for life, okay?"

"I'll get you some pom-poms to match your hairnet," BeeBee whispered in return, and he patted her back before exiting behind her.

Blinking rapidly and keeping her fingers crossed that the waterproof mascara was exactly as advertised, she lifted the microphone back to her lips. "Thank you for playing along with Guess Who?, everybody, and a special thank-you to the people from my amazing town for taking the time to come all the way out here and surprise me. You guys are the best."

Grinning at the group who had been joined backstage by Georgia, she turned her head back to wave at the audience before handing the microphone back to the emcee.

"Thank you, BeeBee," the emcee said. "It sure sounds like you're the buzz of your town."

She was so happy and touched that she didn't even roll her eyes as she walked offstage and into the arms of the people who meant everything to her.

"You should have seen your face." Joe jabbed her in the ribs with his elbow. "I thought you were going to have a heart attack there onstage. For once it wouldn't be my cooking that caused it!"

"But what about the diner?" BeeBee asked before shifting her gaze to Mrs. Van Ressler on his left. "And the inn? The summer-tourist season is in full swing now that the kids are out of school. I can't believe all of you would close your businesses for the day just for me."

Lucas clapped her on the shoulder. "Of course we would, Beatrice," he said with a teasing emphasis on her name. "But we didn't have to. When Georgia called us last night, we started a group text chain with all of the local businesses. Dave Stevenson is looking after the inn, and Renata's daughter is running the diner. My dad can manage the shop for the day without me—"

"And I had planned to be at the watch party anyway, so I already had the bakery covered for the day," Georgia interjected. "Caroline had told me the basic gist of your skit, and Kit emailed us the dialogue." A dimple poked into one side of her cheek as she scrunched her face to one side. "I hope you don't mind us putting our own spin on the stories. We know you were going for self-deprecating humor, but we wanted the judges—and you—to appreciate what you mean to this town."

BeeBee wrapped her arm around Georgia's shoulders. "It was the best surprise anyone has ever given me," she said.

No matter what happened next, whether she won or lost, this was the moment she knew she would never forget.

"We should get back to our seats," Mrs. Van Ressler said, waving her hand back toward the auditorium imperiously. "I paid a young man to save the front row for us, but I don't trust his attention span. His eyes kept darting to the concession stand while we were talking."

"Do we get to watch your cooking challenge?" Georgia asked BeeBee as Lucas and Joe helped Mrs. Van Ressler down the stairs on the other side of the curtain. "I had a slice of the pizza you left at the dairy shop a few weeks ago. It was delicious."

"The kitchens are in the other studio they use for the cooking show," BeeBee answered, nodding to one of the other contestants as she passed them. "They're going to live stream them onto a big screen in here so the audience can follow along though."

"Good luck, hon," Georgia said. She hugged BeeBee one more time before following the others into the audience.

Taking a deep breath in, BeeBee allowed herself a moment to let the happiness roll over her. Once the moment was over, she undid her bowtie and jogged back to the dressing rooms behind the stage. At least she would get to wear sneakers for this part of the pageant.

With half an hour to change, prepare their ingredients and report to the kitchen studios, the dressing room was a mad flurry of flying clothes, hairspray and women loudly convincing other women that their presentations were absolutely not a disaster that cost them the crown. Buttoning the top button on the white overcoat each of them had been given to wear over their clothes, BeeBee tapped a hand on her head, marveling at the fact that not a single hair was out of place. She even had to begrudgingly admit that she perhaps didn't hate the sparkles.

To her right, Emma was nervously running her finger down the printed recipe laying on the counter and muttering to herself.

"Stir the cream vigorously." She wrinkled her

nose. "Then add the vanilla beans—oh wait, I skipped a line." She clapped a hand to her forehead, then looked over at BeeBee and moaned. "I'm going to mess this up, I just know it."

"Well…" BeeBee turned to face her, planting one hand on the counter. "If it doesn't work the way it's supposed to, just make up a fancy word for it. People will eat anything if you tell them it's a French delicacy." She couldn't stop herself from wondering how Bill's dinner had gone. Of course, his food was always amazing. He would probably get job offers from all over the world. But why couldn't the world be here? With her?

Emma giggled, then frowned. "But crème brûlée is already a French word. What do I call it if the blowtorch is too hot and I burn the top?"

"Um, crème brûlée à la cajun?" BeeBee affected her best French accent, which was still pretty terrible. It was enough to make Emma laugh out loud.

"So funny," she said, her laughter winding down with a sigh. "Thanks. I needed that."

"Anytime," she offered and meant it. Bill might have been in Paris for all she knew, but even if he never came back, she was starting to see that her life didn't have to be as lonely as she had feared.

The twelve contestants were divided into three groups of four. Each group was given ninety minutes to prepare their dishes. They had been allowed to prep some of it beforehand. BeeBee carried the cooler with her pizza dough and the toppings into the kitchen along with Emma and two of the other women in the first group.

"This kitchen is so clean," BeeBee whispered to Emma as they waited backstage for the cameras to get into position. "I'm afraid to touch anything. How much do you think they'd charge me if I accidentally broke one of the ovens?"

Emma shook her curls. "You're just trying to get me to laugh so I won't be nervous. As if anyone could break a whole oven."

"You'd be surprised," BeeBee muttered to herself. "You set one little grease fire and the whole thing goes up in smoke."

When the stage manager clapped his hands, they chose stations comprising of a small kitchen island with a butcher block counter, a double-range stove with oven below and a stand mixer. Taking a deep breath, BeeBee laid out her can of tomatoes, herbs, the peppers and the pineapple. When the announcer started the electric clock above them, she bent down to gather a saucepan and the electric grill. She had practiced this so many times that technically she didn't need to look at the recipe. But now, with the stage lights bearing down on the back of her neck and the clatter of the contestants around her, she needed something to reassure her that she would not burn everything this time. She pulled out the recipe and laid it on the counter. Bill's messy handwriting made her smile even as it pulled at the fresh scar tissue protecting the wound on her heart. He had believed she could win, even if that belief couldn't make him stay.

With his words in front of her, it was almost as if she could feel the steadiness of his hands guiding hers as she put the sauce together over the burner on low so the tomatoes didn't splatter everywhere. Once that reached a gentle simmer, she rolled out the dough into a perfect circle. So far, so good. She didn't even look at the other stations or the clock ticking away above her head. All she could focus on was Bill's voice in her head, warm, deep and reassuring her that no matter what everything would be okay.

Once the grill was warm, she placed her pineapple and Calabrian-chili-pepper slices in rows. *Sweet and smoky are a great combination*, he had said even though the first time she had tried this, the smokiness of her charred-beyond-recognition pineapple had heavily outweighed any remaining sweetness.

This was the hard part—keeping one eye on the grill while putting the pancetta in a pan to crisp up. It was the step that always tripped her up as she would focus too much on one element and ignore the others, either burning the things on the grill or over cooking the sauce until it turned into tomato-flavored glue. *Not today*, BeeBee thought to herself with a wry twist of her lips. Today she could do it all, bring home the bacon and fry it up and put it on top of a pizza so delicious even the most determined pineapple haters would gobble it up. Using the tongs, she gingerly turned the pineapples and peppers over. One at a time, the perfect grill marks crisscrossed the produce, and only after the last one was turned did she actually exhale. The smell of the frying pancetta was making her mouth water, and BeeBee used the spatula to slide each crispy piece onto a plate. Then the pineapple and peppers came off the grill. Finally, she actually remembered to turn off all the burners instead of leaving them on to send the smoke alarms screeching to the heavens, a sound she was likely to hear in her nightmares for many years to come.

With the hard parts done to perfection, Bee-Bee actually found herself having fun. This was being live-streamed to the audience after all. Might as well give them something interesting to watch. Picking up her pizza circle, she gave it a little toss in the air and caught it with both hands.

"Salute," one of the girls behind her called

out. "BeeBee, you better be making enough of that pizza to share with all of us. That smells incredible."

"Thanks, Maria," BeeBee said over her shoulder. "All you ladies have an open invitation to visit me in Crystal Hill anytime. I'll make pizza, and you can meet my water buffaloes."

"Ha!" One of the other women laughed. "That's what I call my three big brothers, although I think real water buffaloes probably smell better. Count me in."

Glancing at the clock ticking down, BeeBee left her station and put a hand on Emma's shoulder. "Hey, are you okay?"

Emma turned to BeeBee, her face a mask of terror. "I'm too afraid to do it. If I burn them, that's it. I'm done. I'm too scared."

"Do you want me to help?" BeeBee wiped the tomato sauce off her hand onto her overshirt before offering it to Emma. "I've had a lot of practice with these."

Emma drew in a sharp breath and nodded wordlessly, handing the torch to BeeBee.

Sucking in her lower lip, BeeBee flicked on the brûlée torch, and it fired up with the familiar hiss that Bill's had back in that very first cooking class. She remembered the angle he had used with his strong forearms to keep it just far enough away, how he had slowly and evenly coated the surface of the marshmallows with a light golden brown. She started with the first ramekin, carefully toasting the top until it was just right before moving on to the next one—one at a time until all six were topped with a coating of light brown caramel and the sweet nutty smell filled the air. She turned off the blowtorch and set it down.

"I can't thank you enough, BeeBee," Emma said. "That blowtorch got in my head, you know?"

"I know exactly what you mean," BeeBee said, flexing her hands in and out as they started to cramp. "With my pizza—Oh, shoot, I've gotta get my pizza in the oven."

"I'm fine here—go, go." Emma nodded at BeeBee's station.

Fortunately, she had already preheated the oven, so it was ready to go, but if she waited another minute the thick crust might be raw on the inside. She opened the oven door and slid the pizza stone in before slamming it shut. Tapping the buttons on the timer, she shot a look at the clock above her head. Twenty minutes. Just enough time.

Turning around, she folded her arms and leaned back against the warm oven. The other women were still decorating pastries with frosting, sprinkling fruit with sugar, and the atmosphere had gone from *light and happy* to *pressure cooker* as the time ticked on. Bee-Bee started to clean up her station, checking all the burners to make sure they were off and feeling quite pleased that she had chosen something that didn't require a whole lot of fuss at the very end. An unease nagged at the back of her mind, almost as if there was something she had forgotten. She went through her checklist one more time. The dough had been rolled. She had made the sauce, grilled the produce, cooked the pancetta. Check, check, check. The oven had been turned on. She had put the pizza in.

Shrugging, she finished putting the pots and pans into the sink behind her and went to put the extra ingredients back into the cooler. That was when she spotted the white rounds of buffalo mozzarella waiting with stoic silence for their star turn. There was no time to be angry at herself or rend her tomato-smeared smock in grief. She grabbed the balls of cheese and unwrapped them, pulling out a knife to slice them into uneven rounds right there on the counter. Throwing the oven door open, she tossed a few slices at the pizza in a blind panic just as the stage manager called out a one-minute warning. Closing the oven door, she bit her lip so hard it hurt.

She had made a pizza with hardly any cheese

on it at all. Out of all of the mistakes she had made, even Bill would agree *that* was unforgivable.

CHAPTER SIXTEEN

THE FOUNDATION DINNER had been a resounding success.

The evening had gone by in a blur, with Bill hyper-focusing on his food like never before. It didn't hurt that the ingredients at his disposal were of the highest quality. Food on charter yachts varied tremendously, depending on size, clientele and even what port they were docked in for the season. Tonight, however, it was top drawer from start to finish with even the micro-greens for garnishes smelling as if they had been freshly picked from a garden only moments before. Even his staff ran with perfectly timed efficiency. He felt like a conductor who had been given the chance to lead the orchestra at the Metropolitan Opera House for one night only. When the waitstaff had returned with dessert plates that had been licked clean, it was as good as any standing ovation.

Bill leaned back in his seat the next afternoon. He was back on a boat, albeit a much smaller one this time. Luigi had arranged for a private lunch on a small boat that seemed to operate as a sort of café. It wasn't even large enough to call a yacht, but there was room on the bow for several small tables and chairs and an outdoor pizza oven. The smell of the bubbling cheese and roasting basil made his heart twist, thinking about BeeBee. Tomorrow was the second day of the pageant. He had come so close a few times to calling Lucas and asking how everything was going. But Lucas had made it clear on the drive to the airport that he didn't want to be put in the middle of this because if it came to choosing sides, they both knew where his loyalties were vested. Of course the cheesemaker would choose to be neutral Switzerland.

Putting the doubts and regrets aside, it was a beautiful day. The water sparkled in the afternoon sun, and he sipped a glass of exquisite red wine as they cruised lazily along the shoreline.

"It is beautiful, no?" Luigi asked as he gestured at the vista.

"Very beautiful." Bill leaned forward and set his glass on the table. "So you said last night you had something you wanted to show me?"

Luigi nodded and stood holding on to the table with both hands. Gesturing for Bill to follow him, they made their way to the boat railing, where Luigi pointed at a large villa resting atop the stony cliff face.

"Do you see the big house there?" He turned to ask Bill.

"Hard to miss," Bill replied. The house rose above a twisted grove of green olive trees, its honey-colored stone practically glowing. "What's it called?"

"Villa de Celia," he answered. "Named for the woman I let slip through my fingers all those years ago." His withered hands trembled slightly as he pointed at the house. "It is my favorite holiday home, where I spend every summer and also where I often host events, large dinners, that sort of thing." He raised bushy white eyebrows at Bill.

"Why didn't you host last night's banquet there?" Bill screened his hand over his eyes.

In front of the house was an enormous stone terrace overlooking the water. It would have been the perfect place for last night's gala—a tapestry of stars twinkling overhead, the guests wandering in tuxedoes and formal dresses, the sound of clinking champagne flutes clinking. His chest tightened at the memory of BeeBee walking down the stairs all in white. No matter where he was, she was always with him.

"Ah, you see, that was the plan, but we are in the process of renovating the kitchens," he said.

"Construction takes much longer here than it does in America. I do business in Manhattan as well, and it is a very different pace. You went to culinary school there, yes?"

"I did," Bill said. "That was a long time ago."

"Well, your teachers would be very proud of the meal you made last night," Luigi commented as he took small shuffling steps around to lean his back against the rails. "I have never had such food as you created. I will have to send Captain Lee a bottle of very nice wine as a thank-you for recommending you."

"Thank you." Bill ducked his head modestly. "But, uh, is that why you brought me out here? As a thank-you?"

"In part," Luigi said. "You see, I am, as you say, on the hunt for a new personal chef for this place. It would not be a full-time position. Only for summers and the big holidays—Christmas, Easter," he said, rolling his hand as he spoke as though unfolding the passage of time with the gesture. "I also let out the house to certain very special guests for weddings and other events. A certain actor who played a certain superhero had his wedding here, but I am not at liberty to say his name."

Bill nodded calmly even as his insides crashed about like waves in a storm. This was the dream job, the stability without the tedium of regular restaurant work.

"It would be the same sort of clientele as the gala last night, so the chef would have access to the same quality ingredients and the kitchen would be, of course, state of the art as everything is being redone as we speak," Luigi continued. "There is a cottage onsite that would be provided as living quarters. The position is a sort of on-call, but during the off-season when there are no events planned, you would be free to travel as you please."

"Does this mean that you're offering me the job?"

Luigi swiveled his head and squinted a steely eye at Bill. "Do you want this job?"

"I—" Bill opened his mouth to accept. Why weren't the words coming out? Why was he suddenly struck by a longing that felt something very akin to the homesickness he had felt his very first summer at Camp Herkimer? "I don't know."

"Ha," Luigi crowed, slapping the rail with one hand. "So you are not a complete fool as I was all those years ago. Good, this is good."

The only answer he could manage now was an oh so eloquent "Huh?"

Chuckling, Luigi unholstered his cane from his forearm and started back toward the table. Sitting down, he poured another dram of wine into his glass from the bottle on the table and repeated the move with Bill's glass. "All those years ago, I was too afraid to follow my heart. My family business was here, and if I had followed her to America, I was afraid that on my own, I would fail. So I told myself it could not have been love, that I was saving us both from mistaking a summer romance for something more."

Bill sank slowly into his seat. Boy, did this story sound familiar. "That was very sensible of you."

"If by *sensible* you mean *stupid*, then yes." Luigi raised his glass to Bill with an ironic huff. "Career opportunities will come and go. You are going to fail at something eventually. It's equally likely you might succeed at something no matter where you are. What matters most is the stuff in-between. That's where you spend most of your time anyway. So, ask yourself— how do you want to spend the in-between? What or who makes you the most happy when you aren't really doing anything special at all?"

Sipping his wine, images flashed through Bill's mind. Leaning on a fence post as animals loped down the field in front of them. Messing around in the kitchen and not caring whether the dish came out perfectly because the only people who would eat it was the two of them. Sitting in a rowboat on a lake under the stars and realizing it wasn't the water that was calming his restlessness this time. It was her. It was always her.

"I've got to get back to the States," Bill said, standing abruptly.

Luigi clapped his hands together once. "There you go. I will get you to my private jet. The pilot is used to making the trip to New York for my business there. We have to wait for the boat to finish its route."

"The boat doesn't belong to you?"

Luigi shook his head. "No, my yacht is actually docked in Malta this season. I'm leasing it to some friends there." He jerked his head back toward the deck. "This is what I think they call a popping-up cruise. They go from port to port in the Ligurian region doing lunch and dinner only. It's becoming quite a popular way to run a restaurant here because the costs are low and advertising through the social media is also not expensive. But you're not going to have a big fancy kitchen. Here they do mostly pizzas, salads and light fare using local farm-to-table ingredients." He shrugged. "A lot of hard work, but you could make a living doing it as long as you don't mind spending so much time on the water."

"That's…perfect." Bill turned in a circle, assessing the size of the boat. "It wouldn't need to be a huge yacht. Something with a small kitchen and living quarters. Tables that seat two to four. A floating bar island in the back for wine and light cocktails. Theme nights like Valentine's Day cruises."

Ideas spun in his head like a tornado, gathering strength as they swirled. It would be constantly changing just the way he liked it. And what better place for a romantic pop-up dinner cruise than Upstate New York? Good grief, you couldn't drive ten miles without hitting another scenic lake. It would mean a long off-season in the winter, but he could fill that time in with new projects, new recipes. Maybe he could even continue his Parks and Rec kids' cooking class for something kids could do on winter and spring breaks from school. There were so many possibilities and opportunities. Freedom and roots at the same time. And the best part about his Spartan existence over the last several years was that he had managed to save almost all of the money he made. Salary and tips, which were often fairly generous.

He could do this. More importantly, he wanted to do this.

And even if he failed and he had to do something else, he knew who he wanted by his side through it all.

Putting a hand on Luigi's shoulder, he fought the tide of emotions rising within him to seek the exact right words. "Thank you. For last night and today. This was a life-changing opportunity for me."

The old man chuckled. "It was my pleasure. I will text my pilot and let him know we are on the way."

Bill looked at his watch, then back at the shoreline. "Do you mind if I make a quick stop into the countryside first?"

CHAPTER SEVENTEEN

BEEBEE PEEKED THROUGH her fingers at the TVs backstage live streaming the judges trying each dish, stifling a groan when they got to hers. Two of the uncooked mozzarella rounds had slid off the pizza when she'd set the stone onto the counter, so there was one sad circle of cheese for the whole thing. Her dairy-themed recipe contained almost zero dairy. She threw up her hands.

"Welp, I'm done." Stalking backstage to the dressing room, she plopped into the chair in front of the mirror and began ripping bobby pins out of her head. "No point in even going back in for the interview."

"Don't say that." Emma swiveled her chair around to face BeeBee and put her hand on her knee. "The judges saw you taking the time out from your recipe to help me. They'll take that into account—I'm sure of it."

That hadn't occurred to BeeBee, and she slowed the dismantling of her hair to something less hurricane-like. "I guess so. And there was still a little bit of cheese left, so it wouldn't technically disqualify me."

"Plus, you made everyone smile while we were cooking," Emma pointed out.

"Cooking is supposed to be fun, right?" She swallowed a hard lump as she echoed Bill's words from the cooking class. "And I'm serious about the invite for everyone." She twisted around and leaned her elbow on the back of her chair. "Hear that, ladies? You all have an open invitation to visit Crystal Hill Dairy Farm anytime you want."

One of the other women looked up from unbuttoning her cooking smock. "I'm going to take you up on that. I've never had buffalo mozzarella before, but your pizza smelled incredible. Is it true that their milk is actually easier for people with lactose intolerance to digest?"

BeeBee nodded. "And it's a creamier texture too. Our retail shop makes a really nice yogurt out of it."

"Party at BeeBee's house after the pageant!" Another of the contestants whooped from the mirror in the far corner.

BeeBee turned back around to her own mirror. It was amazing how good she felt despite the complete failure of her recipe. A smile spread over her reflection's face. This was why Jackie had pushed her to enter. She got it now. It had never been about winning the money for Orlando even though that was still the hoped-for result. It had been about finding her people, expanding her circle beyond those who had known her all her life. She needed people who weren't her sisters or her neighbors from town. What was forming here was community without borders or zip codes. It was finding home in the people who understood and supported you, no matter where your life journey led.

"Hey, Emma," she said, plucking what she very much hoped was the last bobby pin she would ever need to use. "Can I borrow some more of your sparkly hair spray?"

BeeBee was spraying a final coat of glitter when a second face popped into the mirror beside her shoulder. Nearly jumping out of her skin, she whipped around to give Kit the tightest hug in the world.

"What are you doing here?" she practically shouted before pushing her back and giving her sister a chastising frown. "You left Lou by herself. You didn't need to do that for me."

Kit rolled her eyes. "She's fine. Her dance partner, Paul, is with her. He'll take better care of her than I would any day."

BeeBee relaxed her face. "Oh, okay, then." Shaking her head, she bit her lower lip. "I... I kind of biffed the recipe."

"I saw." Kit laughed. "Oh, BeeBee. What were you thinking?"

"I wasn't, as usual," BeeBee replied. "But there's still the interview and formal-wear portion to go. Speaking of which, can you help me get into the dress? There's, like, a thousand buttons in the back."

Shedding her chef's overcoat and jeans, Bee-Bee reached for her blue gown hanging up on the rack next to her mirror. It really was perfect for her, the blue-gray satin mirroring the color of the morning sky over her grazing fields. Bill had known exactly what kind of dress would make her feel confident and beautiful. He knew her, all her flaws and fears, and believed in her anyway.

If only he'd known how much she needed him.

She banished the thought, forcing herself to focus on the scripts for the potential interview questions as she pulled the dress over her head.

Kit's perpetually freezing fingers sent a chill through her entire body as she set to work on the buttons. "BeeBee," she said slowly. "There's another reason I came out here."

"Is it to turn me into a Popsicle with your hands because mission accomplished."

"No, not that." Kit finished the last button and BeeBee turned to face her. "We got a call from Salvatore a few hours ago. A third buyer came to him and offered triple what we could pay for Orlando. He accepted the deal. It's over—Orlando is gone."

The cold went from BeeBee's back and spread deep into her core. Yet after the initial shock, she found herself sighing with resignation. "Okay."

"BeeBee, did you hear what I said?"

"Yes." BeeBee repeated the words numbly: "Orlando is gone." Walking back over to the mirror, she adjusted the straps over her shoulders. "We lost him. There was nothing else we could do. We put ourselves out there, we said everything we were feeling and we still lost him."

Kit pushed her glasses back up on her nose and stood between BeeBee and the mirror. Her dark eyes searched BeeBee's face as if looking for signs of head injury.

"You're starting to make me nervous, BeeBee," she said, putting a hand to BeeBee's forehead. "What are you talking about? And why are you so calm? I came to tell you so I could make sure you didn't leap into the lake or try to hire Italian hit men off the internet to go after Salvatore."

Looking down at her bare feet, BeeBee shook her head. "I'm disappointed. More than that, I'm crushed. Orlando was the reason I started doing all this. But even though he's gone, I'm still glad that I agreed to do this. This whole experience has been strangely eye-opening." She lifted her eyes and gave a small, closed-lip smile as she shrugged. "My world feels bigger now. I have new friends who understand me and support me. I feel more comfortable talking to people who haven't known me forever. Thanks to that stupid girdle, I don't get headaches nearly as often, and when Jackie meets some European royalty and falls in love, I can wear heels to their wedding without falling over."

"Speaking of which…" Kit held up one finger, then dashed around the corner. When she returned, she held out a shoebox. "These are for you."

They were high heels, but instead of flashy red satin or sparkling rhinestones, they were a plaid pattern like her favorite work shirts. They were unique and so very her that BeeBee started to tear up.

"No—you'll ruin your makeup." Emma swooped in between them and reached up to dab at the corner of BeeBee's eyes with a tissue. "Oh, those shoes are darling. BeeBee, you are just the most stylish person I've ever met!"

BeeBee and Kit locked eyes over Emma's head and burst out laughing.

"Okay, that's it." Kit held up both hands and turned to walk away. "I'm getting out of here before pigs start flying overhead and BeeBee decides to add pig farming to her repertoire."

She stopped and looked over her shoulder. "Go get 'em, big sis."

BeeBee took the shoes out of the box and slipped them on. Stepping back to look at herself in the mirror, she combed through the waves of hair falling over her shoulders. She looked good, and more importantly, she looked like herself. That was all she needed to be. Although there was one more touch that was missing. Reaching into the pocket of the dress, she pulled out the bandanna Bill had given her. She tied it around her neck and let one hand linger at the pulse point beneath it. The heartbeat that surged under her fingers belonged to only one person and it always would.

Maybe after all this was over, she would do some traveling of her own, perhaps to a port somewhere in the Mediterranean where fancy charter yachts tended to dock. She had never been able to leave the farm before, but now she felt like she had people she could trust to help out, from the people in town who had shown up when she hadn't expected it to the other dairy farmers who knew exactly how hard this life could be. That support meant everything. It gave her freedom.

Later that evening, BeeBee waited backstage as one by one the other contestants took their turn. They walked across the stage to the taped

X, turned in a graceful circle as the spotlight beamed down on them, then glided back to the center where the stool and a microphone waited for them. As they walked, instrumental versions of pop music played softly over the loudspeaker. The judges in the front row stood and asked each of them a question. So far, all of the questions had been on Jackie's list. BeeBee recited her practiced speeches in her head as the other women spoke, trying to focus on her own inner voice instead of paying attention to what the others were saying. But the more she tried to remember the speeches, the tighter her stomach felt. By the time it was her turn, she could barely breathe, let alone walk. Her hands and feet felt numb, frozen with disbelief that anyone had ever thought she, BeeBee Long, could pull this off.

Then the music started up again, familiar notes breaking through the cloud of nerves like warming sunlight. It was "Dancing Queen" by ABBA. Her breath returned in a gasp that was half heartbreak and half hope. Even if it hadn't been forever, she had known the kind of love people wrote songs about.

BeeBee took a deep breath, lifted her chin and walked onto the stage. The clicking of her heels on the floor was instantly drowned out by a roar from the audience. It was so loud that it startled her, and her left ankle rolled slightly, but she recovered quickly. They were cheering...for her. And even though the stage lights made it impossible to see individual faces in the crowd, she could tell it wasn't just her sisters and neighbors hollering for her. It was everyone. People she had never met were rooting for her. The nerves dissolved like sugar in a steaming cup of tea, warm and revitalizing. She stopped on her mark and threw both hands up in the air, waving at the world. It wasn't dignified or demure. It was her.

Going back to the stool at the center, she picked up the microphone and sat, remembering seconds later to cross her legs at the ankle the way Queen Darby had showed her at the seminar. Could that have only been six weeks ago? How was it possible for so much to change in such a short amount of time?

Pausing for a moment, the auditorium felt suddenly very quiet and still. Aside from an isolated cough and the squeak of a chair, BeeBee could scarcely hear anything beyond the roaring of her nerves. This was the final event of the pageant. She should be relieved; after this, one way or another it was all over. Instead, the pressure increased with each thundering heartbeat. She realized with a sudden clarity how much she actually wanted to win.

"Miss Long," one of the judges, a tall man with dark hair and a thick moustache, read from a cue card, "please describe for us something special that sets you apart from other dairy farmers."

This wasn't one of the questions she had rehearsed. BeeBee blinked. They wanted to know what was special about her? She knew what the other contestants would say, what her sisters would want her to say. But Bill had given her the best advice of all—to be honest about who she really was, and if that wasn't enough for them to call her a winner, that was okay.

"There's nothing special about me," she said before holding up a finger to the audience. "No, really it's true. I'm surrounded by special people. My parents, my sisters, the people in my town who have provided me with love and encouragement my whole life. But I'm just an ordinary girl who works hard and makes mistakes and tries to do better next time. What I do have is the knowledge of how special my animals are." The wobble in her voice seemed to echo especially loudly through the microphone, and she looked down, clearing her throat. "A few years ago, I was going through a really rough time. My mom took me out to another farm that was having a liquidation sale of its animals. We found a young female water buffalo that no one else wanted. They don't produce nearly as much milk as regular dairy cows, so there isn't as much return on your investment with them. We brought her home, and I learned everything there was to know about water buffaloes. One thing that none of my research prepared me for was how caring for one animal could heal a heart that had been completely broken."

She touched the frayed end of the bandanna around her neck and looked out into the audience for the one face she knew wouldn't be there.

"I entered this pageant wanting to bring something unique to my town," she continued with a small shake of her head. "I wanted to build a thriving water-buffalo dairy farm that would supply top-quality water-buffalo milk like nobody else. I still do, even though it's looking like it won't work out like I had hoped. But this process has made me realize that what I can share with my town—and the whole state if you choose me as this year's Dairy Queen—is my appreciation for all the creatures, great and small, who provide us with so much more than delicious milks and cheeses and ice creams. They provide us with unconditional love in a world full of hearts that need mending."

As the audience cheered their approval, she stood and set the microphone down, then picked it up quickly. "Oh, also I can whistle on perfect pitch, so I guess that's something special about me." She demonstrated with a high A sharp that sent the microphone squealing in protest. The clapping instantly stopped as everyone, including the judges, covered their ears with their hands.

BeeBee cringed. "Sorry," she whispered into the microphone before setting it gently back onto the stool and walking quickly offstage. But she wasn't really sorry. That whistle hadn't been for them. Wherever Bill was in the world, she hoped it reached him. She hoped it made him smile.

Behind the curtain, Emma, Brittany, Haven and several of the other contestants stood silently with their mouths open.

BeeBee swung her gaze from one end of the line to the other. "What? You all look like you accidentally drank a shot of cow tranquilizer. Funny story about that—"

"What you said up there..." Emma shook her head. "That was...that was *not* what we thought you were going to say. It was so humble."

"So honest," Haven said in an awed whisper.

"So loud," Brittany tugged on her earlobe as if shaking out the ringing. "The whistle, that is. The words were—well, what the others said."

Taking off her heels—pretty as they were, nothing could convince her to wear them a second longer than necessary—BeeBee gestured to Emma. "Your speech was way better. Your idea about using hydroponic technology for sustainable feeding year-round was mind-blowing." She tucked the shoes under her arm and made an explosive gesture by each of her temples with her hands.

"Yeah, but my speech was so technical and dry," Emma replied. "You spoke from the heart."

"Usually that's what gets me in trouble," Bee-Bee said, only half joking. "I'm not sure my heart has made the best judgment calls lately."

As they walked back to the dressing room to wait for the interviews to wrap up, Haven leaned in and elbowed BeeBee in the ribs. "You think you could teach me how to whistle like that? I feel like it would really come in handy."

"On the farm, you mean?"

She tossed her long hair over one shoulder and let out an undignified snort. "No, the animals I can manage just fine. I need the whistle for the toddlers I teach at Sunday school."

Throwing her head back, BeeBee laughed. It felt like someone released a valve and all of her worries and fears were slowly leaking out in a single stream of mirth. "Come over to Crystal Hill sometime for a pizza party, and I'll see what I can do."

They filed back into the dressing rooms behind the stage. All the interviews were over. Now they just had to wait for the judges to make their decision. Dropping her shoes onto the chair at her station, BeeBee reached up and untied the bandanna at her neck. Now that the adrenaline rush had drained, she could feel the cracks inside her again, the fault lines where she had shattered from the loss. It wasn't about Orlando. That was disappointment, an emotion with which she was well-acquainted. No, these were deep fractures. She had flown and she had fallen, yet she knew if given the chance, she would soar all over again just to have seen that view one more time.

Back in the dressing rooms, the food from the contestants' recipes was spread out on a long folding table. Everyone else's looked so impressive compared to her sad little creation. Wrinkling her nose, she held up her phone and took a picture of the feast, even including her own unfortunate contribution.

BeeBee scrolled through her texts and found Bill. He had sent her one last message, but she had been too upset to respond to it at the time. Now all she wanted was for him to be a part of this final experience. Her finger paused on the Send button before deleting the picture. It wasn't all she wanted. She wanted more than just sending pictures and texts back and forth. She wanted him here, with her, by her side through everything.

Even if she had to follow him halfway around the world to show him.

But before she could reach for her sneakers and run straight from the auditorium to the airport like in the movies, the emcee knocked on the door of the dressing room.

"The judges have made their decision," he called out from the other side. "Please line up in your introduction order backstage."

Okay, then. Hopping a plane would just have to wait. It had taken seven years for them to find each other again and it would only take a few minutes for the judges to announce Haven or Emma as the winner.

But as soon as one of her friends was crowned, she was leaving town to claim her pirate king.

CHAPTER EIGHTEEN

BILL WAS EXHAUSTED, rumpled and in desperate need of a shower.

The last twenty-four hours had been a whirlwind of buses, planes and a very long, very quiet ride in Lucas's truck back to Crystal Hill.

"Thanks for picking me up from Saratoga Springs," Bill said as they headed west toward the lowering sun. "It was the closest airport the private jet could drop me off in."

"Uh-huh," Lucas muttered.

"I promise I'm not going to stay with you another six weeks this time," Bill added with an uncomfortable laugh. "It won't take long to work out the details for my new digs."

"Mmm-hmm," Lucas murmured.

"You're really trying to stay neutral here, aren't you?"

"As far as you're concerned, I'm freaking Switzerland."

"Swiss cheese, maybe," Bill said under his breath, shaking his head. "You're really not going to tell me anything about how the pageant went? How BeeBee's doing? Not a thing?"

As they turned off the expressway and through downtown Crystal Hill, Lucas continued to stare stonily ahead. Bill closed his eyes and leaned his head back against the leather seat. It had been a very long day in transit, and not everything had gone as he had hoped it would. Once they were back at Lucas's, he would have a chance to regroup. This was his chance to make things right with BeeBee. It had to go perfectly.

The ride seemed to be taking longer than he had expected though. Wondering if he had actually dozed off, Bill opened his eyes and saw that they were driving through the woods. When the trees cleared, he saw where Lucas was taking him.

"What are we doing here?"

Lucas jerked his chin at the dirt road ahead. "I'm on strict orders to bring you here first," he said as he slowed the truck to a stop in front of the Long house.

"I thought you were neutral," Bill said. He wasn't prepared. He didn't know what he was going to say. He had had a whole thing planned, and it had all fallen apart. There was no way he was getting out of this truck right now.

"Yeah well, there's neutral and there's not

wanting to have the wrath of BeeBee brought down upon you."

"I'm not ready to see her yet," Bill pleaded. "I'm gross, I've been traveling to farms all over the Italian countryside and through two very small, crowded airports on both sides of the Atlantic for over twelve hours. I'm sweaty, I'm tired and I left my bandanna on the yacht, so I'm pretty sure my hair looks like something laid an egg in it. Don't make me do this now."

One side of Lucas's mouth curled upward. "That's life, my friend. You're never going to be ready for it. You just have to jump in with both feet." He opened the driver's-side door, stepped out and turned, clapping his left hand on the top of the truck as he leaned in to give Bill one final burn. "Besides, she likes the smell of barnyard animals. You're perfect."

Bill got out of the car and folded his arms, staring at the house.

"Jump in with both feet," he repeated. "That sounds like a recipe for disaster, and no one knows recipes like a chef."

He was stalling. It wasn't that he didn't want to see her. Since the night of the gala—heck, since the first time he'd seen her walking out of that lake—she had remained in the back of his mind like a prize waiting to be claimed. But this wasn't what he had planned. After his talk with

Salvatore, he had come up with a foolproof idea to show her how much she meant to him. However, none of it had worked out, and now he was here, with nothing but a half-baked idea for his future and a picture on his phone. BeeBee deserved the world. He hadn't wanted to show up with anything less.

Lucas hooked his thumb over his shoulder. "I'm going to the storage out back to collect the water-buffalo milk for my cheese. Let me know when you're done groveling, and I'll give you a ride back to town."

"Well, since it will only be about two seconds before she kicks me to the curb, don't go too far," he called after his friend's retreating form. Sighing deeply, he went straight to the only place BeeBee could be, making sure to close the gate behind him this time. But when he knocked on the doorframe of the barn, the only thing that greeted him was a calf blinking large, dark eyes up at him from the stall for weaning babies.

"Huh." Bill was at a loss. Now that the pageant was over, he'd fully expected her to be back at the barn twenty-four seven. The animals were all milling around the nearby grazing fields, so he knew she wasn't far. He walked back to the house, the sound of several women's voices growing louder as he approached. They didn't sound like the twins, and Jackie wasn't there. Maybe Mrs. Long was holding one of her meetings? He rapped on the door cautiously and pushed it open.

It was indeed a small gathering of women, but they were much younger than Mrs. Long's Bingo for Boys and Girls of America club. Seated on the couches and the floor were several very pretty women in their twenties looking toward the fireplace where BeeBee stood, tapping enthusiastically on a tablet.

"So, it looks like the best time for our next in-person meeting will be around August twenty-eighth," she said as she scrolled down. "But obviously if anyone needs anything before then, we can get through to each other on the group chat. Now about the potluck—"

"Uh, BeeBee?" One of the women piped up as she turned and leaned an elbow on the back of the couch. "There's a man in the doorway."

BeeBee looked up from the tablet, and her mouth fell open.

It never mattered how long it had been. Each time he saw her again, her beauty struck him like the first rays of a new dawn. She wore her usual plaid short-sleeve shirt and overalls, and her hair was in the same long braid draped over her shoulder. Even so, she looked different. Different each time and yet her light, her warmth would never change. She would always be the center of his universe. What was different this time was the bandanna tied around her head like a scarlet headband. His bandanna. She was wearing his bandanna.

"Bill," she said quietly before closing her eyes and giving her head a small shake. "I, um, I mean, ladies, I'd like to introduce you all to Bill Danzig. He's the guy to thank for the pizza recipe we've been enjoying this weekend." Her voice was light, casual even, but the intense shine in her eyes betrayed emotion he was afraid to name.

"Hi." He gave a small wave, then crooked his head and squinted slightly. "I'm sorry to interrupt this, this…" Leaning forward slightly, he asked the girl on the couch, "What is this that you all are doing?"

"Well, it started off as a post-pageant pizza party," a girl with curly hair chimed in from the floor. "But it got late, so it turned into a slumber party."

"I thought slumber parties were more pillow fights and board games," he replied with a small smile, standing upright again to nod at BeeBee's tablet. "This looks a lot more bureaucratic than that."

"It is, actually," BeeBee said, gesturing at the semicircle around her. "As I was showing everyone around the farm, we were swapping tips and ideas, and it occurred to me that we could all really benefit from having a network of women dairy farmers who can provide support and encouragement in a field that for a long time has been a real boys' club that relegated women to either milk maids or moms. So this is the first official meeting of the New York Women's Dairy Farmer Consortium."

His heart swelled with so much love and pride Bill was surprised it didn't burst right out of his chest. "That's an amazing idea."

When their eyes locked, it wouldn't have mattered how big a consortium surrounded them. It was only him and BeeBee.

"Um, do you ladies mind if Bill and I go outside and talk for a bit?" She set the tablet down on the coffee table and stepped carefully between the pile of pillows, blankets and people spread out around the floor.

Bill rubbed his eyes. BeeBee Long, navigating moving obstacles without so much as a stubbed toe. How long had he been gone? Maybe he still wasn't back yet. Maybe he had fallen asleep on the train coming back from the foothills of Positano and this was all a dream he was having.

As he stepped onto the porch and she closed the door behind her, he heard one of the women call out, "Go get him, Your Majesty," followed by a storm of giggles muffled when the door clicked shut.

"Your Majesty?"

BeeBee twisted her lips in a barely repressed grin. "Well, you know that is a title typically used by us royalty, although I don't plan on enforcing it with all my subjects," she said with the lift of her chin that had always been slightly regal even before it was official.

"So, uh, where's your crown?" He shoved his hands into his pockets and jutted his chin at her head, his gaze lingering on the tattered red fabric topping it. "It doesn't match your day-to-day ensemble?"

"Oh, no, it goes with everything," she said emphatically. "The girls were totally right about wearing it everywhere. You should see how it catches the light when I'm bringing the buffaloes in from a wallow." She let out a hearty laugh, then looked down and shook her head before lifting her hand to the bandanna. "I just…like this better."

He sucked in a breath and held it there for a moment, not daring to let it out because then he might wake up. "You know, between you commandeering my first mate's truck and kidnapping me to bring me here, you've got the makings of a pretty good pirate." He reached out and took the hand lingering on her head, lowering it gently in his. "My pirate queen."

She kept her eyes on his face as she took a step away from the door to stand even closer to him. "I think the piracy was a one-time thing for me. The farm is where I belong."

"And I belong with you," he said. His voice rumbled with the deep emotions he could no longer hold back. This wasn't the moment he had planned, the way he had hoped to sweep her off her feet and win her heart once and for all. But this was the moment to tell her how sorry he was for leaving. "BeeBee, I don't expect you to forgive me for taking the job in Italy, for going away when you needed me with you. But I came back because you deserve an apology. You deserve to have everything you want in life, and if there was a way for me to give that to you I would. I wanted to come back to you with this big grand gesture to make up for it all." He looked down at their entwined hands and squeezed hers hard. "But I failed. I couldn't get him for you—I tried."

"Bill, what are you talking about?"

"Orlando." He swallowed hard, dropping his shoulders. "I wanted to bring him to you. I had it all worked out, even got the private jet pilot to agree to clear out the cargo hold for him."

"Oh" was all she said.

"But when I got out to the farm, Salvatore told me he had sold him to another bidder," Bill went on. "He said the guy offered him—"

"Triple what we could pay," she said softly, stroking his knuckles with her thumb. "I know. He called Kit the day of the pageant."

"I'm so sorry," he said again, taking her other hand in his and bringing both to his chest, drawing her into him. "For leaving, for not being able to get your water buffalo for you. For looking like laundry that got taken out of the dryer too soon—although you were the one who ordered Lucas to bring me here without showering, so technically that one's on you, Your Highness." He lifted her fingers to his lips to kiss them, thrilling at her touch once more. "I'm sorry you worked so hard and it was all a waste."

She chuckled and lowered her head to touch her forehead lightly to his. "Oh, Billamina. None of this was a waste." Allowing a breath of space between them, her shining eyes captured his gaze and locked it with the key only she possessed. "Somewhere along the way I realized how wrong I was."

"About what?" he murmured, spreading her fingers to nestle his cheek in her palm.

"About everything," she whispered. "I thought that when people left a place, it meant they were leaving me. I thought that my home was here, this place and the only way I could have the life I wanted was to gather everything and everyone important to me here in this very small, wonderful bubble. But that's not how any of it works. My home is the people who matter in my life, no matter where they are. And the more I reach out to those people, the bigger my home grows. And when people leave, they take a piece of me with them. It doesn't matter then how far away they are. I tried to force things to happen my way, in my time and place because I was afraid of being left behind." BeeBee's lips curved in a small smile. "I thought I needed something special like Orlando to make people want to stick around. But now—" she turned her head and looked back into the window where the shadows of the other women moved and danced in the fading light "—I know that I'm enough, just me and my stained jeans and my old boots."

"You're more than enough." Bill pulled her back to him and wrapped his arms around her. "BeeBee, you're everything."

He bent his head to hers and kissed her, pressing his lips into hers with both forceful heat and tender sweetness creating that perfect balance for a kiss that would never grow stale. When they finally broke apart, her softly blurred gaze and flushed cheeks drew him in once more to kiss her gently on her eyelids, her temples and the corners of her lips that turned up just for him.

"You were right about one thing though," he whispered against her cheek. "About me, that is. I was afraid that if I stayed in one place, then I would stay the same person. The guy people love for a season and then they get sick of. But I forgot about the best part of sticking around—second chances." He took a deep breath and looked deeply into her eyes. "I hope it's not too late. I want to be the person you choose, just like you chose Crystal Hill as your place. I'm not perfect and I'm going to make mistakes. But being by your side every day isn't something I need to earn. It's what I need. You're what I need. I just didn't think I deserved you."

She ducked her head and laughed softly, pulling back to extend her arms while keeping her hands tucked safely in his. "I think the two of us deserve each other," she said, smiling up at him with love beaming out of every corner of her face. "A hopelessly klutzy queen and a bumbling pirate without a ship. Although I guess you'll have to go back to sea pretty soon here, huh?" She bit her lip and inhaled, her eyebrows furrowing before she glanced back up at him with concern. "How long do we have before you go back for the rest of charter season?"

"I'm actually not going back for the rest of charter season," he said, exhaling deeply. "While

I was in Italy, the head of the foundation took me to lunch on a pop-up cruise. It wasn't like a big fancy yacht or any of the charters I've been working on. It was more like a catamaran, the kind you see in Florida or Hawaii. The boat goes to a different port every week and uses local produce for simple lunches and dinners."

"Is this your way of telling me you're moving to Italy?" Her bottom lip disappeared entirely.

"Italy is one of the most beautiful places in the world," he said emphatically. "But I happen to think that the scenery around here is just as stunning." He looked down at her meaningfully.

Blinking as if opening her eyes first thing in the morning, BeeBee's hand traveled up his arm to clutch the sleeve of his T-shirt. "Here? You mean it?" The smile that broke across her whole face felt like it reached through his chest and pulled him into her. "But how? You'll need a boat and a captain and permits. It's going to take a lot of time and money."

"Well, those are all questions I had hoped to take a little time to figure out before I saw you and blurted all this out," he said, the sound of Lucas's heavy footfall kicking up gravel behind him. "Then someone hijacked me and came straight here." The footsteps skidded to a stop and the sound faded away in the direction of the milking stand. "I don't have any concrete details to give you. Right now, it's only a loosely formed idea, and despite the very high chance of complete failure, I'm going to use my savings and all my energy to make it happen. At the moment, though, I only have one thing to offer." He gently pulled her hand from his sleeve and placed it over his heart. "It was always yours anyway," Bill whispered.

She brought her face to his, pausing with her lips half an inch away. The fragrance of hay mingled with something sweet and floral rising from her hair which inexplicably glittered in the last streaking light of the sun. "I love you, Captain Bill."

"And I love you, my queen."

EPILOGUE

Nine months later

BEEBEE SURVEYED THE sloping hills wound with ancient vines. The briny scent of the sea hung in the air along with a hint of citrus from the lemon trees that grew in emerald clusters along the coast. The russet-colored buildings in the valley below took on a coppery gilding from the reflected light of the midday sun.

"Okay, so I guess people weren't completely exaggerating about the scenery here," she grudgingly admitted, turning back to face Bill as he leaned against a fence post and grinned at her. "But I still say there's nowhere in the world more beautiful than Crystal Hill."

"Whatever you say, Your Majesty," he said.

Technically, she was still Queen of the Dairy for another three months. But her duties were starting to wind down as preparations were beginning for this year's pageant. This time she would be leading the seminar, and she already had an introduction planned that would have the other contestants rolling on the floor laughing. Hopefully. She might have to plant a few of the consortium members in the audience as insurance gigglers. Her friends had become more like sisters over the last year, and they had relied on each other for more than just laughter as the winter had been especially tough. Leaning on each other's resources had made a world of difference.

Prosperous for Bill too. Even if she didn't have the seminar, they wouldn't be able to stay in Italy for more than a few days. Captain Billy's Wandering Dinner Cruises had its soft launch next week. True it was only for a select few residents of Crystal Hill, but they wouldn't hold back their criticism, especially as they had quickly adopted Bill as one of their own. His cooking classes had been the hit of the winter, both for kids looking for activities during their break from school and adults hoping to add some new recipes to their holiday entertaining menus. Plus, the money from the teaching had been enough to pay his rent for a room at Mrs. Van Ressler's while he'd completed the renovations on the SS *Dairy Queen*, his initial request to name it *Beatrice* having been met with threats of beheading. It was a beautiful boat, an old two-level yacht that Bill had found with the help of Mr. Giordano's contacts here in the States. Although, it had taken almost all of his savings to buy and refurbish it, Lucas and Everett, the town plumber had donated their time to help with the renovations.

The boat—and the name—was perfect anyhow. Everything wonderful in her life was thanks to the pageant. She wouldn't be here in Italy now without it. Despite losing out on Orlando, Bill's efforts to track down Salvatore almost a year ago hadn't entirely been in vain.

The night they had reunited, Bill had told her how he had traveled inland to find Salvatore's farm and begged him not to sell BeeBee's precious water buffalo. They had sat in the barn with the baby calf and the two adult female water buffaloes who'd looked after him as if he were their own. Stroking their thick, dark hair, he had smiled over them at BeeBee with so much love and hope in his eyes she'd thought she might burst from the joy of it all.

"When I told Salvatore I was here for you, he lit up. He said he had tried to tell your sister about it, but the signal was bad and they had a hard time communicating." He had pulled out his phone, scrolled through and held up a picture of another water buffalo. This one's horns were slightly akimbo and he had a droopy eye. His bearing was as comical as Orlando's had been regal. "It turns out, Orlando has a brother."

BeeBee had yanked the phone out of his hand. "He's—"

"I know, I know," Bill had interrupted with a grimace. "He's kind of unfortunate looking and half the size of Orlando. They sold him to another farm on the coastline that shelters unwanted farm animals since there was some doubt over whether he was quality breeding material."

"He's perfect," BeeBee had breathed at last. "Does he have a name?"

"He does," Bill had answered, his grin broadening. "And you'll never guess what it is."

Now, the farmer was leading the water buffalo toward them with a bridle around its neck. It ambled with a sort of jerky gait, stumbling slightly over the rocky landscape. As BeeBee clasped her hands to her chest, Bill walked over to her and enveloped her in his arms from behind her. Bending down, he hummed softly in her ear, one of the songs they had danced to so long ago. As always, an electric thrill went through her at the comfort and warmth of his embrace. It was a feeling that never got boring, and she knew it never would. It was the feeling of peace, of harmony, of being loved exactly as she was.

Turning her head, she didn't whistle it. Instead, she sang the refrain right back to him. It didn't matter that she was on the completely wrong key. In fact, the mistake made their secret language even more perfectly their own. Especially perfect since this particular ABBA song was also the name of the water buffalo smiling back at her.

"Fernando," she sang through a mist of happy tears. "Welcome home."

* * * * *